The Langdon Codex

R. P. Poe

I hunt for sign of you in all the others,
in the rapid undulant river of women,
braids, shyly sinking eyes,
light step that slides, sailing through the foam

-Pablo Neruda

In the broken window
The broken boats will come in,
The life boats
Waving their severed hands,
And I will love as I ought to
Since the beginning

-W. S. Merwin

One

Now I don't know but that I half-expected trouble when I returned home after so long. My cousin, Griggs, had come back to the island, and I knew how he found mischief wherever he went, or mischief found him. I can't say which. Onward Cates had made his way back as well, a happenstance that would prove crucial. But I knew nothing of it at the time.

The more I thought about it, the more I began to believe you can never truly escape the circumstances of your beginning. Such places inhabit you from birth, hidden somewhere deep inside like a grain of sand until that day you discover the essence of who you are, a pearl white or black, bad or good. And what you learn changes everything.

But the good or bad in people didn't concern me at that moment. Instead the orange light of the ship channel appeared through the windshield like a false dawn, silhouetting a row of palm trees. Their narrow trunks seemed to me impossibly fragile and impermanent on such a storm-riddled coastline. I couldn't help but be reminded of the fugitive and disconnected state of my life. So, I breathed in the warm air, hoping it might once again make me part of the place, the place of my birth and now my return.

Peering up at the low clouds streaming past, their round forms lit from within like Chinese lanterns, I recalled an odd paradox that often occurs when life turns dark. All at once the world takes on a special sort of beauty, sharp-edged and clear, as if everything near and far has suddenly come into focus. What was there all along gains a meaning you never imagined, leaving you with a feeling close to affection, love even, and a hope for something better. Or so it seems.

The causeway emerged from the darkness and the car bumped onto the first section, the tires clicking along the concrete in a rhythm as familiar as sunrise, as known to me as my uncle's face. Flashes of pewter and bronze reflecting off the bay's windblown surface winked through the guardrail. A seagull swept past the headlights and vanished.

At the causeway's end the road spilled onto the island, passing through and out of a tunnel of live oaks. Within minutes I had turned onto the main boulevard. To my right the Gulf of Mexico's dark expanse stretched south, hidden beneath a starless sky. Yellow-green oilrig lights floated in the void like fireflies.

The seawall stood empty at that late hour save for a lone figure, head down, shoulders hunched against the coursing wind. The restless sea rose and fell below him. Blowing mist blurred streetlights into halos of silver.

I turned left onto Rosenberg and followed the wide boulevard inland. Palms and oleanders dotting the avenue's grass-covered esplanade vibrated before the breeze just as I remembered them. To my right a row of two-story frame houses, most perched on hidden piers to avoid floodwaters, loomed over the neighborhood as if keeping vigil over my ill uncle.

The familiar pink and white stucco home Griggs had nicknamed the Ice Cream House signaled my turn onto O Street. I pulled to the side midway down the block. A clutch of acacia trees beyond the curb framed a short walkway leading to an unadorned frame house. Though near midnight the porch windows blazed like lighthouse beacons. My aunt Fiona was waiting up for me.

I sat for a moment and pondered the cause of my return, the mysterious illness that had left my uncle pale and exhausted and, more importantly, unable to work. With typical certainty of purpose Fie had called to demand my immediate return. As his twin sister she no doubt felt she had a right if not an obligation to do so. In her view the

2

family, and by extension the family business, a musty and sprawling downtown furniture store founded by my grandfather, required my attention. I sat for a moment trying to conjure an image of the place but the thought of selling tables and sofas day in and day out left me lightheaded and nauseous.

I refocused on the house. Fie and Whit began sharing the place after they were widowed years earlier. Little had changed since my last visit. Beneath the scattered streetlights, the home's white shiplap siding shone a muted blue-gray, a shade not unlike a Confederate uniform my uncle August might say in admiration. The screened-in gallery, stretching the length of the house, buzzed with fluttering moths.

I climbed out of the car and made my way along the sidewalk, up the broad stairway and across the porch, pausing before door. Then without knocking I stepped through. The living room spread before me bright as daylight and crowded with plantation heirlooms and antiques passed down from generation to generation, all looking just as I'd imagined them. Family photographs still littered side tables and shelves.

I spotted my aunt beneath a yellowed reading lamp, a book in her lap, her forefinger pressed to the middle. Erect against the seatback, she sat unmoving in robe and slippers. Only the angle of her head gave her away. She was sound asleep.

I pushed the door closed with a thump and she jerked upright, eyes wide, blinking over her reading glasses into the blaze of light. Her gaze drifted to where I stood waiting. She blinked again and her composure returned at once as she studied me with her coal-dark eyes, finally motioning me into the room with a brusque wave of her hand.

"Well, you're here," she croaked. She set her glasses aside and seemed to soften, as if she had suddenly remembered the reason for my coming. "What time is it, dear?"

"I'm sorry to wake you, Fie." I glanced at my watch. "It's coming up on midnight."

"I was only resting my eyes from this interminable story." She snapped the book closed. "I'm intent on finishing the tome but Mister Joyce makes a practice of cramming more words into one sentence than a hive has bees.

"Now, I've set a cot in the study until we can get hold of a proper bed for you. Your dresser is still in there along with a wicker chair your uncle Augie stole off some poor fool, and then there's my old bedside table…"

"No… Fie…" I stammered, "I can't..."

"Whit and I have it all taken care of," she said dismissively. "Well, if the truth be known I did the lion's share. But there's plenty of room for the three of us so you need not..."

"I've rented an apartment." I blurted out the lie without thinking. There was no turning back. "I move in tomorrow."

I could only hope I would find a place that quickly. Her black eyes scrutinized me as if she sensed the ruse. Then she gestured around the room.

"This house was good enough for your grandfather and, after he willed it to us, good enough for your uncle and me. But for a man who thinks he knows what's what in this world it fails to measure up. Is that what I'm hearing?"

"Now Fie, you know good and well it's not like that."

"I hate it when my brother is right," she grumbled. "He said a young man needs his own place. I just can't understand such attitudes."

"I'm here," I said, looking for a diplomatic way out, "aren't I?"

"Oh," she sighed, "I suppose that counts for something."

"Fie, you have to understand. I'm past thirty and…"

4

"Don't patronize me, Duncan Osay," she snapped. "I was there when you were born. Not a week later I held your mother's hand as she took her last breath. Then I took you, a six-day-old baby boy, an orphan no less, into this house."

"I know the story, Fie," I muttered.

"After all that, you don't think I would remember your age?"

"I appreciate the offer, Fie. But I'm not a child. I need my privacy."

"Men and their privacy," she replied. "That's exactly what Whit said."

She raised herself with a groan, standing straight-backed and erect even in her night clothes. Then she motioned me over with a snap of her fingers.

"Come and give your aunt a hug so I can go to bed."

I started toward her then stopped at the shuffle of footsteps in the hall. Seconds later my uncle appeared in the doorway, his mottled face pale, an unlit cigar wedged between his fingers. His free hand gripped a tattered book.

Steadying himself on the doorjamb, he peered at me with watery eyes. Wisps of gray hair sprang from his scalp. A yellowed undershirt and boxer shorts peeked from beneath his half-open robe.

"What are you doing here?" His voice was a rasping near-whisper.

"That's a fine way to greet your nephew," Fie complained, "after he's been up half the night driving himself down here."

"But why is he…?" he started. "Oh… yes, I remember now. You've come to help with the store."

Fie frowned as he absently raised the cigar to his lips. Catching himself, he glanced at her and then lowered his hand with a pained look.

"I don't imagine you'll be staying long," he added.

"Well, I…" I hesitated, unprepared for his changed appearance.

5

"What I mean is," he continued, "I'll be feeling better any day now. I won't keep you long."

"I'll stay long as you need," I replied and regretted it at once, my shame over not coming earlier clouding my judgment.

"Well, Griggs is covering the store but we do have a repair scheduled for pick-up in the morning."

"Griggs is working for you?" I said in disbelief.

He gave his head a slow nod, sticking the cigar between lips for an instant before jerking it free.

"I had no choice," he muttered.

"But you know how he is."

"He's not like he used to be, Dun." He dismissed my complaint with a wave. "He's finally grown up. You'll see."

"But even his own father," I replied, incredulous, "refused to hire him."

"My brother is an idiot. Besides, Onward will keep him in line."

"Onward is back?"

His eyes narrowed and he thrust the cigar between his teeth.

"You would know that if you bothered to pay us visit once in a while."

"I get down here often as I can," I replied, feeling defensive.

"I wouldn't call once in two years often."

"I have responsibilities."

"You sound downright proud of yourself."

"When's the last time you paid me a visit?"

He plucked out the cigar and glowered at me.

"You think that has anything to do with this?"

"You don't understand, Whit."

"I understand you don't have time for your old aunt and uncle."

"That's just wrong, Whit."

"There's always an excuse out there if you're looking to find one."

"Whit," Fie barked, "stop such talk! You Osay men must have some genetic predisposition to contrariness. Can't you be in the same room for two seconds before you start to arguing?"

"Well, I'm through with arguing," he snapped. "If a man can't smoke, he might as well sleep."

He turned and disappeared down the hallway. Fie sighed and lightly touched my arm.

"Best to get some rest, sweetheart," she whispered as she stepped past. "He'll be in better spirits tomorrow."

I watched after her, wondering what sort of mess I'd gotten myself into. The past seemed to be rushing toward me like a rogue wave. Or so I thought. But if I'd known then what was to come, I would've picked up my bag and walked right back out that door.

Two

The next morning I skipped breakfast and gulped the last of my coffee as a car horn blared from the street. I was glad to get away before my uncle was awake. I hustled through the honey-colored daylight, reminded of the many mornings I had passed the same way as a boy. Moments later I stood before a panel truck emblazoned with the family name. I peered inside.

Onward Cates sat clutching the steering wheel, his gaze fixed on the street ahead. Puzzled by his unsettled look, I climbed in. He shot me a quick glance, shifted into gear, and pulled away from the curb without so much as a single word, just a long, slow "uh-huh" under his breath like the first few notes of a gospel song, a song of troubles. I felt like I had stepped back in time.

I had known Onward since before memory, since before I knew even my own name. Or so it seemed. His was, of course, impossible to forget. He had come from Mississippi to work the store as a teenager, only sixteen at the time. I was ten. Despite his young age, Onward always made time for me no matter what else might need tending. His reddish-brown skin, like tea with cream, didn't stop me from thinking of him as the older brother I never had.

His family still lived in the place of my ancestors, a small town on the Mississippi Delta, one of a handful spared during the Civil War. Plantation-style homes and buildings, many beautiful despite their disrepair, still lined its tree-shaded streets. As often happens in the rural backcountry, the town was slowly dying. A nearby paper mill was all that kept it alive.

Onward had returned home only once in all the years since his arrival. That was for his father's funeral. To everyone's surprise he dropped out of sight right after the service, vanishing for months without notice or explanation.

8

I glanced at his furrowed profile, wondering about his strange disappearance and, even more so, the cause of his return. That my uncle had taken him back held no mystery. The paths of Onward's family and mine threaded together like the stitching of an heirloom quilt. But where had he gone, I wondered, and why?

The truck slowed and he pulled to the curb in front of a two-story, four-columned house painted canary yellow. Stained glass fleur de leis filled the first-floor windows with patterns of purple and red. Compared to the house my aunt and uncle shared, it was a mansion.

A figure moving behind the stained glass caught my attention and, seconds later, a young woman appeared in the doorway. Framed by a curtain of black hair, her face shone the color of ripe peaches. She waved us forward and vanished inside, leaving her image floating before me like a vision. Onward groaned and climbed from the truck, snapping me out of my trance.

"Heard about this place before, sure enough," he said.

"Heard what?"

"Some things about this lady here."

He paused to look over the house, his expression still troubled. I decided I had to know why.

"What's on your mind, then?"

"If you weren't so impatient," he snipped, "I'd tell you."

"I don't mean about her," I ventured, "I mean about you."

"What about me?"

"You seem bothered."

"The only thing bothering me," he grumbled, "is Dun Osay."

"But…"

"Now, about this lady here…"

"Why won't you tell me?"

He faced me, clearly annoyed. His refusal made me push harder.

"Tell me what it is," I pressed.

"What're you talking about, Dun?"

"Something's troubling you."

"They say she lost her husband early on," he continued, turning back to the house. "That was in the war. They say she never was the same since."

"You're not going to tell me what's wrong?"

He pivoted, glaring at me.

"I tell you what's wrong, Dun" he snapped, "not a damn thing. Now, let's go."

He started to turn and then hesitated, studying me as if for the first time, his eyes softening, the look of consternation replaced by affection and then, finally, resignation. He sighed and motioned toward the house.

"Come on, then, we got a job to do."

Deciding to let it go, I followed him up the walkway and into a wide, high-ceilinged foyer partially blocked by a wooden crate. I glanced about the adjoining rooms, hoping to spot the woman. She was nowhere in sight.

Instead, an older woman rounded the crate, coming nose to nose with Onward and nearly jumping out of her skin. He did a sort of dance while she stumbled backwards, spilling the drink in her hand. I could see she was heading for a fall, but he reached out in a flash and caught her.

Then it was his turn to jump. Seeing his dark hand around her pale wrist, he flinched and let go almost too soon. Somehow, she managed to grab hold of the crate. Onward had no blush to his brown skin but she turned five shades of red, one right after the other, all matching her tinted hair.

"Lord God Almighty, a… a colored man…" she stammered, "a colored man in my…"

Onward stood statue-like, his eyes wide. She gripped the crate, panting, looking like she might faint any moment. I could smell the whiskey on her breath even from where I stood. She raised the tumbler to her lips and then stopped as her gaze settled on me. I saw her mind was working.

"You are Mr. Whit Osay?" she said, lowering the glass.

Struck speechless by her appearance, I gave my head a slight shake. Wearing a white turban and an emerald-green gown that stretched to the floor, she looked like she'd stepped out of an old movie. She raised the glass again, drained it and threw back her shoulders, studying me coolly.

"There was no mention of a…" she cut her eyes at Onward, "of a…"

"I'm Dun Osay," I interrupted, "Whit's nephew. I apologize for not calling out and saying so first thing."

I glanced around the room, hoping the younger woman might show herself.

"I guess we gave you a fright," I added.

"Why, no, it's just…" She shot Onward another glance. "I was expecting someone else. My name is Victoria Langdon. And I've forgotten my manners. You must let me make it up to you, Mr. Osay. Come into the sunroom while I find you something to eat."

She disappeared down the hallway. I found the invitation both familiar and reassuring. Such formality was commonplace during my childhood. The island had a deep and long-standing connection to the South.

Fearing I might miss my chance to meet the younger woman, I started down the hall but Onward blocked my way.

"Dun, listen here." He leaned in, speaking under his breath. "We best get on back."

"We have time for a short break," I whispered.

"We just got started."

"You were early so I missed breakfast."

"Whit won't like it."

"He won't care long as he doesn't know."

11

"The shop has a load of work waiting," he added, "backed-up work, a week or more worth of it."

Out of patience, I started to push past him when Mrs. Langdon reappeared in the hallway. She brushed back her copper-colored hair and adjusted the turban.

"Come now, Mr. Osay, my granddaughter has decided to join us." She stood unsteadily, peering down the hall. "Oh, my, from this distance you remind me of someone I once knew quite intimately, a dark-eyed and handsome young man."

Her words left me unnerved but I wanted to meet her granddaughter so I motioned Onward forward. Before we had taken two steps, she raised a hand to stop us.

"Your helper can wait on the porch, Mr. Osay. There's a comfortable chair just outside the door. My cook will bring him a plate."

Unbelieving, I stared at her and felt my chance slipping away. I could no more leave Onward standing there, much less exile him to the porch, than I could rob a bank. An image of the younger woman flashed through my thoughts and I struggled to keep hold of it even as the vision faded. A part of me wanted to walk down to that sunroom and not look back. I had no responsibility for such mindless prejudice. Why should I have to pay for the failures of the past, a past I had nothing to do with?

I turned to him, feeling put-upon and resentful. I could see right away he knew me better than I knew myself. He leaned in close.

"You gone on, now," he said under his breath, "you go on like you want to and meet that girl, see what she's like up close."

"I don't know what you're talking about," I lied.

"We'll make up the time later."

"I'm just hungry is all."

"Go on, then."

I hesitated, unsure what to do. The good or bad in people again crossed my thoughts. Telling myself I had no hand in the despicable ways of this world, I started down the hall again when the self-satisfied look on Mrs. Langdon' face stopped me cold.

I pivoted and peered into Onward's dark eyes, eyes the color of black walnut, the drawn corner of one giving him a thoughtful yet melancholy air. My own reflection peered back. I turned and straightened myself.

"The truth is, Mrs. Langdon," I called to her, "Onward here is my partner. I believe we'd better just load up the crate and be on our way."

"But, you…" she said, flustered by my reply. "You're not hungry?"

"I had a big breakfast," I answered, surprised at how easily I managed the lie.

She walked back down the hall, pausing at a sideboard to refill her glass, then stopped and eyed me. After a moment, she reached for the crate.

"This box contains a family heirloom, Mr. Osay," she announced. She ran her hand along the rough planks. "The desk was sent by an agent handling my father's estate. He advised that we leave it in here as it is in need of repair.

"But this is no ordinary desk. The Civil War musket round that killed my great grandfather passed through the front right corner. My grandfather repaired the shattered leg himself. Years later, after financial ruin caused by Reconstruction, he shot himself while sitting before it. My father, a boy of only nine at the time, found him.

"You see, Mr. Osay, I believe spirits inhabit such old and revered objects, objects of tradition, objects that carry the past within them. The past must be honored, Mr. Osay, traditions must be maintained or we slip into disorder and anarchy. Do I make myself clear?"

The blood burned beneath my scalp. I knew she meant to say, in the roundabout way of rich people, that Onward would never be welcomed in her house. But I wasn't about to give her the satisfaction by letting on I understood. Instead, I let my gaze wander to the adjacent doorway where a three-foot high statue of a black boy stood as if awaiting orders. An iron ring dangled from his hand. She followed my eyes.

"There before you is just such an example," she continued. "That colored stable boy once stood at the entrance to my family home in Jackson. I set it below the stoop here in honor of my relations but vandals kept painting his face in white, so I was forced to move him to a less desirable location. This is the sort of disorder I refer to, Mr. Osay."

That about did it for me. Biting back my anger, I took a step closer.

"Mrs. Langdon, 'mam,'" I said in an exaggerated drawl, "we'll have your heirloom desk fixed up good as new and back here in short order. You can take my word, the word of a gentleman, on it." I managed a strained smile. I made a point of looking up and down the hallway and adjacent rooms, still hopeful her granddaughter might appear. "Then you can find the perfect place for it somewhere here in your beautiful house."

"Yes, well…" she paused, clearly puzzled by my change in demeanor, "I understand Mr. Whit Osay to be the best and most reliable at this sort of work."

I gave my head a solemn nod, hoping for a way to steer the conversation back to her granddaughter, when an idea came to me.

"Please give my apologies to Miss Langdon. Or I can tell her myself, if you like."

Seeing what I was up to, Onward gave his head a quick shake. Then, to my surprise, she appeared from behind the crate.

I thought I caught the trace of a smile cross her lips, but only for a second so I couldn't be sure. Her indifferent gaze seemed to look at me and past me at the same time, a manner that left me perturbed and speechless. Yet I could not turn away. Her hazel eyes had a softness that pulled me in and held me.

14

Onward cleared his throat and nodded toward the crate to get my attention. I ignored him, hoping the old lady would introduce us but she just waited there with a sour look on her face, saying nothing. I could see it was up to me to get things started but before I got a word out she moved beside her granddaughter, pulling her close.

"Mr. Osay was just leaving, Isabel," she said coolly. "He is evidently a very busy man."

Onward took hold of the crate and tested its weight, snapping me to attention before I made a complete fool of myself. I dragged my gaze from Isabel.

"That would be right, 'mam," I replied in a matter of fact tone. I positioned myself beside the crate. "Onward and I have a load of catching up to do."

Mrs. Langdon stepped aside as he tilted the box toward me and lifted one end. Moments later, we had it loaded and secure. He angled the truck away from the curb and I watched the yellow house fade into the distance, wondering what excuse I might find to return.

A deep chuckle drifted from the driver's seat. I turned to find him grinning at me.

"What are you so happy about?"

"You get back on this island less than a day and already you got yourself in love with some lady."

"I was just looking," I countered.

"Looking is right. Your eyes nearly fall right out of your head with all that looking."

"Well, you were no help, scaring the life out of the old lady like that."

"Thought she was getting robbed, she did."

We both laughed at the image, neither of us wanting to put into words the tired and stale bigotry we had just witnessed. Despite my lingering anger, the raven-haired Isabel roamed my thoughts. But how or even if I would see her again I could not imagine.

Three

The van slowed and turned away from the center of the island, rousing me from my daydream. My uncle's store had been located downtown, just off Post Office Street, ever since my grandfather had founded the business sixty years earlier. We were heading the opposite direction, into one of the older and poorer parts of town. I watched the scenery change and, rather than ask, decided to wait and see what he had in mind.

The large, stately homes soon gave way to smaller houses on tiny lots, the front lawns dotted with orange and lemon trees, loquat and fig. Garden plots lined with sweet potatoes, okra and peppers filled side yards. Here and there a dilapidated two-story house rose from the street like a monument to peeling paint and rotting wood. During Prohibition, the once-grand buildings had been home to a succession of brothels and speakeasies.

We made another turn and moved alongside a fence flecked with bits of lint, some the size of grapefruit. Beyond the chain-link, rows of car-sized cotton bales bound in gray canvas stretched to the edge of a battered wharf, recalling the island's slave-holding past. Giant machines now did the work of those many hands.

The road changed from asphalt to crushed oyster shell as we passed an abandoned warehouse scattered with discarded wooden boxes used for shipping tea. A rust-streaked freighter, the deck still empty, waited nearby. Half a block farther a row of shotgun houses came into view. Their narrow forms crowded each other like a book of multicolored matches. I turned to Onward, my curiosity finally winning out.

"You forget the way back," I quipped, "or what?"

"I got to go check on my Uncle Tarp. Won't take long."

"He's still alive?" An image of a wizened face, black as ripe plums, came to me. "He's your granduncle, isn't he?"

"Tarp is my grandfather's brother, the only one besides me to leave Mississippi."

"I always wondered how he got that name," I said, half to myself.

"There's a story to it, sure enough." He perked up. Onward loved to tell a story. "Tarp's mother worked a trawler out of Mobile. She was some kind of woman, stubborn as a mule and just as tough. That's where he got born, on the boat.

"Well, the only thing at hand to wrap him up in was a gray blanket the crew used for throwing dice, quarter a game. She called for it and then let the men come inside the cabin. First thing they told her was he looked like a little tarpon fish wrapped up tight like he was. The name just stuck."

"Why do you need to check on him?"

"He got this crazy idea from some preacher," he scoffed. "Thinks he got the power."

"The power?"

"Decided he turned prophet, hears directly from the Almighty. Tarp's always getting some idea or another in his head. Once he does, he can't put it down, just chews on it and worries it night and day. But old as he is, I'm afraid his mind is going. So, I got to check up on him now and again."

"You think he's gone senile?"

"Tarp can quote the Bible verse by verse. He knows the time the sun will rise on a given day to the minute. He can tell you the name of every star in the sky, no matter the season. So, I don't know." He glanced at me and gave his round head a slow shake. "Whatever you do, don't say even one thing about the weather, rain in particular, or else he'll go on so you won't ever get him to quit."

He pulled the truck next to a whitewashed, low-slung cottage wrapped in a mass of morning glory vines. The wide flowers shone iridescent blue in the scattered light. Under a sprawling live oak, a battered metal bucket held half a dozen bamboo poles fitted with cork and fishing line. Tattered throw nets drooped from a trio of sawhorses.

Onward slipped from the truck and moments later we stood before a narrow mahogany door, the center bowed out in a smooth arc. The name 'Feldberg' crossed the top in ornate script. I gave him a quizzical glance.

"Washed up in his yard last hurricane," he said in a matter of fact tone.

I peered at the strange form, finally recognizing the shape.

"The door is from a coffin?"

"From the lid, sure enough," he nodded. "The storm took his old door so he had to make do."

I grimaced at the thought of a coffin bobbing amid floodwaters where we now stood.

"Was anyone inside?"

Before he could answer, the door flew open and Uncle Tarp appeared wide-eyed and panting. His gaze finally settled on Onward and a look of disappointment replaced his surprise.

"Onward, I should've known it was you," he muttered. "That deep voice of yours rattle the windows."

"What'd you mean, uncle?"

"I thought old Feldberg had come to me from beyond the grave, come to take me across the River Jordan. Instead, it's only my grandnephew and some young man."

"We didn't mean to give you the fantods." Onward nodded in my direction. "You remember Dun Osay, don't you?"

He peered at me as if trying to decide if I was real or ghost. I figured the fantods still had hold of him.

"Your name's not Peter?" he finally said.

18

"What're you talking about, uncle?" Onward sighed. "I just told you this is Dun, Dun Osay."

"Look like Peter to me."

Unsure how to respond, I glanced at Onward. He kept his eye on the old man.

"Tarp, there's no Peter in the Osay family," he said, exasperated. "You know that."

The old man leaned in, studying me again.

"You're not Peter?"

"No sir, Mr. Cates."

"No need to call me nothing but Tarp." He took a step back and a wave of recognition slowly crossed his face. "Are you Mister August's son or Mister Whit's?"

"My father was Jimmy Osay."

He ran a hand along his jaw and considered my answer. The white stubble of his beard glistened against his blue-black skin.

"Yes, yes, I remember," he nodded. "Mister Jimmy was the youngest of the boys. His was a sorrowful story, truth be told. Got killed in that war, war that took too many young men, good young men, before you're even born if I remember right."

"Yes sir, that's right."

I gave my head an exaggerated nod, glad to move to another subject. But he leaned in and studied me again.

"You sure your name's not Peter?"

"I've been Dun my whole life."

I glanced at Onward again. The old man shifted his gaze, for a moment lost in thought.

"Why do I want to call you Peter, then?" he said to himself. "Unless… unless… yes, that must be, it sure must be."

"Uncle, we got to…" Onward began. I could see he wanted to steer the conversation elsewhere. "We have work…"

Tarp raised a hand to stop him and turned his red-rimmed eyes back on me.

19

"Listen here, Dun Osay. God gave me a message and I mean to tell you it." He waved a crooked finger in my face. "No way to get around it, you will deny your brother three times over, as the Apostle Peter did Jesus, before a week's time gone past."

"But I don't have a brother," I replied, not knowing what to make of the pronouncement.

"You sure about that? Can't never tell who might be kin in this mixed-up world."

His eyes grew wide and he glanced at Onward as if expecting a reprimand. I shook my head in answer, not knowing what to make of him.

"Someone like a brother, then," he added, shooting Onward another glance.

"And I'll deny them?"

"Uh-huh, three times over, just like Saint Peter."

"Three times…" I repeated, unnerved by his grave tone. "What will I deny them of?"

"Can't say for sure but got to be important," he nodded solemnly. "Wouldn't come to me like it did otherwise ways."

Onward nudged me aside and stuck his head through the door.

"Uncle, what's that I smell?"

"What?" He glanced over his shoulder. "Oh, I'm frying up a chicken. You want some?"

Onward pushed past him and disappeared in a rush. Tarp ambled after him. I followed reluctantly, still rattled by the strange conversation. Moments later, I found Onward standing at the kitchen sink, a sizzling frying pan in his hand. Smoke drifted below the ceiling like a rolling fog. He lowered the pan and glared at his uncle.

"Tarp, you can't leave a stove untended when you got something on," he barked. "The grease in that pan was about to light up, take this place with it. Then what would you do?"

Tarp straightened himself and poked a finger in Onward's chest, his face rigid with anger.

"Don't you talk to me like I'm some six-year-old child, goddammit!" He whirled around and started pacing the floor. "I got a stored-up lifetime of being treated less than a man and I don't need a goddamn scolding from you or anybody else to remind me what I put up with. You hear what I'm telling you nephew?"

"I hear you, Tarp," he muttered, head down.

"This is my house and I do what I like in my own house. Nobody going to tell me how to live my life, where I go and don't go, where I sit and don't sit, what fountain I drink from, what fountain I got to stay away from. That day is gone, you hear me?"

"Yes sir."

He stopped before Onward and peered at him with a fierce intensity that slowly faded.

"Your daddy," he finally said, "he was a good man."

Onward flinched at the mention of his father. Tarp leaned closer.

"He raised you up to respect your elders. Tell me I'm right."

"You're right, Tarp," he answered. "I mean no disrespect when I care about your safety."

He turned and started pacing again, more stooped with every passing, and then stopped and eased himself onto a chair.

"Alright, then," he sighed, "no harm done. Besides which, not me that's to blame anyhow, no sir. That old witch next door put a hex on me after I sprayed her dog with the water hose. Did his business in my garden for the last time. Got him good too.

"But now I'm hexed and everything's gone bad," he added, "breaking and burning and such. Lost a fishing pole to a fish just this morning."

He faced me as if a thought had suddenly come to him.

21

"You like to fish, Dun Osay?"

"I like it fine if it isn't too cold or rain..."

The words had left my mouth before I could stop myself. Onward pivoted, glaring at me.

"Now you listen here, young Osay," Tarp announced, pointing to the ceiling. "When you go out in that rain, you watch out for the mud pools. Mud pool will eat up your car lickety-split, you along with it, drown you like a rat in a barrel of molasses.

"Mud pool not easy to see neither, no sir. That rain gets to falling and there they come, deep as a river and just as ready to take you under. They hide and wait, wait and hide, looking for people to come along that don't know better. That's why I tell you now. You got to be on the lookout or else they take you, you and your car both.

"Now if the weather goes too low, you got to watch out for that black ice. Black ice will hide and wait too. You never see that black ice and before you know it..."

"Tarp, we got to go now," Onward broke in. He waved at the sink. "You may be able to do something with the chicken but I don't know."

Tarp stood and peered into the sink.

"That chicken's just fine, good and done," he mumbled to himself. He lifted the pan and sniffed. "Makes no never mind if it's a little crispy."

"You stay with it next time," Onward added, "and it'll be just right."

I followed when he started for the door. At the street he paused and turned to me as if he had something to say, the same mix of consternation and affection I had seen earlier crossing his broad face. I stood by waiting for him to speak. Instead he motioned me to the truck without another word.

Fie

Seeing Dun in the doorway the night of his return nearly brought me to tears, he so looked like his father, Jimmy. In that brief moment a memory of our last summer in Mississippi swept over me as if it was the river itself, swift and unyielding. The recollection still held a vivid clarity despite the intervening years.

Throughout childhood I and my brothers, Whit, Jimmy and August spent two weeks of every July with our extended family in Mississippi. Our stays were accompanied by a slew of traditions, watermelon on the back lawn, homemade ice cream, cards after dinner. My last visit captured the moment before adulthood responsibilities crowded out the simplicity of youth.

As the youngest of the four Jimmy always enjoyed a freedom I could only dream of. My role as oldest, if only by about three minutes, was to lead by example and if that failed, by force of will. Ours was a family of matriarchs. There was no halfway in my mother's view, only success or failure.

That final summer was unusually wet even for a place as storm-prone as Mississippi. Nearly every afternoon the sun would vanish and the sky fill with clouds, soon followed by the roll of thunder. Before long lamps were required to fix supper or read despite it being the middle of the day.

For us young people the inclement weather was a curse, but to my considerable annoyance Aunt Sophie, my mother's sister, seemed to thrive amid the gloom. I suppose it was the romantic in her. Once the rain started she would inevitably grab a book and migrate to the veranda. I expected my vacation to be sun-filled and littered with flowers, not to mention boys. Instead, the few blooms that dared show themselves were soon beat to nothing by the daily deluge, and boys were scarce as sunshine.

Like the dismal weather, Jimmy was not his usual self that summer. His military draft notice had arrived in the mail just before our departure. There was no question he would be called up. Because Whit and Augie had been spared the draft I naturally assumed Jimmy had no reason to worry. That was my first lesson in the power of self-deception.

The prospect of Jimmy going into combat weighed on us all but, for obvious reasons, particularly on him. By that point the war was widely regarded as a perverse form of Russian roulette. Photos of the dead and wounded were routine on the nightly news. Jimmy adopted the attitude he had nothing to lose, thumbing his nose at the few rules we were supposed to follow and coming and going however he pleased. Needless to say, I was perturbed by the change.

True to form, I did my best to rein him in but to little effect. Though he was never unkind in ignoring my direction, the snub hurt nonetheless. He had always been my favorite. Adding insult to injury, his brothers took his side. Looking back, I can see how my self-importance deserved taking down a notch or two. But of course I was too proud to see it at the time.

As if Jimmy's rebelliousness was not enough, Augie suddenly became nearly impossible to live with. He'd always had a surly streak. But midway though our visit he went from testy to downright belligerent. I was at a loss to understand why and he made it clear he had no intention of explaining.

Some nights he would sneak off to drink beer with the neighbor boys and return later spoiling for a fight. Other times he would just sulk around the house. Either way he could explode for the smallest of reasons. Although he directed most of his anger at Jimmy, we all got a share at one time or another.

Whit looked on with a bemused lack of concern, as if he had expected to spend his vacation in a lunatic asylum. I knew he would come to my defense if Augie went too far *but otherwise he kept clear of the fray. I found his natural-born talent for toleration infuriating, mostly because it was a quality I did not share despite being his twin.*

In an attempt to maintain my sanity, I began spending more time with Aunt Sophie. In those days it was common for families to hire a cook, and Sophie's cook, Bea, had been with them since before I was born. She had a daughter, Viola, only a few years younger than me so I soon found myself helping around the kitchen just for the female company. I'd had about all I could stand of the male gender.

Since Bea planned the meals, she shopped for groceries as well. One morning as she and Viola were about to leave on a shopping expedition I decided to ask if I could join them. I was hoping a change of scene might boost my sagging spirits. Up until that point my vacation had been a disappointment, to put it mildly.

Despite the fact that I had been so bold as to invite myself along, Bea and Viola accepted my intrusion with grace. Our first stop was the home of her middle sister, Opal. A third sister, Ophelia, lived in Mobile. Their family had known mine for generations though I had no way of knowing how many. My mother refused to discuss her side of the family, a mystery I was a long time in unraveling.

Opal was known for her homemade butter and when we arrived she was just finishing up a fresh batch. She set Viola and me to packing a large tub while she and Bea drank coffee and gossiped. I did my best to listen in.

Now and then I ventured a glance at Viola. I sensed she had something on her mind and was trying to decide whether to tell me. I could not imagine what.

By the time the tub was nearly full I had heard nothing memorable from either Bea or Opal, to my considerable disappointment. A juicy bit of gossip would have done wonders for my morale. The mere thought of returning to my aunt's house with nothing to show for it depressed me.

I had about given up hope of any excitement whatsoever when the back door swung open and a gray-haired woman in a purple dress and sequined hat stepped through. She took one look at me and frowned, muttering under her breath a musical "umm, umm, umm" in descending notes. Leaning close to Opal, she whispered something out of hearing, glancing at me all the while. Then she eased into a chair and sat back, signaling she had news to tell.

I could see Viola intended to listen in so I gave her a knowing look and we slowed our work, doing our best to prolong the stay. After the usual preliminary small talk required of polite conversation in that part of the world, the woman pressed her palm to the tabletop. I tried not to be too obvious in my eavesdropping.

"One of our local girls has got herself in the family way," she began.

Viola flinched, locking eyes with me for an instant before catching herself. Bea and Opal gave her a worried glance. The woman nodded solemnly.

"Uh-huh," she hummed. "That Dewberry girl is already showing."

The sisters took a breath and leaned across the table as if to better hear.

"Nobody is saying who the father is," she added, "but I bet you can guess."

Bea raised her eyebrows in answer.

"That's right," she continued. "Everybody knows Leon Jackson's been snooping around that house for months."

"Her mother must be beside herself," Opal replied.

"She's got a relative in Nashville," the woman nodded, "a cousin I believe."

"She's going to have the baby there?"

"She may already be on the train."

"Being sent away is a hard lesson," Bea sighed, "but I can understand their decision. Her parents must feel they have failed her."

"Lordy, I'm glad sister Ophelia isn't here with us right now," Opal cackled. "She'd be going on about a woman's right to decide what happens to her own body and how parents fool themselves instead of teaching their daughters the facts of life."

"Nobody around here is fooled," the woman said, shaking her gray head, "no matter what that family might go and do."

Thunder rumbled outside and Bea stood, motioning us to seal the tub. When I set the lid in place Viola's hand touched mine and I felt her fingers trembling. She raised her eyes. For the briefest of moments she looked at me as if we had just shared a secret. Only years later would I come to understand why.

Four

The small houses and shotgun shacks disappeared behind us, replaced by ever-larger homes. Ropes of cloud streamed overhead on the coursing wind. The warm air carried hints of honeysuckle and gardenia.

The rich fragrance recalled an image of Fie perched on the porch swing, her preferred daytime reading spot. Whit had always kept a well-tended gardenia bush just off the front steps. When I was a child the lush aroma would surround us as we whiled away a Saturday afternoon on the veranda.

The truck passed along a shade-dappled street lined with live oaks. Strands of Spanish moss dangled from their blackened limbs, drifting before the restless breeze like smoke. Seagulls rose and floated briefly on the turbulence before vanishing over the treetops.

At an intersection, I caught sight of a small sign midway down the block. Suddenly, I remembered my need to find an apartment. I grabbed Onward's wrist and pointed to his left.

"Go that way."

"Might as well waste some more time," he muttered. "You find yourself another woman to chase after?"

"Worse than that." I craned my neck, trying to keep sight of the sign. "I need to find an apartment right away."

"You're not staying at home? You got to know your Aunt Fie will want you there."

"I'd go nuts, Onward."

"You tell her that?"

"Are you kidding? I told her I already had a place to live."

"You're a brave man, lying to Fie," he chuckled, "brave or stupid."

"Well, right now I'm not feeling so brave."

He pulled alongside the curb before a white two-story house. A row of sky-blue columns edged the porch and balcony, reaching to the roofline. Floor to ceiling windows, seemingly without blinds or curtains, flanked the front door.

I hopped from the truck, searching for the sign, finally spotting it hidden behind a squat palm. The hand-lettered ad read 'Garage Apartment for Rent'. I started for the house and then stopped as a man stepped through the door.

Wearing plaid pants and a silk bowling shirt, he resembled a conventioneer on his way to happy hour. A thin mustache edged his top lip. He brushed back a thick matt of hair, smiled and motioned me closer with a shy wave, as if anything stronger might offend.

Before I'd taken a step, the door again opened and a younger man moved onto the porch. Short and wiry, in cutoff jeans and flip-flops, he seemed the opposite of his companion. A torn half-shirt barely covered his chest. He sauntered to the stairs and squinted at me.

"If you're one of those macho surfers," he sneered, "you can forget renting the apartment."

Wondering what I had walked into, I glanced toward the truck. Onward sat unmoving behind the windshield, his face impassive. I guessed he figured I deserved whatever I got.

"Ronny, be nice," the older man muttered, "or you'll convince our guest we're uncivilized."

"Surfers think they're so buff in their tight wetsuits," he continued. Bleached hair jutted from the top of his head in tiny spikes. "It makes me want to puke."

"You're only jealous because I can't help but watch when they pass by."

The man brushed back his hair again and descended the stairs, moving toward me with a smooth grace that belied his round form. He gave my hand a light squeeze.

"Ronny comes from up north," he whispered in a lilting drawl, "and has yet to learn the value of our southern

29

ways. A little hospitality makes life go down easier, yes it does. I'm Moon Thibodaux, recently relocated from New Orleans."

For reasons I could not explain, I took an immediate liking to him. Within minutes I had told him the entire story of why I needed an apartment. He took me by the arm and led me up the stairs and through the door.

An immaculate room stretched before us, the hardwood floors polished to a high sheen, the walls scattered with abstract paintings. Spare and uncluttered, the place resembled an art gallery.

He ushered me through the kitchen, down the back steps and across a small yard to a two-story garage. An outdoor staircase stretched from the alley to a small landing. Overhanging the stairway, a stout palm cast the porch in a greenish glow.

He pointed me up the stairs. Moments later we stood inside the apartment, two rooms and a small kitchen, all tastefully furnished. Green storm shutters covered several windows. The hardwood floors shimmered beneath the overhead light. This place, too, was immaculate. I was lucky to happen upon such a find.

"Warm and cozy, don't you think, Dun?" He smiled and then flashed an exaggerated frown at me. "But I'm sorry to say there's no air conditioning. That's why Francine put in storm shutters, to let the breeze in on rainy days, of which we have an unfortunate abundance. I, myself, am a child of the sun."

"She was the previous tenant?"

"Not exactly. Francine was my aunt. She grew up in the main house." He paused to survey the room. "This building was used as servant's quarters, slavery being gone by then, thank goodness. The area below us was once a stable.

"When Francine passed this last spring, I inherited the house along with her small fortune."

He stared out the window, for a moment lost in thought, and then turned, bending close to my ear.

"I'll tell you a shameful secret, Dun Osay," he whispered. "Though my inheritance was modest, it left me no longer in need of gainful employment."

"You don't have to work?" I said in disbelief.

All at once, the directionless state of my existence again enveloped me. On the surface, it made little sense. I had a job teaching English at a small Catholic school. And I'd known several women, though none for long. There was nothing wrong with the work or the women. The problem resided within me. Moon took a step back.

"Oh my, that look on your face," he whispered, putting a hand to his mouth. "Is that disapproval? It is, isn't it?"

"I have no business judging anyone," I muttered.

"You don't think it's shameful to be so rich?"

I shrugged, not knowing what to say.

"I believe I might," he continued. "I sometimes think I need a vocation but I have no idea what I would do."

"Take it from me and find something you enjoy, and then throw yourself into it."

"Yes, well, if only life was that simple." He suddenly jerked to attention and gestured around the room as if seeing it for the first time. "But then fate intervenes, Dun! Circumstance takes control and, like it or not, work becomes optional."

"That's hard to imagine."

"Yes, in more ways than you might think. Overnight you become everyone's friend, especially among those who care nothing about you.

"On the other hand, the beautiful people suddenly and inexplicably find you appealing." He pressed his back to the wall, stretching out his arms with dramatic flourish. "I won't lie and say I'd rather be a wallflower. One must adjust."

"You don't mind that their friendship is a sham?"

31

"Oh, Dun, you are the innocent one." He dismissed my question with a wave, resuming a normal pose. "Anyone will deceive to have what they want if they think they can get away with it."

"There's a depressing thought," I said, half to myself.

"Don't kid yourself, Dun, the honest soul is a rarity. Everyone has their secrets. Most people are just out for themselves, an unpleasant yet unavoidable truth."

"But you put up with it anyway?"

"Ah, yes. You see, above all else, I want to be wanted. Being wanted gives me purpose."

His words filled my head with a throbbing ache. Suddenly, I needed to be out of there.

"I'll take the apartment," I said as I brushed past him.

"Did I say something wrong?" he called after me.

The following morning, having spent a restless night in my new home, I stood before the downtown post office. I had arranged for my mail to be forwarded there temporarily. Also serving as the customs house, the stone building shone white against the cerulean sky. Scattered clouds drifted overhead on a steady breeze.

I walked up the sidewalk and paused before the ornate bronze and glass entrance. Palm trees flanking the doorway rattled nervously. I pushed through and into a high-ceilinged room that ended in a long counter crowded with people despite the early hour. The mailboxes were in an adjacent room to the right.

I angled across the polished tiles, my head down as I fumbled with the box key. The cramped space was busy with people. Dodging the main part of the crowd, I slipped along the wall and found the box. The tiny, glass-fronted door opened with ease. A single envelope rested inside. Lifting it out, I held it to the light, spotting the Catholic school's return address on the top left corner.

I pondered for a moment why the school might write. I still had vacation time left. Unsealing the flap, I pulled

32

out the single sheet of letterhead and quickly scanned the few lines. The school was combining classes to save money. My position had been eliminated. Unbelieving, I read and reread the message.

I forced my eyes from the page. The bustling crowd surged by me. I envied their sense of purpose but I could not watch and instead shifted my gaze back to the letter, seeing nothing, hearing nothing.

When I finally looked up again Isabel Langdon stood before me. I blinked and looked again. Her hazel eyes held none of the casual indifference of our first meeting. She brushed a strand of silk-like hair from her lips, tucking it behind an ear. All at once I was mesmerized.

"You're Dun Osay," she announced as if I had forgotten my own name. "You came to my grandmother's house yesterday to pick up a crate of furniture."

"I remember," I managed.

She studied me and then moved in close, as if to shield me from the crowd.

"You don't look so good." She nodded at the envelope. "Bad news?"

"I just moved into a new apartment," I replied, managing to split the space between truth and lie, "and I didn't sleep so well."

Telling her the whole truth would make me out a failure. Or so I thought. The last thing I wanted was her sympathy.

"The school where I teach English," I added, raising the envelope to bolster my claim, "wants me to know they have my classes covered while I'm gone."

Gone permanently as it turns out. Another half-truth.

"You must feel gratified to know you're helping to make a better future for your students, not to mention the world."

Her words settled over me like a cold rain. Suddenly, I felt the sting not only of my lost job but of my failure to appreciate it. I had seen teaching as just a salary, a job less important, less impressive than what I'd always imagined myself doing. I wondered how else I had blinded myself to what the world had to offer. The list of possibilities seemed endless.

"I thought you restored furniture for a living," she added.

"I came here to help with the family business," I replied, relieved to finally tell the truth. "My uncle is sick."

"He must really worry you." She leaned close and peered into my face. "Are you sure you're okay?"

I had no answer. This was not the sort of second meeting I'd hoped for.

"I'm so sorry," she said, checking her watch. "I can see you're having a bad day. But I can't be late for work again."

She disappeared through the doorway. I stood unmoving, dazed by all that had happened. In the time it took me to read the letter my previous life had vanished like a puff of smoke. I could see little reason for returning to what until then had been my home. Suddenly I felt disconnected from all I had known. I needed something tangible and solid to grab on to. So I began pushing through the crowd toward the one certainty I could think of, unfortunate as it might be, my uncle's store.

Five

Later that afternoon, I stood by as Onward pried open the crate. The desk Mrs. Langdon had described slowly came into view, damaged on one corner and scarred from use but otherwise intact. The opaque finish, crossed by web of miniscule cracks, held a blackish-brown hue.

I bent for a closer look. In a few well-worn spots I could make out the unmistakable grain of black walnut, dense and linear. Onward whistled between his teeth. He knew better than most the potential beauty hiding beneath the old varnish.

We slid the desk onto the cement floor. Located in the back of my uncle's furniture store, the room served as an on-site repair and refinishing shop. I knelt before the brass-handled drawers, lifting them out one by one and checking for cracks or loose joints, the first step in our ritual. Once I had finished repairing any damage, Onward would strip off the old varnish, sand and re-stain the bare wood and apply a new coat of varnish.

He disappeared down the hallway, leaving me to my work. I set the drawers on end one by one and stood, suddenly struck by a subtle difference. While the front panels were identical, the inside of the top drawer was several inches wider than the other two.

I knelt again and reached into desk, palpating the inside wall and finding a rectangular extension extending upward from the bottom. A narrow recess lined the upper edge. I slipped my index finger into the space and pulled, lifting off a thin panel and setting it aside. I reached back in and traced the outline of a metal container.

Within seconds, I had the box cradled in my lap. I grabbed a rag and rubbed the tarnished lid. An oval of silver emerged from the surface. I rubbed another spot and a maze of gold filigree appeared along the outer edge. That such an heirloom must be worth a small fortune crossed my thoughts, followed by the near certainty Mrs. Langdon had no awareness of its existence, and then by the pitiful state of my finances. If the box should disappear, she would never know the difference.

I forced the notion from my mind, instead flipping open the latch and lifting the lid. A sheaf of yellowed papers covered with a cramped longhand lay before me. A spiral of cotton thread bound the pages together. I guessed the book to be a diary or journal of some sort.

I tossed the papers into a nearby drawer and again turned my attention to the silver box, trying to imagine who might want it and how much they'd be willing to pay. I had almost convinced myself that finding a hidden treasure gave me the right to keep it. Then Fie's voice intruded on my daydream, arguing to the contrary like a spare conscience.

I decided I needed time to think and Whit's old filing cabinet offered the perfect hiding place. I stood but before I could take a single step Griggs walked into the room. I sat and slipped the box back inside the desk, trying to look nonchalant. If I hadn't already realized my mistake, his furrowed brow would have told me. The hint of a smile crossed his lips.

Nothing about him said he'd been away from the island for long. With his sun-bleached hair and chiseled features, he looked every bit the carefree beach bum. But I knew beneath that laidback demeanor lurked a shameless opportunist.

Growing up together, Griggs and I were closer than any brothers. I looked up to him in all ways that mattered, and for good reason. He was clever, adept at every sport, and always seemed to have several girlfriends at once, a feat I could not in all my wildest dreams imagine. My love life had been a long series of fits and starts, with me keeping my guard up as if I expected a bad end, and the girls all eventually tiring of my game. Little had changed in the years since.

I studied his slate-blue eyes, trying to remember the last time I'd seen him. His indifferent and irresponsible ways frustrated me more often than not, but looking at him now I knew I'd still do most anything for him if the need arose. I owed him. He'd stepped in for me more times than I could remember.

But there was another more powerful reason for my loyalty. Growing up, I'd witnessed the way his father treated him, belittling his dreams, criticizing his every move. That he had retreated into a devil-may-care irresponsibility made perfect sense. In his place, I might have done the same.

He pulled a paint-splattered wicker chair over and sat, peering at me with the same mixture of curiosity and mirth I remembered so well. An image of a bug under a magnifying glass flashed through my thoughts, followed by annoyance that he still had such an effect on me. I squinted back at him, trying to banish the thought.

"It's been a while, cousin," he said in his smooth drawl, "but you haven't changed a bit."

"You mean other than the crow's feet."

"They just give you character, Dun. Besides, the ladies love them."

"I wouldn't know," I muttered, irritated that the conversation had so quickly turned to my shortcomings. "Not everyone is as lucky with women as you."

Without thinking, I glanced at the desk. He sat back and eyed me.

"So, are you going to tell me?"

"Tell you what?"

"You know what."

"No, Griggs, I don't."

"You never were much good at lying, Dun," he smirked. "Your face tells the story whether you like it or not."

"I don't follow," I stalled, unwilling to give in.

"I'm your cousin, Dun." He leaned closer. "Don't you trust me?"

"Of course I trust you."

"Then come clean."

I took a breath, unnerved by the familiar exchange. The words seemed plucked straight out of our childhood. He nodded toward the desk.

"What'd you have in there?"

I could see that stalling further was pointless so I turned and retrieved the box, setting it on the floor between us. He ran his fingers over the top as if they could tell him how the heirloom came to be. Then he lifted it, testing its weight and feel.

"It's valuable?"

"Solid silver is my guess." I motioned toward the desk. "I found it in a hidden compartment."

"It has to be worth a bundle," he whispered before glancing down the hallway. "Does anyone else know?"

"No." I grabbed it from him. "I don't like that look, Griggs."

"So, there's a silver box," he mused," and no one knows it exists but you."

"And now you," I muttered.

"But the owner doesn't know?"

"I don't see how."

"What are you going to do with it?"

"Don't get any ideas, Griggs. This is my problem and I'll figure it out."

"Problem?" He sat back, grinning. "How can finding a priceless treasure no one else knows about be a problem?"

I nodded toward the store.

"Aren't you supposed to be at work or something?"

He glanced at the hallway and then jumped up, frantically searching the room.

"Someone's coming," he hissed. "Hide it quick!"

I bolted across the room and jerked open the filing cabinet, slipping in the box. An instant later Whit strolled in. He eyed me a moment and then faced Griggs, his expression morphing from suspicion to annoyance.

"You were due back twenty minutes ago," he grumbled.

"I've been in here helping Dun," he lied, somehow managing to sound both convincing and offended.

Whit looked at him askance.

"It's true, Uncle Whit." He rapped the desktop with his knuckles. "He needed my advice on how best to handle this repair. Tell him, Dun."

Whit waved off the excuse before I had a chance to speak. He pointed Griggs down the hallway.

"Since you're in such a generous mood," he snipped, "go find Onward. He's the one that needs your help now."

Griggs ambled off muttering to himself. Whit started for the exit.

"Come on, Dun," he called over his shoulder. He almost sounded happy. "You're giving me a ride."

Six

I made the turn onto Broadway but instead of south and the way home, Whit pointed me north toward the ferry landing. When I gave him a quizzical look he just motioned the truck on without explanation. Minutes later, we bumped onto the near-empty boat. I parked along the bayside gunwale and followed him to the bow.

The channel stretched away from us toward the open water of the bay and on to the loading docks and warehouses of the port. To the southwest, the brackish waters of Chocolate Bayou meandered between salt grass marshes and mangrove swamps, finally merging with the Gulf at San Luis Pass.

As a boy, I spent summer days roaming the shallows of the pass in search of blue crab and flounder, just as Whit had when he was a boy. I glanced at him, puzzling over our destination. His eyes held a feverish intensity I'd never before seen.

The ferry engines rumbled beneath the deck, belching a plume of black smoke into the air. Clouds of silt roiled the surrounding water. With a lurch, we moved past the dockside pilings and into the gray-green channel. To our right a pair of orange marker buoys marking the deeper water tilted southward on the outgoing tide.

I was reminded of the many times he and I had made the crossing. Something about the wilder, less crowded peninsula had always drawn him, had always seemed to lift his spirits. I wondered whether he needed a boost just then or if he had another purpose in mind.

Whit was as close to a father as I would ever know. Joining with Fie to raise me rather than hand me over to the authorities, he had taken on his role without question or complaint. His gruff manner scared me as a child and often landed him in hot water with her, but he could be patient and kindhearted at the most unexpected moments.

I suddenly found myself wanting to tell him of the silver box, to ask what he would do if he had been the one to find it. His unconventional views, more like a man in his twenties than his sixties, often surprised me. But the urge soon passed, cancelled by my indecision.

I studied the approaching shoreline, feeling the strangeness of my return, subtle yet undeniable. Like the island, the peninsula seemed different from what I remembered, familiar yet changed, known yet mysterious. Whether the difference resided within me or otherwise, I could not say. Either way, I found it unsettling.

As if sensing my troubles, Whit pointed me toward a faded red building perched above the water on an army of wooden pilings. Colored lights stretched from corner to corner. Music drifted from the wooden deck, rising above the engine roar for an instant and then vanishing on the wind. The distraction worked. Now firmly back in the moment, I breathed in the salt-laced air.

We exited the ferry and turned off the highway, bouncing down a rutted shell road between scattered tidal pools and sand dunes. Dense stands of prickly pear cactus dotted the windswept slopes. Seagulls lined the flats like penny arcade ducks.

The dunes soon parted and the weathered building reappeared, pinkish-gray and sagging. I parked beside the stairway. A sign over the door read 'Last Chance Bar' in alternating black and red letters.

I wondered again why Whit had brought us to the peninsula and, especially, to this dilapidated bar. Before I had a chance to ask he was out of the truck and up the stairs. At the top step, he paused, red-faced and panting. I offered my hand but he reared back, giving me a look that meant he would tolerate no pity.

Instead, he pointed me inside. I pushed through the door and into a windowless space filled with pool tables and barstools. A blend of cigarette smoke and neon cast the room in a garish red, as if the air itself was tinted with

41

color. Across the dance floor, two men bent over a billiard table glanced at us distractedly before returning to their game.

Whit moved to a corner booth and grabbed an empty beer bottle from a nearby table, waving it at the bartender. Then he pulled a half-smoked cigar and book of matches from his shirt pocket. His face flickered beneath the flame, briefly regaining its natural color before fading back into the red haze.

"Should you be doing that?" I frowned.

Ignoring the question, he rolled the cigar between his fingers and eyed me as if deciding how to begin.

"You're wondering what we're doing here," he finally said.

Two beers appeared before us. He pushed a bottle toward me and lifted the other, taking a long pull.

"You spent the day with Onward," he continued. "How does he seem to you?"

"Why are you asking?"

"Do you make a habit of answering a question with a question?" He blew a thin stream of smoke into the air.

"No, do you?"

I disliked being argumentative but I hated talking about Onward behind his back. Whit leaned across the table.

"I can't put my finger on it, but ever since his trip to Mississippi he's been different."

"Different in what way?"

"He seems evasive and secretive, like he's hiding something."

"You don't trust him?"

I thought again of the silver box. He gave his head a quick shake.

"I wouldn't put it like that. It's just… he seems like he has something on his mind, something troubling. You can see it in his eyes."

I remembered the expression I had noticed first at the Langdon home and, later, when leaving Tarp's house.

"Why not ask him?"

"Onward doesn't take well to snooping. Besides, you two have always been close. I thought he might've said something."

I shook my head in answer, annoyed by his probing.

"You're sure?"

"Yep, I'm sure"

"You noticed nothing out of the...?"

"You're asking me to spy on him," I interrupted, incredulous.

"Don't go overboard..."

"How could you even think I would do something like that?"

"Okay, okay, I get the message." He waved off my complaint. "What about you, then?"

"What about me?"

"When are you going to get your life together?"

I stared at him, taken aback by the unexpected comment and all that it implied. That I had yet to tell him I'd lost my job only made it worse.

"Since when do you get to be the judge of how I live?" I snapped. "Fie was right. You're just itching for an argument."

"That's not true," he said with a sigh, "... or fair."

"Then you think I'm a failure."

"You know I didn't mean it like that."

"What other meaning can there be?"

"I'm interested. Is that okay?"

I shrugged.

"What work is it that you do?" he asked.

"I teach." I had no choice but to continue the lie. "You should know that by now."

"I don't recall ever hearing you talk about work."

I had no answer, knowing he was probably right.

"Don't you like what you do for a living?"

"I suppose so."

Unable to get past the notion I should be doing something more with my life, I sounded less than convincing. Besides the teaching job, which paid next to nothing, I had clerked at a shoe store. Before that, I drove a delivery truck.

"How about female companionship?"

Seeing Griggs again had only highlighted my other big failure, women. The last thing I wanted was to discuss my love life.

"What about it?" I muttered.

"Anyone in the picture?"

"No one serious just now." I tried to sound unconcerned. "I'm pretty busy."

"You said that the last time I asked."

"Did I?" I stared at the floor, my thoughts so twisted I could barely muster an answer. "I don't remember."

He leaned closer, looking pained.

"Don't spend your life alone, Dun," he said, his voice just above a whisper. "It's no way to live. Trust me, I know. Find someone you want to share your time with, someone you can confide in, or before you know it you'll end up out of time."

His words knotted in my chest. I tried to tell myself his comments were the misconceptions of an old man, but their truth seemed inescapable. My head felt incredibly heavy.

A pair of red shoes appeared beside the table. I looked up to find an attractive, middle-aged woman in a purple dress smiling down at me. She slipped beside Whit and peered into my eyes as if she knew me.

"I can spot you Osay men anywhere," she said in a difficult to place accent, "so handsome with your dark hair and blue eyes."

She turned and flashed Whit a smile, lightly touching the side of his face.

"You are looking better, I think, Whitford."

"Don't spread it around," he said, putting a finger to his lips, "or they'll put me back to work."

"But it is true."

"My dark hair vanished long ago, in case you haven't noticed."

"Yes, but I still remember when we first met." She took his hand and pressed it to her chest. "You were some kind of a man then, and, in case you haven't noticed, I still think this."

I sat speechless, unable to imagine him as anything but old and uninterested in romance, much less sex.

"Dun, I want you to meet Connie," he announced as if reading my thoughts.

"Connie is Whit's name for me." She offered her hand. "My real name is Consuela Menendez. But I think you, as an Osay, shall call me Connie also."

"Connie is an old acquaintance," he added.

"I am not so old," she said, frowning. "I have known Whit many years, but first as a friend and customer. After my husband died, we became more than friends. It will be ten years next month."

I wondered at how little you can really know of someone. They had been seeing each other a decade yet I had no idea. Whit leaned across the table.

"Connie's the only person I've ever met who can speak five languages. She's an executive for a Dutch shipping company."

"Whit, you make me sound too important," she protested. "It is a job only."

"Say something dirty in French," he whispered loud enough for me to hear.

To my relief, she ignored him.

"I was born in Mexico," she continued, "but my father was German so I heard many languages from a young age. When this happens, it is easy to learn."

The jukebox suddenly started and she jumped from her chair, grabbing his hand. I cringed at the thought of him trying to dance in his weakened state. Yet moments later, he was moving with her across the dance floor, slow but without obvious difficulty.

Deciding I needed another beer, I started for the bar. An instant later the door flew open, filling the room with sunlight and temporarily blinding me. I stopped in mid-stride and waited for the dim, red-tinted room to reappear. Instead, a woman's face emerged from the haze, a face framed by a loose mass of sun-streaked hair, familiar yet changed, like the world I had just passed through. A smile spread across her lips, moving to her blue-gray eyes, eyes that held me with a knowing look.

"Dun Osay," she whispered.

I stood transfixed, my mind awash with images from my past, some sun-filled, others sultry.

"Marti Finch," I finally replied with a voice that seemed not my own.

She grabbed my hand, pulling me to a corner booth and squeezing in next to me. She smelled of soap and lavender. I stared at her, unable to speak. Long-neglected memories skipped along my thoughts like light across water. Years had passed since I had last seen her, more than I could say, but I knew for certain she had never looked so good. I blinked and looked again.

I had known Marti my entire life. She had grown up a block away, on the corner of 26th and Avenue P, and we had shared many of the same classes in school. I remembered her as a thin and freckled tomboy, but the woman before me was filled-out and radiant. Her eyes held the same merry confidence I remembered.

"Dun Osay, is it really you?" she said, breathless. "What on earth are you doing in the Last Chance, of all places? I figured by now you'd be travelling the world, writing stories for some magazine."

"Fie sent for me," I muttered, dismayed that my life in no way lived up to her image. "Uncle Whit has been sick, so I'm taking time off to help with the business."

"You mean the furniture store?"

"Not exactly travelling the world," I replied, "but unavoidable."

"You're a good soul to offer your help," she said softly, laying her hand on mine. "I hope he'll be well soon."

Her touch sent a jolt through me and I wondered for an instant if she could see me blush in the crimson haze. Determined to avoid any more talk of my life, I slipped my hand free and gestured toward the bar, where the group she had come in with stood drinking.

"Who are your friends and why are you all wearing the same…" I suddenly realized the pink jacket she had on was in truth a white lab coat. Her name, embroidered across the chest pocket, was followed by the letters M. D. I looked up into her face, unable to hide my surprise. "You're… you're a doctor?"

"Don't look so shocked, Dun."

"I don't mean to…" I backpedaled. "It's just that..."

"Never mind," she huffed. "Besides, I'm still in school. We're about to begin our hospital rotation."

"You always did like dissecting frogs."

"That's what you remember about me?" She winced. "I must've been a complete nerd."

"I remember other things too."

"Tell me."

"The time you asked me to walk you home from that terrible party and we got to talking about how cruel and fake people can be… and talking and talking."

"So, by the time I got back the dorm mother had locked me out."

"She gave me the evil eye when she finally let you in."

"The old witch made me pay for that mistake the rest of the semester." She leaned into me playfully. "What else?"

47

"You and your sisters spotting me on the porch steps, all alone on a Saturday night. You backed up the car and talked me into going to a concert right then, no time to even put on shoes. I was barefoot, the music was earsplitting and everyone around us was smoking pot."

"I hate to think how many brain cells I lost that night. I could use a few of them back just now."

"Being picked up by a carload of good-looking girls was the sort of thing that happened to other people, not me."

I sat back, surprised at the admission, the opposite of my usual guardedness. She gave her head a slow shake.

"You could've had any girl you wanted, Dun."

"You must be thinking of my cousin."

"I know exactly who I'm …" Her eyes flew open and she jumped from the seat. "I have to go."

She hurried across the dance floor without another word, greeting a bearded man in a lab coat with a quick kiss. She glanced my direction once before the group migrated out the back door and onto the sundrenched deck beyond. I watched after her, stunned by her sudden appearance and, equally, by her quick departure. I could still feel the heat of her skin.

Whit suddenly entered my field of vision, moving across the room with Connie, his arm hooked in hers, a sly smile on his lips. He winked and nodded toward the exit. They were leaving together. I didn't want to know where.

I puzzled over his condition, one minute pale and exhausted, the next nearly normal. Was his illness an act? If so, why? The idea of Whit deceiving those closest to him seemed impossible to imagine, even ludicrous. Perhaps he had something to hide. Perhaps, as Moon Thibodaux claimed, everyone had their secrets.

My thoughts jumped to the hidden box and I realized at once I had made my decision. I would return the heirloom. Marti's commitment to making something of herself, to pursuing her dream, had inspired me.

I hurried toward the exit, wanting to put the temptation out of reach as soon as possible. I paused at the cackle of laughter drifting from the deck and a wave of disappointment passed over me. Then I stepped into the brilliant afternoon.

Seven

I parked behind the store, slipped out of the truck and stopped in mid-stride. The shop door stood half-open. I moved closer and peeked inside. The room appeared unmolested as far as I could tell.

Mumbling a quick prayer, I hurried to the filing cabinet and jerked open the top drawer. The silver box was gone. I yanked open the other drawers in quick succession, finding nothing but varnish-stained rags and cans of glue.

Trying to keep a lid on my growing anger, I hustled along the narrow passage toward the store. I hoped to find Griggs inside. But other than a half-eaten burrito hidden behind a bedroom dresser, there was no sign of him.

I hurried through the maze of end tables and dressers, headboards and mattresses, following the rumble of Onward's voice. The store was otherwise empty. Beyond a bedroom suite complete with sleeping mannequins, I found him bent over an overstuffed chair. An old woman, her skin a shade darker than his, sat facing him. He turned at my approach.

"Mrs. King," he announced, motioning at me, "this is my friend Dun, Mr. Whit Osay's nephew."

She rose from the chair, nodded solemnly and started for the exit in a stiff but determined shuffle. Onward watched after her.

"Mrs. King needs a new reading chair," he said as she disappeared through the door, "but she always has to think on it awhile before she decides. Been coming here twenty-odd years and…"

"Where is Griggs?" I interrupted.

"How would I know that?" He frowned. "I'm not his daddy."

"I need to find him."

"He in trouble again?"

"I've got to talk to him right away."

50

"He's not in trouble?"

"I just have to ask him something."

He eyed me with suspicion.

"Sounds important, this question you got."

"No, not really." I tried to act unconcerned. "It's just a simple question is all."

"Just a simple question," he repeated. "What's this simple question about?"

"Nothing important."

"Nothing important, huh?" He stepped closer. "What're you and him up to, Dun?"

Ignoring the query, I glanced around the store.

"When did you last see him?"

"Griggs comes and goes as he pleases," he replied, eyeing me again. "Surely does look like you got something important to ask him."

I gave my head a quick shake to put him off.

"You don't have any idea where he is?"

He sighed and moved to the chair, in no hurry to answer.

"Left half hour ago," he finally said. "Claimed he had to see to something, something that couldn't wait."

"Where is he living now?"

"I'll say long as you tell me what you two got yourselves up to."

"We're not up to anything."

"You sure about that?"

Seeing I had no choice, I made my way to the front door and flipped the 'open' sign to 'closed'. Then I pointed him toward the shop. Moments later we stood before the filing cabinet. I knew I'd have to tell him about the box if I wanted his help.

Griggs' tiny bungalow sat perched on the edge of a stagnant canal. Rainbows of oil drifted on the tea-colored water. A defunct boat repair shop filled the opposite bank, its weed-choked yard littered with empty barrels and

51

rusting equipment. Their shadows cast ominous shapes through the dying light.

Onward had listened in silence as I told him of the heirloom and my intention to return it, interrupting only after I failed to mention my initial reluctance. Somehow, he knew. Or maybe, as Griggs claimed, I was an easy read.

A part of me hoped so. I recalled Marti glancing back at me before vanishing into the bright light of the afternoon. I hoped she had caught in my expression a wish to see her again. To what point, I could not say. She was clearly involved with the bearded man.

The rattle of Griggs' approaching sedan drifted over the trees. Seconds later the car rounded a dense stand of oleanders separating the yard from the street. He climbed out and leaned against the fender, regarding me with an innocent grin.

"What brings you to my humble abode, cousin?"

I gave no reply, unwilling to play his game.

"You've been waiting for me?"

I said nothing. He nodded his own reply.

"You have been waiting. You're probably wondering why I'm not at the store." A trace of worry crossed his face. "You're not going to tell Uncle Whit, are you?"

"Tell me where it is, Griggs."

"Tell you where what is?"

"You know what."

"Is this a riddle?" he replied, the grin returning.

"I'm not kidding."

He eyed me for a moment and then nodded toward the bungalow.

"How'd you know where to find me?"

"Don't change the subject."

"I was just wondering. Why not tell me?"

"Onward gave me the address."

His smile vanished.

"I never should've told that spook," he grumbled.

"Don't talk about him like that!"

52

"Everyone knows you can't trust them."

"What's gotten into you, Griggs?"

Surprised by his harsh words, I wondered again if you can ever really know a person. I'd always assumed he despised his father's casual racism. He leaned back against the car, resuming his usual indifferent gaze.

"I don't know what you mean, cousin."

"Never mind," I grunted. "Where is the box?"

"You mean that silver box?"

"Tell me what you did with it."

"It's not where you left it?"

"Don't play stupid."

"Are you saying someone stole it?"

"You know what I'm saying, Griggs."

"Do I?"

"You shouldn't have taken it."

"You think I have the box?"

"Stop screwing around," I shouted, taking a step toward him.

"Okay, okay." He pressed himself to the car. "I know a guy. He's checking to see what it's worth."

"I don't care what it's worth."

I was angrier at him for not telling me than for taking the heirloom.

"That box is solid silver with gold inlay. It cleans up real nice. Are you're sure you don't want to know its value?"

"It belongs with the owner."

"But we found it."

"I found it, Griggs. And now I'm returning it."

"You can't be serious."

"Get it back, Griggs."

"But Dun," he pleaded. "What about discovering hidden treasure, finders-keepers and all that? They say possession is nine tenths of ownership."

"What they say is not my concern. I say the box belongs to the old lady who owns the desk, not me, not

53

you." I pointed him into the car. "Now you're taking me to it."

"All right," he muttered, "I'll take you."

He started and then pivoted, his face brightening.

"Maybe she'll pay us," he blurted, "for finding a priceless heirloom."

"Not everything is about money, Griggs."

I pointed him back to the car. He ignored me.

"That's easy for you to say. You're not broke."

The pitiful state of my bank account again crossed my thoughts. A chance for some quick cash, maybe a lot of it, stirred inside me. The idea was tempting, disturbingly so.

"Keeping the box would be wrong," I said, in part to convince myself.

"Are you absolutely sure?" His eyes held a strange intensity, as if he sensed my indecision. "That box could be worth a small fortune. Think what you could do with all that money."

"You can't be completely broke," I countered. "You have a job."

I realized to my chagrin I was speaking as much to myself as to him.

"It's worse than that, Dun."

He dropped his head. His usual confidence had vanished in an instant. Perplexed, I peered at him.

"What do you mean?"

"I'm in debt to some bad people." He put a hand to his mouth as if the words had made him ill. "I need to pay them back, and I need to do it soon. If I don't…"

He left the thought unfinished. I could see he wanted to let it drop but I needed to know more.

"What bad people?"

"You don't want to know."

"How much do you owe?"

"Too much," he muttered. "I don't know how I'll ever repay them in time."

"What will they do if you don't?"

54

He shook his head in answer. The look in his eyes gave me a shock. Griggs rarely showed any sort of real emotion, especially fear.

"We'll figure out something," I replied, motioning him to the car. "Now, let's go."

Minutes later we were bouncing down a rutted alleyway, the sedan sounding as if it might fall apart at any moment. I glanced over at him and began doubting my decision. The good or bad in people again crossed my thoughts. Was selling the box less wrong than returning it? After all, he needed the money. His life might even depend on it.

A rich old lady with no awareness of the heirloom's existence, an old lady who already had a house full of antiques, had no need of another. How was giving the box to her better than bailing Griggs out of trouble? He had plenty of need; we both did. Without telling him, I decided to try to sell it if we could.

"You really think it could fetch a good price?"

I tried to sound half-interested in his answer. He slowed the care and eyed me.

"You're going to sell it, aren't you?"

"Don't get ahead of yourself, Griggs."

"I knew you'd come through for me, cousin," he yelled, jamming the accelerator to the floor.

We rounded a weed-choked curve and a row of abandoned military barracks appeared, graffiti-covered and rotting. He pulled alongside a flat-roofed building partially hidden behind a wall of bamboo. Iron bars crisscrossed the windows. I peered through the windshield in disbelief.

"You brought the box here?" I glared at him. "Is your friend a drug dealer?"

"You worry too much, Dun," he said, dismissively. "This is his storeroom. He deals in used furniture, personal items and electronics."

"Legal or illegal?"

"A little of both."

I followed him past the bamboo and up a short set of stairs to a narrow landing. He started to knock but seeing the door ajar instead pushed through. I followed him inside. Pale sunlight reflecting off the bamboo filled the room with a green glow.

A wall of battered cabinets and wardrobes split the space in two, blocking the view between us and the opposite wall. Television sets and stereos littered the floor. Griggs craned his neck, trying to see around the clutter. The warped floor creaked beneath his feet. Then a weak groan drifted from the far corner.

We glanced at each other and started pushing our way through the maze of castoffs, eventually stopping before a quilt-draped cot. A figure stirred beneath the spread. Griggs pulled a corner aside and a man's face appeared, one eye blackened, his lip split.

"Don't hit me," he shrieked, raising his hands to protect himself.

A pit opened in my chest. I knew then the box was gone. The man watched us through his fingers, his face a mix of fear and confusion. I pulled a chair next to him and sat.

"We're not going to hurt you." I leaned toward him and motioned over my shoulder. "You remember Griggs, don't you?"

He pulled himself upright with a groan and draped his legs over the edge of the cot. His feet barely reached the floor. Zigzag strands of hair stretched across his baldness like cracks in an egg. He pointed me to the corner.

"If you don't mind," he whispered. "I believe my eyeglasses ended up over there."

I found the glasses beneath a nearby dresser. He eased them onto his swollen nose and blinked at me.

"I'm nearly blind without them."

His eyes flashed large beneath the thick lenses. He attempted a smile and then winced, reaching for his jaw.

Griggs moved beside me. The little man rubbed the knot beneath his thin beard and squinted up at him.

"When I agreed to the deal," he said, pausing to run his tongue over the split in his lip, "I failed to mention the fact that precious metals such as gold and silver are outside my area of expertise."

"Wait, wait, wait," Griggs interrupted. "Are you telling me you lost the box?"

"I lost nothing," he replied as if insulted. "The box was taken from me at gunpoint, along with a Rolex, a car stereo and my own rare coin collection. They wanted only what was transportable and easily converted to cash."

He watched warily as Griggs pivoted and began pacing the floor.

"How could you let yourself get robbed?" he yelled. "This is what you do."

"Do you think I ask for such treatment?" He pointed to his swollen eye. "If I hadn't had to go outside my usual contacts to help you, none of this would have happened."

Griggs paused and stood glaring down at him. "You're blaming me?"

"As I said, my expertise does not include gold and silver."

"What does it include," he shouted, "ineptitude?"

"You have no reason to get yourself in a tizzy," he snipped. "The barbarians assaulted me, not you. Besides, I paid you a fair price. No one made you come here and..."

I raised a hand to stop him. He gasped and pressed himself against the wall.

"Don't hit me!" he shrieked.

"He sold you the box?" I yelled.

He cowered behind the blanket. I quickly scanned the room but Griggs had disappeared.

"The correct term is 'pawn'," he answered in a shaking voice, "and, as I said, for a fair price, half up front and half after I concluded a sale. Please believe me."

57

Jumping from the chair, I stumbled through the maze. I found Griggs slouched against the wall, staring out the open doorway. He would not face me.

"You pawned the box?"

"I needed that money…" he turned and yelled into the room, "all of it! You won't tell the old lady, will you?"

"You lied to me, Griggs," I replied, shamed by my moment of weakness, "and I believed you. I should've known better."

"You don't understand, Dun."

"I understand perfectly. Anything is justified if you need it to be. That's the way it's always been between us."

"You don't really believe that."

A bitter smile twisted my lips. He looked at me expectantly but I turned and started for the door, too disappointed to speak.

Fie

When Onward first came to us he was rail thin and terribly sad. My heart hurt for him. The more I saw of him, the more determined I was to help, to understand why he had left his home. In that way I hoped to make him feel welcomed. But as much as I probed and prodded he never offered an explanation, never mentioned his home or family. I was at a loss what to do.

So I began bringing hot lunches to the family store where he worked alongside my brother, Whit. Cooking was one thing I could do. Sensing he was too proud to accept charity, I convinced Whit to act as if I had been bringing him lunch for years when in truth the thought had never crossed my mind. I was far too busy with my own work to worry about my brother eating right.

Onward proved to be a hard worker from the start. The day to day regularity of work suited him. At some point Whit noticed he had a talent for working with wood, so he took every opportunity to teach him the particulars of furniture repair, the various hardwoods, the delicate nature of lacquer. Within weeks he was restoring entire pieces on his own.

But it was his way with Dun that most endeared him to me. Their age difference never stopped him from taking time to answer Dun's many questions or to offer encouragement when Dun felt unsure of himself, which in my view was worrisomely often. Onward had patience to spare and seemed to enjoy their time together as much as Dun himself.

He lived in a weather-beaten cottage owned by his granduncle, Tarp Cates, near a little used part of the old harbor. In my view the area was not suitable for a teenager new to town. And Tarp's long shifts at the shipyards took him away from home for long stretches, leaving the boy on his own much of the time. But despite the drawbacks, he eventually seemed to settle in.

Still, his sadness remained. Our efforts made little difference. I sensed he was stuck in a sort of limbo, caught between his past and future, belonging to neither.

Then one afternoon Whit called from the store. He had found Onward passed out on the shop floor and burning with fever. We did not hesitate to take him into our home.

We set a cot in the dining room for Dun and put Onward in his room. By the time we had him in bed he was senseless with fever. The doctor said there was little to do other than let the illness run its course and keep a close eye on him. Whit and I took turns sitting bedside.

From the beginning I read to him regardless of whether he seemed awake or asleep, Faulkner for his sense of place, Hemingway for adventure, Dickens for the humanity of his characters. Now and then I'd pause to find him staring at me, his glassy eyes unblinking. I had to fight to keep from tearing up.

Eventually, the fever broke and though terribly weak he was able to sit up. I thought our time with books had passed but he still asked for them. He seemed interested in little else. Once or twice I even had to bargain to get him to eat, ten pages for a bowl of broth. I could see the stories had captured him.

Then one morning after we'd finished Faulkner's Go Down, Moses, he began talking about himself, about the way the story reminded him of home, of his family. Though he never said much, I sensed he had little choice in leaving.

I also noticed that while he talked of his father with affection, he scarcely mentioned his mother, Viola. Recalling her name conjured an image of my last summer in Mississippi. Young and pretty, she had her whole life ahead of her, a life presumably full of hope and promise. Yet something had happened to derail that future.

When I asked him about her he grew subdued and eventually retreated to talk of books and writers and the deep forests and bottomlands of the Mississippi Delta. Despite his words, the pain in his face was impossible to miss. I vowed then I would return to Mississippi and see what I could learn about the cause of his leaving. Perhaps then I would know how to go about easing his sadness.

Eight

Furniture repair is more art than science, more educated guess than simple formula. The level of difficulty rises when restoring antiques. Stains and varnishes long out of use must be approximated in texture and hue. Wood type and grain must be matched as close as possible.

All of that crossed my mind as I knelt beside an antique cherry table, trying to repair a deep gouge in one of the legs. The stain was proving a difficult match. If I failed to concentrate I would make the problem worse. The parallel with my own circumstances was unavoidable.

I could hear Onward behind me, putting the finishing touches to the Langdon desk. One of the file cabinet drawers opened and closed, followed by another, and yet another. I figured he was looking for a polishing rag or touchup brush. Then he ceased rummaging.

I focused on the repair. After several minutes, I realized he had become unnaturally quiet. I thought little of it at first, figuring he was absorbed in his work, but finally my curiosity won out. I turned to find him bent over the desk, peering at a sheaf of yellowed papers, the same papers I had taken from the silver box.

"Look here what I found in Whit's old filing cabinet," he said, facing me. "I wonder who put it there."

I told him the story as quickly as I could, anxious to be free of it. The sheaf was yet another reminder of my poor judgment. He thumbed through the pages for a moment and then tapped the cover with his finger.

"What'd you think it is?"

"Just some old papers," I muttered, in no mood to discuss it, "probably a diary or journal. I wasn't much interested in finding out then and I'm even less interested now."

"You going to give it back?"

"How am I going to do that, Onward?" I griped. "I'd have to explain how I found it and that would surely lead to questions, questions I can't answer, questions I don't want to even think about. I'm ready to forget the whole mess, the sooner the better."

"I can sure understand that. Not going to be easy though, with your eye on that girl." He tapped the papers again. "Mind if I take it home and see if I can make heads or tails?"

"No, I don't mind," I replied, glad to have it out of my sight. "Just don't tell anyone where you got it."

I wasn't surprised by his interest. I knew he had a room full of books at home, books on everything from physics to history, botany to astronomy. Biographies were his favorites, other than novels. His tiny house had barely enough space for a table and chairs, yet he always had room for another book.

On home deliveries he inevitably gravitated to the bookshelves, poking around the titles while I hobnobbed with the owner. Any library sale or bookstore drew him like a bee to honey. If I came across a paperback or magazine in the store, the odds were it belonged to him.

Strangely, he seemed an unlikely booklover. He never used what he learned to impress. Instead, his was a quiet and personal love affair with the printed word. He could talk at length on all sorts of topics, but it was not his nature to do so. I would have to ask, and then ask again.

I envied his pure and straightforward love of reading. I'd once had something similar. But somehow my affinity for words had been short-circuited, lost beneath the grind of day to day demands, a casualty of my directionless existence.

An hour later we closed the store for the day and loaded the repaired desk into the panel truck. Onward had just started the engine when Griggs appeared at his window. He and I had hardly spoken since the box was stolen. He threw open the back door and climbed in.

I had no wish to cross paths with Mrs. Langdon again, unable as I was to forget my role in the heirloom's loss. But I couldn't pass up a chance to see Isabel. I hoped to make a better impression than I had at our last encounter.

We turned the corner and the looming yellow house appeared through the windshield. As we unloaded the desk and carried it up the stairs and onto the broad porch, I found myself wondering why Griggs had come along. Two of us could easily manage.

Before I had a chance to knock the door flew open and Isabel stepped through. She gave me a quick smile and then turned to Onward as if she had something to say, but her grandmother's voice called from down the hall, asking for her. She shrugged and slipped back through the door, taking time to point us to the adjacent study, where a place had been cleared for the desk.

Once we had it in place Onward headed for the truck. I stood by waiting to settle the account. Griggs wandered the room, keeping one eye out for Mrs. Langdon. I found myself again wondering why he had decided to come along when the sound of footsteps echoed down the hall. Moments later Isabel reappeared. She glanced over her shoulder and hurried to where I stood.

"I only have a minute."

I turned to Griggs, giving him a quick nod toward the door. Instead, he looked Isabel up and down.

"Nice work, cousin," he said, grinning. "She's a peach."

"Aren't you supposed to be helping Onward?"

"At least introduce us."

"Isabel Langdon," I said grudgingly, "this is my cousin, Griggs."

"Don't mind him, Isabel. He's always had a hard time enjoying life."

Her gaze drifted over him and she smiled shyly. I felt my face burn with a jealous anger.

"You can go now, Griggs," I snapped.

He gave her a quick wink before slipping out the door. She peered into my face.

"You're looking better than the last time we met."

"That definitely was not my best day," I muttered.

A part of me wanted to tell her I had lied, that I had lost my job and could no longer call myself a teacher. But her beauty held me back, my hope for her approval outweighing my honesty. More than anything I wanted to buy time, time enough to get my life on track, to make a good impression before the truth of my actual circumstances came out. I hoped by then I could claim something more than an aimless existence, something to be proud of.

"How's your uncle?" she asked.

"About the same, I suppose."

"So, you'll be around for a while longer?"

"It looks that way."

"Maybe we could…"

Mrs. Langdon suddenly appeared. Isabel stepped away, assuming the affected indifference of our first encounter. Her grandmother pulled her aside and leaned close, speaking under her breath. Isabel glanced at me, turned and vanished through the doorway.

Mrs. Langdon bent over the desk, running her hand over the smooth finish. Then she stood and studied me a moment.

"Please tell your uncle the work is satisfactory, Mr. Osay," she said coolly. "You may send the invoice at your convenience."

"I have it right here." I held up the paper. "We can settle up now."

"The payment will have to wait," she replied, snatching it from my hand. "My accountant handles all my finances. You may see yourself out."

She hurried off as if glad to be rid of me. Disappointed, I ambled to the street where Onward stood waiting in the shade of a sprawling live oak. Griggs was nowhere in sight. We checked the truck and searched up one side of the street and down the other. No sign of him. I again puzzled over what he was up to.

We were about to leave without him when he appeared at the window. He rounded the truck and climbed in as if he'd been the one waiting. I shifted in my seat and eyed him.

"Where've you been?"

"A pretty lady I know lives close by," he said distractedly. "I decided to go see her."

I faced the windshield, unsure whether to believe him. Griggs was rarely forthcoming, a habit of his difficult upbringing. But this time, for reasons I could not explain, I found his evasiveness especially troubling.

After returning the truck I rushed home to change clothes. Uncle Augie had invited the family, meaning me, Fie and Whit, over for dinner. Since Griggs and I had scarcely spoken, I had no idea if he'd be there. Considering the tension between us, a part of me hoped not.

Fie stood in the living room looking peeved and impatient. Wearing her usual high-collared dress and low-heeled shoes, she clutched her purse in both hands. The fingers of one hand tapped out an agitated rhythm.

"You are keeping a close watch on your uncle," she said, scrutinizing me with her coal-black eyes, "aren't you?"

"Why would I want to do that?" I replied, unsure what she had in mind.

"He has been venturing to the store against the doctor's orders. Surely you've seen him."

I had seen him downtown only the one time, before our trip to the peninsula.

"Once or twice," I hedged.

"That's puzzling." The tapping ceased. "Only once or twice, you say?"

An image of Whit and Connie on the dance floor flashed through my mind and I suddenly grew uneasy.

"I'm often away on deliveries," I added, hoping the excuse might satisfy her, "so I could easily miss him."

"You don't have an idea where else he might go?" She looked at me askance. "You and Whit aren't in cahoots, are you?"

"What would he and I…"

"Tell me," she demanded. "Is he sneaking off to smoke again?"

"Fie, you can't expect me to…"

At the sound of footsteps she raised a hand to stop me. An instant later Whit stepped into the room. He eyed each of us in turn.

"Whatever you two are guilty of," he announced as he started for the door, "I don't want to know about it."

Uncle Augie's house was a rambling, bayside monstrosity on the island's west end. To get there, we had to cross an arched, one-lane bridge and pass through a manned security gate. The guard eyed my rusted sedan with disdain, taking his time to note my license plate number on a clipboard while Whit grumbled about his brother's ostentatious lifestyle.

Augie had split from the original business years earlier, going on to open a chain of upscale furniture stores on the mainland. Much to Whit's chagrin, he used his financial success to become a key figure in the island social scene, donating his way onto numerous boards and charities. In the process, he divorced Griggs' mother to marry a woman half his age.

Though I was less than sure whether Griggs would make an appearance at dinner, I knew his sister, Babs, would be there along with her son. After her husband left, she had returned to the insular safety of island life. The last time I'd seen her, her sense of defeat was palpable.

We followed a wide boulevard lined with palms and oleanders. Beyond the sprawling, manicured lawns, tile-roofed mansions of stucco and stone lined a web of saltwater canals that all led to the open bay. The sun-scattered water winked between the houses.

I slowed as we approached Augie's orange and vermillion two-story. A Confederate flag fluttered above the circular drive. Augie had always been inordinately proud of his heritage.

Fie hopped from the car even before I had cut the engine. She paused at the flagpole and frowned skyward. I could see she was preparing herself, much like a soldier before battle. She and Augie were often at odds.

Augie's wife, Sheila, answered the doorbell in a tight, low-cut dress. I tried not to stare. Though they had been married for nearly a decade, I still had trouble imagining the two of them together. She was only slightly older than me.

She ushered us into the living room where Augie stood at the wet bar mixing drinks. Griggs slouched in a nearby chair. Noticing me, he raised his glass in a silent toast or, perhaps, a peace offering.

Before I could respond Augie rounded the bar, blocking my view. He handed me a cocktail, took me by the arm and ushered me out the back door. The bay stretched away from us, its dark surface etched by a coursing wind.

"Now that's some view." He motioned toward the shoreline. "This is what you call the good life."

"You have a nice house," I replied, not knowing what else to say.

"Damn right I do."

He sipped his drink and stared into the distance. I stood by wondering why he had brought me out there.

"I had to put in a lot of hard work to get where I am now," he finally said. "Unfortunately, Griggs doesn't know the meaning of the word."

"Maybe he just hasn't found what suits him," I replied, looking for a diplomatic way out. I wanted to avoid discussing their fraught relationship.

"Or maybe he's just lazy," he muttered. He turned to me. "What line of work are you in?"

"I've been in education for a while now."

Another of my half-truths.

"A school teacher," he snorted. "Don't waste your time working as some low-paid do-gooder, Dun. You can do better."

"The world needs good teachers."

"Sure, sure, but you need a business of your own. That's where the money is."

"I'm keeping my options open," I added, hoping he might drop the subject.

"By the time I was your age I had two kids and a mortgage." He clasped my shoulder and leaned in close. "Just because your uncle Whit can't make a decent go of it doesn't mean starting your own company is a dead end."

"The store is doing alright," I replied, feeling defensive. In truth I had no idea.

He grunted and turned back to the bay. I drained my glass and rattled the ice, thinking I might use the empty glass as an excuse to leave. Before I had a chance, he grunted again.

"I hear you and Onward are back working together." He kept his eyes on the water. "It's just like old times."

"That's right," I answered tentatively, unsure what he was getting at.

"My brother likes taking chances, don't you think?"

"I don't follow."

I wondered if he, like Whit, was fishing for information about Onward. His gaze shifted from the shoreline back to me.

"The fact is, most of them aren't worth hiring," he said in disgust. "That's God's own truth."

"Who do you mean?"

"The coloreds, of course, who do you think? I've found them nothing but shifty or lazy, or both." He sipped his drink and studied me. "I figure it's the white blood in Onward that makes him a decent worker."

"What on earth," I replied, baffled by his pronouncements, "are you talking about?"

"Just look at how light-skinned he is compared to his daddy or old Tarp."

"That doesn't mean anything," I scoffed.

"You don't think some plantation owner could've knocked up Onward's great grandmother back in the slave days? He sure as hell could've, and many did just that."

"Onward works hard." I struggled to corral my anger. "He takes pride in a job well-done."

"I wouldn't go that far. He's still a colored."

"He's a man just like you or me."

"You can't be serious," he sneered. "Don't you know that scientists have done the research and found they aren't as smart as us? On the other hand, they're wily enough to steal you blind if you give them too much leeway."

"That's nothing but racist propaganda," I countered.

"Dun, I think you've been brainwashed. Don't believe everything you read in the damn newspaper." A wry grin crossed his lips. "You haven't taken to hugging trees, now have you?"

To my relief, Sheila appeared in the doorway, waving us inside. I had forgotten my family's propensity for prejudice and racism. Augie drained his glass and started for the house. I waited, wanting no more of his talk.

Once he disappeared inside I felt I could breathe again. Griggs waited for me just outside the door.

"He didn't waste any time cornering you," he muttered. "What did he want?"

"Explaining would only ruin your dinner." I held open the door. "Best to forget it."

Sheila motioned me to a chair next to Griggs and across from Fie, with Whit at one end of the table and

70

Augie at the other. Babs and her son, Riley, had already taken their seats.

We passed around the covered dishes and bowls, baskets of bread and condiment trays. When our plates were full Augie raised his hand to quiet us. Head bowed, he muttered a rapid-fire prayer. As usual, I could make out less than half the words.

Other than the clink of silverware on china, the table grew quiet for a time as we turned our attention to the meal. A stout woman in cap and apron, her clay-colored skin dark against her white blouse, moved about us removing dishes and refilling glasses. Suddenly, Augie's voice broke the silence.

"What are doing with that plate, boy?" He leaned across the table. "Didn't I tell you to stop that nonsense?"

I looked to my right. Head down, Riley sat unmoving, his fork suspended over his plate. Babs cast a nervous glance at her father. Griggs stirred next to me.

"I will not allow such prissy behavior at my dinner table," he continued. "You're not one of those light-footed boys, are you?"

Fork still above his plate, Riley gave his head a quick shake.

"What the devil are you going on about, Augie?" Fie scowled. "Let the boy have his meal in peace."

"A man eats his food all together," he grumbled, "not one damn thing at a time."

"Who gave you that harebrained idea, John Birch himself?"

I glanced at Riley's plate. He had finished his peas and started on the mashed potatoes. The rest of his meal, clearly untouched, remained pristine. He had yet to move a muscle.

"You listen up, boy." Augie rapped his finger on the table. "You're in my house now and I want to see you take a bite of meatloaf and mix it in with those potatoes and stick it in your mouth."

"August Osay, you stop talking to him like that this minute." Fie sat erect, her gaze unwavering. "What is the matter with you, a grown man who should know better? He's just a boy."

"I won't have my only grandson turn queer on me. He needs a stern hand… or the back of one."

"Daddy," Babs offered, her voice a near-whisper, "he just likes to eat his meal one thing at a time. He's particular."

"I call it peculiar and I won't have it. You're going to end up with an oddball for a son if you let him do whatever he wants."

"But Daddy…"

"You see what happens when you can't keep a man around?"

"Leave her alone!" Griggs shouted, tossing his knife and fork onto the table.

"No one asked for your opinion," he snapped.

"It's hard enough raising a boy on her own without you adding to it."

"What would you know about raising a kid? You're stuck in perpetual childhood."

"Just maybe," he sneered, "that has something to do with having a bastard for a father."

Sheila gasped. Griggs rose abruptly, kicking the chair from the table and storming out the patio door. Augie stared at the empty chair, his face crimson.

"You are a shameless bully, August Osay." Fie's voice shook with anger. "Your son and grandson deserve your approval not your disdain. Let them be who they are. And stop making me ashamed to be your sister."

Without a word Whit stood and moved to where Riley sat. Clasping his shoulder, he motioned him to stand and then ushered him out the front door. I watched after them, trying to decide whether to follow. An awkward stillness filled the room.

As if reading my mind, Fie turned to me and tilted her head toward the patio in a wordless message to follow Griggs. Relieved to have an excuse to leave, I slipped out the patio door. To the north a wall of clouds towered over the flat horizon, their ragged tops edged in gold. I wondered if fall was finally about to arrive.

I found Griggs in the boathouse sitting beside an open cooler of beer. His bare feet stirred the dark water below. He emptied the can in his hand with one long swallow and tossed it onto the ice before fishing out two more and handing one to me.

He turned back to the bay. Neither of us wanted to speak. I watched him for a moment, recalling the many such scenes I had witnessed over the years, hoping against hope that this was the last.

Nine

By the time I reached my apartment I had worked myself into a dark humor. The disappointments and troubles of the last week had finally caught up with me. A little voice inside my head kept repeating 'nothing ever works out', as if I needed convincing. I did not.

I parked next to the wall of honeysuckle separating Moon's house from the neighbors. The dense vines blocked what little twilight there was left so that I had to feel my way along the alley. When I reached the stairs I found Onward waiting on the landing, the sheaf of yellowed papers in his lap. Even in the broken light I could make out a troubled look beneath his calm demeanor. He stood and motioned me up the stairs.

Long as I'd known him Onward always had a peculiar response to excitement. The more things heated up, the calmer he got. The smallest aggravation might set him to cussing and pacing, but anything important would have the opposite effect. So much so that I worried anytime I saw him especially subdued or tranquil, the way he seemed at that moment.

He stepped aside without so much as a hello while I unlocked the door. I knew better than to ask what had brought him there. He would say only when he was ready.

I switched on the overhead light and he set the papers on the dining table, letting his gaze wander over the small apartment, finally settling on me. He nodded toward the kitchen.

"You got something to drink around here? You may need it by the time I'm done."

Anxious to hear what he had to say, I retrieved two beers from the refrigerator, popped off the tops and handed him one. He eased into a chair and took a long pull. I sat opposite him.

"You found yourself something here, Dun," he said, running his hand over the papers, "something big, something nobody in this world will believe unless they see it for themselves."

"What are talking about, Onward? No one cares about an old journal."

"Did you read it?"

"Enough to decide that's what it is, a journal or maybe a diary."

"Well, you're not too far from the mark. It does read like one. But it's a whole lot more."

He sat back and admired the yellowed sheaf, sipping his beer. After all that had happened, I was low on patience so I reached for the stack but he batted my hand away.

"Are you going to tell me about it," I complained, "or did you come only for the free beer?"

"You got to know the American writer," he finally said, "name of Mark Twain."

"Of course," I snorted. "Everyone knows he wrote Tom Sawyer, Huckleberry Finn and the rest."

"Huck Finn is thought to be his greatest book, one of the greatest novels ever written by an American. You recall how the story ends?"

I should've known. I had read the book three times over. But that was many years in the past.

"If I remember right," I replied, half guessing. "Jim is set free and Huck decides to head west before Tom's Aunt Sally can civilize him."

"Both Huck and Jim get their freedom, sure enough." He lifted the stack and thumbed through the pages. "What would you say if I told you there's more to that story?"

I peered at the rough paper, the frayed string binding, the slanted scrawl, and his meaning slowly settled over me. The silver box had served a purpose far greater than the value of its silver and gold. By protecting the fragile papers, it had preserved a priceless work of American literature.

"You're telling me Mark Twain wrote that book, a book no one knows about, a second book about Huck and Jim?"

He flipped to the end and pointed at the bottom of the page. Written below the last sentence in oversized letters were the initials S. L. C. A note beside them read 'do not publish'.

I stared at the page, trying to sort through my racing thoughts. Was it possible the stack of papers before me was truly a lost sequel to The Adventures of Huckleberry Finn? If so, Samuel Langhorne Clemens, better known by his pen name, Mark Twain, had written a book no one knew existed until I had stumbled across it, a book he then declined to publish. Why would he? Was the novel too ahead of its time? Charles Darwin delayed publishing his theory of evolution because he knew the reaction from the religious community would be swift and strong. Perhaps Twain faced a similar dilemma.

I flipped the stack and began deciphering the faded longhand, chiding myself for so easily dismissing the papers as worthless. I had given them a quick scan and no more. My usual curiosity had been short-circuited by the silver box and my own shameless greed.

"How much have you read?"

"Enough to know Huck is grown when he and Jim get thrown together again, somewhere west of Mississippi, might even be Texas."

"Could it be a fake? Maybe one of Mrs. Langdon's relatives was in the forgery business."

"Don't believe so. I have a book of Twain's letters." He ran his finger under a sentence. "Writing here looks just the same as in those pictures."

I suddenly realized the book created even more of a dilemma than the silver box. What would I do with a priceless manuscript? If I kept it hidden, I'd be denying the world a sequel to one of the great American novels. If not, the lies would multiply exponentially.

The sound of breaking glass shattered the quiet, followed by shouts and then screams, all coming from Moon's house. I locked eyes with Onward and then jumped from my chair, making for the house as fast as I could manage the stairs. We reached the back door in seconds.

I burst through just as shards of a smashed vase skittered past the kitchen doorway. I rushed into the living room, spotting Moon slumped on the floor, one hand to his face, the other raised to protect himself. Ronny stood over him, a thick leather belt at his side.

Onward brushed past me in a blur, stepping between the two men. Ronny raised the belt but Onward made no move toward him or away. Instead, he pointed to the door.

"You leave now and don't make more trouble for yourself. Maybe then you can get past what happened here."

I knelt beside Moon. Ronny lowered the belt and began pacing, pausing to glare at one or the other of us between rants.

"Don't you talk to me like you think you're better," he sneered, pointing a finger in Onward's face.

"I'm just a man, no different from you."

"You're different all right. No colored will ever be better than me. You hear what I'm telling you, boy?"

Onward flinched at the word but his voice remained steady.

"I make my share of mistakes like all men do," he replied. "You don't need to make this one any worse than it already is."

"You hear that, Moon?" He peered past Onward. "Who does he think he is talking to me like he's my daddy? No colored man has a right to talk to us like that."

A hateful smile spread across his lips. Onward motioned at Moon.

"This man here needs tending to."

"He doesn't want help from your type. That right, Moon? You tell him."

Moon mumbled an answer, wincing with pain. Onward motioned toward the door.

"You leave so we can fix him up right."

"How many times do I have to tell you, he doesn't want your help."

Tired of his arguing, I moved next to Onward.

"You leave now," I said, surprised by my own anger, "or I'm calling the police."

Moon groaned, shaking his head. He grabbed my hand and pulled me close.

"I don't want him going to jail," he whispered. "Please, tell him that I'm begging him to leave. I'll see him later, after I get myself cleaned up."

"You sure that's what you want?" I peered into his swollen eyes. "After what he did to you, I'd enjoy seeing him hauled off in handcuffs."

"Do as I ask, Dun, please," he pleaded. "He doesn't mean to do it. He just gets so angry. But I don't believe I can live without him."

I stood and faced Ronny. I could see he had overheard us. The hate-filled smile returned.

"He asked so nice, how can I refuse?" He started for the door, calling over his shoulder. "Now, I'm going to get drunk."

An hour later, we left Moon asleep on the couch. We walked back to the apartment and Onward paused at the gate, pointing his chin up the stairs.

"You keep that book until you decide what to do with it."

"I can't decide anything right now," I muttered.

I had scarcely thought of the manuscript since we left it sitting on the table. An image of Moon's battered face suddenly filled my mind.

"Onward, I can't for the life of me figure what makes a person so hateful."

"There's hate, evil too, roaming around this world." He peered at me with the same mix of affection and consternation I had seen earlier. "Makes a man appreciate what he has, the people close to him."

"I suppose so. But I'll never understand such meanness."

"You figure that out," he said with a half-hearted chuckle, "and you better write your own book."

Ten

Unable to get Moon's battered face out of my thoughts, I decided to go check on him the following morning. I paused on the landing and surveyed the gray clouds streaming overhead. The storm of the evening before had passed well to the north, amounting to little. A warm breeze drifted past smelling of the sea.

I crossed the lawn between the apartment and house and stopped to listen for voices. I had no interest in meeting up with Ronny again. I might do something I would regret. Instead, the lilting whine of accordion music drifted from the kitchen window, nothing more.

I found Moon sitting at the table with a glass pressed to his cheek. His bruises had faded to a yellowish-purple. Before him, a cutting board littered with lime wedges and a half-empty bottle of gin sat alongside a scattering of containers. Seeing me, he hid his face behind a napkin.

"Don't look at me, Dun. I fear I'm not fit to be seen."

"To tell the truth," I said, sitting opposite him, "you're looking better than I expected."

"You don't find me nauseating?" He lowered the napkin. "I'll put a bag over my head if you like."

"I'm here to talk to you, Moon, not a bag." I studied his face. "How does it feel?"

"I spent the morning with my head in the sink. Aunt Francine always swore by Epsom salt and ice water for bruises. That is, along with liberal quantities of her special gin and tonic recipe." He sipped the sweating glass and returned it to his cheek. "Would you like to join me?"

"It's a little early."

"Francine was like a second mother, you know," he continued. "She never married so she spent a good deal of time in New Orleans with mother and me. She taught me everything she knew about New Orleans cooking. That's how I got to be such a food fanatic.

"Francine preferred the company of women to men," he said, winking, "if you get my drift. That is, excepting yours truly. I think that's why she had no problem with my peculiar lifestyle. My mother and her relations acted like either I had the plague or I didn't exist. But Francine was the exception. She accepted me as I was and always treated my friends like family. I suppose to her we were a family of sorts.

"You remind me of her, Dun. You take a person as they are without judgment or prejudice. I saw it in your eyes the moment we met. And I saw it again last night."

"What was that all about, Moon?"

"Oh, you know how love is."

"What he did to you is not love."

"Tempers flare over the smallest of things," he replied, waving the napkin through the air, "when passions are high."

"But, Moon, anger is no excuse for violence."

"Ronny doesn't mean to get that way. It just happens. Beneath all that macho is a sweet man. I just get under his skin sometimes."

"Moon, you did not do that to yourself." I pointed at his face. "You could've been seriously hurt."

"Oh, Dun, you're worried about me," he said, patting my arm. "I'm touched, really I am. But Ronny and I will work things out like couples do. You'll see."

He drained his glass and stood.

"Now, I must leave you. I'm meeting him downtown for a make-up lunch. A bottle of wine and a good meal, and all will be well again."

He disappeared through the doorway. I watched after him, puzzling over the disconcerting vagaries of love. Moon's willingness to forget what Ronny had done to him was beyond understanding. Yet my thoughts quickly turned to Isabel, and I wondered if I would ever see her again or even if I wanted to, knowing the secret that stood between us. If I'd known then what the day held in store, I would surely have given it more thought.

Later that morning Onward angled the truck away from the curb and we passed along a street crowded with live oaks, their intertwined branches locked in a dark and intricate struggle. Blue-gray clouds beyond them tumbled on a freshening wind. The heavy air felt electric yet oppressive, mirroring my mood.

My mistake, I realized too late, had been in hiding the box from Whit. He would have returned it without hesitation, the manuscript still inside. Instead, an heirloom was lost forever and I was saddled with a problem I had no idea how to solve. I consoled myself with the thought that Mrs. Langdon would never know the difference.

Onward pulled to a stop beside a café wedged between a bait shop and fish market. A battered wharf stood just beyond. Shrimp boats, their idle nets reaching into the air like waterlogged wings, rocked against the pilings in slow rhythm.

We found an empty table against the far wall. Seconds later a short, wiry man appeared before us, his mahogany-colored skin lined and leather-like. A half-smoked cigarette dangled from his lower lip.

I peered at him, again overcome by an odd combination of familiarity and strangeness. Though it had been years since I had last seen him, Carmelo Puglia looked just as I remembered only smaller and somehow shrunken, as if his features had fallen in on themselves. He grabbed Onward's hand and gave it a violent shake.

"My best customer," he announced, beaming.

He held a notepad in one hand. The other gripped a broken pencil. He squinted at me through a cloud of blue smoke and jabbed the air with the pointed stub.

"You look like a boy I knew, the son of Jimmy Osay who got raised by his aunt and uncle. It's been so long since I saw him, I don't think I can remember his name."

82

"Well, Mr. Puglia," I replied, recalling his game, "I'm still Dun."

"Dun Osay, is that truly you in the flesh? I thought you forgot all about old Carmelo."

"No, I didn't forget."

"And so, you don't forget where the good food is too. Maybe somebody reminds you." He gestured at the room. "Miss Fiona, she comes in here once a week for the lasagna."

"Then that's what we'll have."

Onward nodded his agreement. Carmelo pointed the pencil at the adjacent row of booths.

"All the good-looking ladies come here to eat. Very nice. You see that table over there, so beautiful."

I looked past him and felt the blood drain from my face. Sitting at a booth with three other women was Isabel Langdon. I wanted to turn my head, hoping she might not notice me, but my eyes seemed to have a will of their own.

She shifted her gaze and spotted me. Without hesitating, she slipped from the booth and moved toward us through the maze of tables. My throat tightened with shame. That I had once come close to selling the silver box seemed beyond belief, the decision of some low and selfish version of myself, a decision I now wished I could change or at least forget. Finding the Twain manuscript had only deepened my guilt.

She stopped beside the table. Onward glanced up and, seeing her, jumped from his seat. He looked from her to me and back, awkward in his surprise. She waved him back into his chair with a shy smile.

I glanced at him, wondering what he must be thinking. Then I shifted my gaze to her seemingly flawless profile. A part of me wanted her to leave but the rest wanted the opposite. She kept her eyes on Onward.

"I know how my grandmother treated you," she offered. "She's old but that's no excuse. I want to apologize."

"No need," he replied, his eyes on the table.

"I wish there wasn't," she continued, "but… well, I'm sorry for what happened."

"Truth is," he said, looking up, "I already forgot about it."

I watched him with a touch of envy, realizing that putting such treatment from his mind, acting as if it never happened, left him his dignity. I wondered if she could see it too. She turned and leaned toward me.

"I've got to get back to my friends," she said, her voice just above a whisper, "but I was wondering if you'd like to meet later for a drink."

As much as I wanted to see her, I hesitated to answer. Would I be able to put out of mind what I'd done? I had no idea.

"There's a place called Leroy's just around the corner," she added without waiting for a reply. "I'll be there at six."

She flashed a quick smile and turned to leave. I glanced at Onward, feeling I should say something about their exchange but having no idea where to begin. I sensed that he felt the same. Instead, I watched her move across the room, knowing I would still carry my secret when we next met.

The corner bar Isabel described appeared through the windshield. Unfortunately, the nearest parking space was three blocks away. I parked and hurried along the elevated sidewalk, knowing I would be late. I hoped not too late.

Leroy's entrance, a roughhewn plank of driftwood painted bright purple, opened onto a narrow alley crowded with trashcans and empty liquor boxes. I took a breath and pushed through. A dozen faces turned my way, none of them Isabel's.

I stood for a moment and pondered my nervous state, trying to figure what had me so agitated. Onward would tell me my feathers had stopped shining, meaning I'd lost

84

confidence in myself, most likely due to the secret I carried, or my mounting list of failures, or both. He'd add that the past is beyond reclaiming so I had better forget about it if I wanted even the ghost of a chance with Isabel.

I swallowed hard, hoping I could pull it off. I was about to go looking for her when a waitress in black leather shorts, combat boots and a skin-tight blouse approached me. Her eyes were dark with mascara. A silver ring pierced her bottom lip.

"You must be Dun," she said, her little girl's voice disorienting given her appearance. "I have a message from Isabel. She said to tell you she's running late but please wait. She'll get here as soon as she can."

She disappeared through the kitchen door. I wandered the café intending to find a quiet table but my thoughts kept returning to the Twain manuscript. I had stayed up half the night reading it. Though I was midway through the book, I still had trouble believing he wrote it. Now and then I would run my fingers beneath the tilted longhand, trying to picture him scribbling away in Huck's unmistakable voice.

Titling the novel simply "Finn", he began with Huck, now in his thirties, again crossing paths with the freed slave, Jim. The setting is a small town in Indian Territory, part of what would eventually become Oklahoma. Huck discovers Jim by chance, deathly ill and living in a decrepit hotel, and decides he must help him.

The more I read, the more determined I was to return the manuscript. The idea of keeping such a treasure hidden was almost as shameful as taking it in the first place. I had to find a way.

A sudden hand on my wrist pulled me from my trance, and I turned to find not Isabel but Marti Finch smiling up at me. Her blue-gray eyes flashed with mischief. An image of Isabel danced through my mind but still I could not look away.

She pulled me down onto the seat next to her. The woman sitting opposite watched us with interest and a knowing smile crossed her lips. She stood and collected a scattering of papers from the table.

"Good luck with your rotation," she said to Marti. "Call and let me know how it went."

She flashed me the same smile and then started for the door. Marti leaned into me playfully.

"Dun, where were you off to just now?" she chuckled. "You trudged past us like a zombie."

I peered into her eyes, eyes that made me want to tell her everything, the stolen box, the Twain manuscript, my shameful part in it all. I felt sure she would listen without judgment or prejudice. But I said nothing, pride and fear overruling all else.

Suddenly, I found myself wanting to reach over and run my fingers through her hair, feel the heat of her skin, taste her breath. Her unadorned beauty, earthy and sensual, was nothing like Isabel's dark glamour. We locked eyes and a rose-tinted blush spread across her cheeks as if she had guessed my every thought. I felt the heat of my own blood on my face.

With difficulty, I reminded myself that she was involved with someone. I had no reason to entertain such fantasies. I looked away, trying to hide my disappointment.

"What's wrong, Dun?" she asked. "Is it your uncle? Has he taken a turn for the worse?"

I shook my head in answer.

"What then? Won't you tell me?"

I wanted to answer but could find no foothold, no beginning. My thoughts were a mishmash of conflicts and desires. Yet something about her warm presence, the concern in her voice, compelled me to speak.

"I lost my job," I muttered.

I looked up at her, surprised by my own words. Once I started, I could not stop.

"Up until a day or so ago," I continued, "I was an English teacher at a Catholic high school. It didn't pay much, and I didn't appreciate the importance of teaching, but the work gave me purpose, something to call myself. Now all that is gone."

"Dun, you're more than any job." She took my hand and leaned closer. "Don't you know that? I look at you and see a man I've known most of my life, a man I admire not for the job he holds but for who he is, for his compassion and sense of humor, his intelligence and honesty."

I cringed at how far I felt from her description.

"You wouldn't say that if you knew everything."

"I know enough. None of us are perfect, Dun. I have my own long list of mistakes and regrets. But they're not all of who I am. The same is true for you."

"It's just that..." I paused, searching for the right words. "I want to get on with my life, Marti, to feel like I'm doing something that matters. Instead, I feel like I'm only wasting time."

"What you're doing now matters, Dun. Your aunt and uncle need you."

Suddenly, she looked past me and dropped my hand. I followed her gaze. Isabel stood frowning down at us. Her face held a mix of confusion and annoyance.

"You didn't get my message?"

"No, I... I mean, yes... but then I ran into..."

"I'm Marti," she interrupted, "an old friend. He's trying to say we keep running into each other."

"A friend?"

"Since before grade school. I grew up a block and a half..." She stopped as a pager buzzed on the tabletop. Grabbing it and the remaining papers, she nudged me out and followed. "I have to go. I'm on call."

She moved past Isabel and hesitated, turning to me and mouthing 'I'm sorry'. Then she hurried out.

Isabel studied me with cool detachment. I tried to guess what she must be thinking, coming upon the two of us sitting close, Marti's hand in mine. I sat and motioned her to do the same. She eyed me warily.

"Is it true?"

"Please sit, Isabel. I can explain."

"Just answer the question and then I'll decide if I'm going to stay or leave."

"Marti and I are friends," I replied, unable to rid my mind of her blushing face, "like she said."

"Friends don't usually sit so close."

"We've know each other a long time."

"Why did she leave in such a hurry, like she had something to hide?"

"She's in medical school. You saw the pager. Being on call is part of her training."

"And I suppose holding your hand," she sneered, "was so she could take your pulse."

"We were discussing something important."

"What about?"

I had no reason not to tell her but something held me back.

"It's personal."

"You can tell her but not me?"

"Like I said, it's personal."

"Fine," she said, glaring at me. "I get the message."

"But Isabel…"

"And trust me," she said, starting for the exit, "it's very personal."

Eleven

A biting wind gusted past the pier, sending its metal light poles into plaintive song as if dueling flutists played somewhere out of sight. I turned my collar to the gale. Spits of rain splattered the wooden walkway, staining the sun-bleached pine blue-black. The first true cool front of the year had arrived early in the afternoon while Griggs and I were still at work.

He moved along the rail, stopping to check each catch, chatting with the fishermen. A pair grizzled brothers, identical twins beneath their unkempt beards and layers of raingear, offered us coffee. A few yards away, a lone woman handed him a slice of homemade pound cake and told him of her exceptional luck a week earlier. We moved on and he handed me half of the cake, motioning down the pier.

"Funny how different we act when the weather is against us." He turned his gaze to the scudding clouds. "For a short while people have a sense of camaraderie, something to pull together against. Once the sun returns, it all vanishes."

I stood for a moment and surveyed the pier, suddenly seeing what he meant. Groups huddled together all along the walkway, sharing conversation and steaming cups, going out of their way to untangle lines or help land a catch. A teenager baited the hook of an old man in a wheelchair.

I studied Griggs' profile. Though an average student at best, his insights into people never ceased to surprise me. Of the two of us he had always seemed the shrewder and, in his way, smarter. I couldn't help but admire him even when he used that knowledge for his own selfish purposes.

After the clash between him and his father, we had assumed an unspoken peace, both of us willing to accept the other's faults and foibles. My sympathies had always been with him. Having Augie as a father was beyond imagining.

Earlier, as we were leaving work for the day, he had yelled over the wind that I should follow him. I asked where to but he gave no answer and instead waved me to my car. I climbed in and turned the engine, wondering how many times I had acted out my part in an identical scene.

With that thought in mind, I caught up with him at the pier's end. The mud-stained water rose and fell below our feet. He rested his elbows on the guardrail and faced the open sea.

"What are we doing here, Griggs?" I leaned close to be heard over the wind. "In case you haven't noticed, it's starting to rain."

"You've forgotten who you are, where you came from," he replied, his eyes still on the water. "I'm helping you remember."

I stepped back, struck by the truth of his words. He'd always had an unnerving knack for seeing right through me, as if he could read my every thought. I did need to remember. Though I was again living on the island, I had yet to absorb the purpose of my return, yet to find the meaning.

I took a breath and surveyed the unbroken horizon, trying to capture a sense of the place, the salt-laced air, the broad sky. A corduroy-like set of swells rose above the outside sandbar, their steep faces dark and windblown, their tops feathering. They seemed to pause and hover in place. Then they pitched forward with zipper-like perfection, collapsing onto themselves in a mass of foam and spray.

Griggs and I had spent countless summers roaming this same beach, fishing from this same pier. Within those days, time had seemed suspended, irrelevant even. We moved from moment to moment completely immersed in the world around us, our day to day life basic and elemental. Though I knew those times were gone forever, I wanted to make that connection to a place once again. But I had no idea how. He pushed himself from the rail and grabbed my shoulder.

"Let's go." He pointed me toward the street. "You're in need of another sort of sustenance."

Minutes later we stepped into the cramped confines of Tidewater Oyster Bar. Perched on a weathered bayside dock, the tiny café overlooked a curving breakwater and the ship channel just beyond. To our left, a marina filled with yachts, shrimpers and fishing boats stretched alongside the jetty.

We sat at the bar and watched gloved men in rubber aprons shuck one ice-covered tray of oysters after another. The window behind them framed the marina entrance, where a half-dozen pelicans circled the main channel, diving into the green water each in turn. Scattering shad skipped along the surface like silver coins.

An oyster-filled tray and two bottles of beer appeared on the counter between us. Griggs turned to me and raised his bottle.

"May you find," he said, grinning, "a pearl in every oyster."

"Or even just one." I tapped my bottle against his.

"Dun," he mocked, "you have to think big to get anywhere worth going to, even if it's only where you came from."

I dipped an oyster in red sauce and let it slide down my throat. The fresh saltwater taste lingered on the back of my tongue as if I had just swallowed the essence of the sea itself. I wondered how many trays of oysters we had shared over the years. Far too many to remember.

The bartender, a slender blonde in a strapless top and denim shorts, eyed Griggs as she moved about the counter. He pulled out a roll of bills and pulled several free, making sure she noticed him drop them into the tip jar. She sauntered over to where we sat.

"I'm off in five minutes," she whispered.

"I'll be here," he replied, grinning. "Any chance you could find a girlfriend for my buddy?"

She glanced at me, nodded and turned to leave. He leaned across the bar, watching as she disappeared through the kitchen door.

"Now that's what I call sustenance, some for me, some for you."

"Not for me, Griggs."

"Come on, Dun, she has a friend."

"I'm not interested."

"Have some fun for once," he pressed. A salacious grin crossed his lips. "Or have you forgotten how?"

"No, I haven't forgotten how."

"Oh, I understand," he nodded. "This is about that babe I met at the big yellow house. What's her name?"

"Isabel Langdon."

"You must have it bad for her, cousin." He squinted at me. "Doing the wild thing yet?"

"Don't talk about her like that."

I cringed, hearing how prudish I sounded.

"She's a fox, cousin. It's only natural."

Hoping to change the subject, I motioned at the bills.

"I thought you had money problems."

I made no effort to hide my suspicion. He stuffed the roll back into his pocket.

"Some people owed me," he muttered, avoiding my gaze, "and finally paid up."

"Is that the truth?"

His eyes flashed with a brief anger before returning to their usual indifference.

"Like I said," he said as if predicting the weather, "you've got to think big."

"Well, I hope you know what you're doing."

The blonde reappeared, a purse over her shoulder. A dark-haired woman stood behind her. Griggs gave his head a quick shake, sending her back into the kitchen.

He slid off the stool and joined the blonde, winking at me as they pushed through the door. Watching them, I was reminded of my hapless last encounter with Isabel. Was there a chance she might be willing to try again? I decided I had to know.

The sky had cleared by the time I stepped onto Mrs. Langdon's high-ceilinged porch. Sunlight speckled the floorboards with bits of gold. I rang the doorbell and silently rehearsed what I wanted to say. I could only hope Isabel would answer the door. I would have little chance of getting past the old woman.

The heavy latch clicked and the door swung open. Isabel stood at the threshold eyeing me. I searched her face trying to gauge her reaction. That she had yet to slam the door on me seemed encouraging.

"I'm sorry we got crosswise," I began. Then I nodded toward the porch steps. "Will you sit and talk?"

She glanced inside the house, pulled the door closed and started down the stairs, motioning me to follow. We turned at the sidewalk, saying nothing as we walked into the indigo shade of late afternoon. The scattered oleanders and palms rattled before the shifting wind.

Midway along the street she stopped and turned, peering into my face as if unsure how to begin.

"I only have a moment," she said, glancing toward the house. "My grandmother has made it clear she wants me to have nothing to do with you."

"What do you want?"

"I'm sorry I got angry when I saw you with your friend. It's just that… she's very pretty and, well, the way she was looking at you. Is it true she's just an old friend?"

"Not only that," I nodded, "she's involved with someone."

She glanced at the house again.

"We're still getting to know each other, Dun, but so far I like what I see."

"Maybe I'll improve with time."

"Like wine," she added with a smile.

Her grandmother's voice drifted over the oleanders. She took my hand and drew me close, letting her lips brush mine with the hint of a kiss. Then she pressed hard into me before pulling away and disappearing past the bushes. Breathless, I ran my tongue over my burning lips, half-expecting to taste blood.

A close-up image of Isabel, her flawless skin the color of fresh peaches, roamed my thoughts as I drove to my apartment. A low sun streamed through the broken clouds. The wind had already shifted to the south again. Our taste of fall would be brief.

I parked in the alley, climbed out and rounded the honeysuckle, still lost to my thoughts. When I reached the gate, I looked up and suddenly felt as if I'd stepped back in time. Onward was sitting at the top of the stairs again. He stood and motioned me up with an impatient wave.

"Grab the Twain book," he said, passing me on his way down, "and meet me out front."

Minutes later we pulled up to a high, vine-draped wharf edging a narrow inlet. Dense stands of mangrove and salt grass rimmed the opposite shoreline. Beyond the thicket, the open bay stretched to the horizon, its sunset-filled surface an undulating maze of tangerine and azure. A lone palm rose above the water like a sentinel.

Onward explained on our way that he had enlisted the help of an old friend, a retired freelance journalist and rare book collector. The man assured him he could tell us if the manuscript was genuine. Then maybe I could figure a way to return it.

The story had filled my sleep with restless dreams. Jim's freedom, fragile and illusory, echoed the later bigotry of Jim Crow and segregation. He had eventually gone on to find work as a buffalo soldier in West Texas and marry again, a woman half-white and half-Choctaw. Huck had

94

ceased his aimless wandering to live near his friend. I couldn't help but imagine the public's reaction had Twain decided to publish. I also found myself wondering what Onward thought of the story.

I climbed out of the panel truck and surveyed the pointed spit of land. Other than the wharf, I could see no sign of life, no house or trailer. I was astounded that such an isolated place still existed on the island.

I followed Onward up the weathered steps and through a slim gap in the wall of vines. A wooden deck opened before us, descending to a waterside landing and walkway. A mildewed houseboat sat moored to the far end.

I peered at the floating wreck, wondering what sort of book expert would live in such a place. We climbed down the creaking stairs and onto a waterside dock, where a ship's bell hung from a forked pole. Onward pulled on the rope. The high-pitched peal echoed down the inlet in a series of diminishing notes. Moments later a man emerged from the cabin. A wild mass of silver hair framed his broad face. He waved us on and disappeared inside.

"Now don't let old Gibson put the scare in you." Onward leaned in, his voice a near-whisper. "He can be a little different."

"What do you mean by 'a little different'?"

"Got to live by his own rules, do things his own way."

His vague answer only added to my uncertainty.

"Are you sure about this?"

"Gibson, he knows his books," he replied, pointing me onto the boat, "knows them good."

Moments later we stepped inside the cramped cabin. Books and papers crowded the shelves and every corner but one. It held a small table and manual typewriter. The man sat bent over a shortwave radio, screwdriver in hand.

Putting the tool aside, he sat back and flipped a toggle switch. The radio crackled and then settled on a monotone reporting of offshore barometric pressure, water temperature, swell height and wind speed. He listened intently, taking little notice of us.

Onward sat on the tattered couch and idly thumbed through the manuscript. I wandered the bookshelves to see what they might tell me. Right off, I noticed an unusual title, On the Nature of Things, by the Roman poet and philosopher, Lucretius. The ancient text, lost for centuries, is known for claiming that matter is composed of atoms, and happiness is found in seeking beauty and pleasure rather than fearing death. The book was considered heretical by some.

The shelves also held texts on physics and alchemy, paganism and Christianity. Carl Sandberg's five-volume biography of Abraham Lincoln sat next to Graham Greene's The Power and the Glory. Gibson was clearly a man of ideas.

The radio crackled again and the weather report was replaced by the pulsing rhythm of reggae. He had dialed up a station in Jamaica. He stood and ambled to the refrigerator, pulling out several bottles and setting them on the counter. He had yet to say a word.

Popping off the tops, he wedged the bottles between his thick fingers and moved back into the room, handing us each one. His quick eyes darted between the two of us. He raised his beer in a silent toast and then took a long pull.

"Three thousand years of brewing expertise went into what we now enjoy," he announced, holding the bottle to the light. "Think of it. There was a time in the dark and distant past before the existence of beer."

"Uh-huh," Onward replied, "must have been some dark ages, sure enough."

"Now, there's a sobering thought," Gibson added, grinning. "So, what have you brought me? Something mysterious, I hope."

Onward handed him the manuscript and he thumbed through the pages, pausing to squint at select passages. His lively eyes jumped from line to line, paragraph to paragraph. After a moment, he looked up and brushed back his cloud of hair.

"Looks like a codex."

"A codex?" I asked.

"A codex is a handwritten and bound manuscript, usually ancient." He tapped the cover with his forefinger. "And you think this is a lost sequel to Huck Finn?"

I nodded.

"It'll take time to be sure, but if you are willing to leave if with me…" He turned and vanished through an adjacent doorway, reappearing seconds later with a metal lockbox. "As I was saying, if you'll leave it, I'll store it in this fireproof case and hide in the cabinet above the refrigerator."

"Agreed," I answered, "as long as you're willing to keep it a secret."

"If this is what you think it is then secrecy is the only way to ensure its safety."

"But based on what you've seen so far, what do you think? Did Twain write it?"

"Handwriting is only one part of the puzzle. The phrasing, the word selection, and above all, the story itself will tell the truth of authorship."

I turned to Onward and he nodded his agreement. Gibson sat and cradled the manuscript in his lap, flipping to the first page and beginning again.

"I'll be in touch when I'm ready," he muttered without looking up.

Onward shrugged and we started for the door, the crimson glow of dusk lighting our way.

Twelve

After a restless night dogged by a slew of fleeting dreams - Moon's battered face, the manuscript in flames - I drove the few blocks to my childhood home, pulled to the curb and cut the engine. Fie waited on the front steps. Seeing me, she checked her watch and called through the door. Whit appeared at the threshold, frowned at her and ambled down the stairs. She tailed him impatiently.

She had asked me to ferry them to an appointment with Whit's longtime doctor and childhood friend, Hanley Curtis. Whit was not happy about the arrangement. As far as he was concerned, there was no point in covering the same ground yet again. Fie, on the other hand, had little toleration for his defeatist attitude. In her view a cure for his mysterious condition was there to be found. It was only a matter of persistence.

I had known Hanley my entire life. Compact and balding, he wore wire-rimmed glasses and used a long black and gold holder for the three cigarettes he allowed himself each day, only while at the office. His gray suits always seemed a size too large.

Mrs. Kopeck, his receptionist, had worked for him since before I was born. I figured she had to be in her eighties. She blinked at us through thick bifocals as we filed into the waiting room.

Turning to her appointment book, she flipped through the pages, first one way and then the other, her face pinched with worry. The door to Hanley's office stood half-open, the room empty. I wondered if Fie had misremembered the time. Mrs. Kopeck blinked again, her finger pressed to the date.

"The doctor…" she started, "well I… today he…"

Before she could finish the thought, Hanley strolled through the door and turned toward his office, motioning us to follow.

"I know, Mrs. Kopeck," he called over his shoulder, "I'm not supposed to be here."

He set his bag on the desk and sat on the edge, turning his attention to Fie.

"My Fridays are usually reserved for hospital visits but I make exceptions when necessary."

"We're sorry to disrupt your routine, Hanley," she replied. "I felt this just couldn't wait any longer."

Onward had told me Hanley, a longtime bachelor, had always been sweet on Fie. He bent toward her.

"Well, Fie, I'm glad to have the benefit your company," he smiled, "even for a little while."

Whit snorted and paced the floor impatiently. Hanley leaned closer.

"I'm willing to wager," he added, "you had to twist the stubborn mule's arm to get him in here."

"Jackass is the word I'd use," she deadpanned, "but mule is close enough."

"And you've brought along reinforcements." He nodded my direction.

"You remember Dun."

"Of course." He shook my hand. "I have something to ask of you after we're through here. Now, if you'll excuse us."

He took Whit by the shoulder, led him into an adjacent examining room and closed the door. We moved back to the waiting room where Mrs. Kopeck busied herself with a stack of files. Fie settled onto an overstuffed couch and peered out the lone window. I sat beside her.

The second-floor looked out onto the hospital grounds, tree-filled and splattered with sunlight. Men and women in white uniforms and lab coats moved between the buildings singly and in pairs. I imagined Marti among them. The way she had been looking at me when Isabel arrived at the bar haunted my thoughts. Whatever her intent, Isabel saw it too and had taken offense.

Mrs. Kopeck gathered a stack of folders from her desk and vanished through the doorway. Fie turned from the window and studied me with her black eyes.

"Dun, something has been bothering you these past few days," she announced with authority, "and I'd like to know what it is."

She sat back waiting for a reply.

"I'm tired is all," I hedged. "We've had a lot of catching up to do."

A part of me wanted to tell her of my lost job and my worry over Griggs' sketchy choices. But I knew better. Once I started, she would have one question after another, her quick mind seeing through my omissions and evasions. Still, I reminded myself she had always been the one person I could count on for advice. Her no-nonsense practicality brooked no illusions. All at once an idea came to me.

"Fie, if I ask your opinion will you answer me without turning it into an interrogation?"

"Why do you assume I would do such a thing, Dun?"

"Is that an answer?"

"Yes," she replied with a sigh, "I will answer without interrogation, as you so kindly put it."

"Imagine you discovered something valuable," I began, "maybe even priceless, something that belonged to someone else. Then you lost it without them knowing it ever existed in the first place. What would you do?"

"What sort of priceless thing?"

"That was a question, Fie," I reminder her.

"You must give me some idea of what you have in mind."

"Let's say you found a painting by Vincent Van Gogh, a painting no one knew existed, maybe the very last painting he ever did. And you decided to keep it for a while, maybe longer than you should have. Then it was gone, stolen. The painting didn't belong to you but you had

100

it when it was taken, and only you know it ever existed. What do you do?"

"Why, I find a way to get it back and return it to the rightful owner."

"How do you do that? It was stolen. It's gone."

"If you lose a priceless work that the entire world should have a chance to see, then you are responsible for getting it back. You have a moral obligation."

"But you don't know who took it or what became of it or where to start looking."

"Every problem has a solution. You must be determined enough to find it."

I stared at her, unable to excuse myself from the unfortunate logic of her answer. I was responsible for the silver box and, more important, the manuscript. I had to find the solution she insisted waited somewhere out there. She leaned her elbows on her knees and peered into my face.

"Dun, does this have anything to do with what's bothering you?"

"Fie, I can't..."

"Has it something to do with Onward? He's seemed troubled ever since his return. Never once has he explained where he was for those months after his father's funeral."

"Onward is a private man, Fie. You know that. He's not likely to bring up personal matters without good reason."

"You're not him, Dun."

"Fie..."

"Then won't you tell me about yourself? How is your teaching?"

I turned my eyes, ashamed my sense of humiliation and defeat had forced my silence. If the tables were turned I'd want her to trust me with the truth. I might have attempted an answer but Whit's voice called from behind.

"What's that I heard about teaching?"

"Not that it's any of your business," she replied, "but I was just asking Dun about his job."

"What the devil for? He has a job right here."

"It's only temporary," I grumbled.

The thought of working in the store for the rest of my life depressed me beyond words. He sat beside her and waved a finger at me.

"I wouldn't count on that. At the rate I'm going, I may have to retire."

"But Whit, you can't expect me to…"

"I hate to break up this family meeting," Hanley called from his office doorway, "but I need to talk to Dun."

Relieved to end the conversation, I joined him. He closed the door and motioned me to a chair.

"Whit gave me permission to talk with you." He resumed his spot on the corner. "So I can speak freely."

"Okay," I replied, unsure what he meant.

"A doctor has to have a patient's permission to discuss his or her condition."

I nodded my understanding.

"I know Fie asked you back home," he continued, "to help him with the store."

He placed a cigarette in the holder and held a heavy brass lighter to the end. The thin paper crackled before the flame. Clenching the tip between his teeth, he leaned back and folded his arms over his chest. A trail of blue smoke drifted past his eyes.

"So, you see him on a regular basis?"

"More or less," I answered. "Is that what you wanted to ask me?"

"In part it is." He studied me a moment. "Do you have a clear idea why he needs your help?"

"If you're asking whether I understand what's wrong with him I'd have to say no. Sometimes he seems okay, other times not at all."

"Whit is my friend," he said with a sigh. "I hate to see him like this."

"Like what, Hanley? You're worrying me."

"Neither he nor Fie will believe me, but from a purely physical standpoint there's not a thing wrong with him."

"I don't understand."

"I've done every test in the book, consulted with every specialist I know. There's no illness."

"It's all in his head?"

"As a doctor, I wouldn't put it like that. He doesn't fit an actual diagnosis like depression."

"What then?"

"Whit believes he's dying. I suppose in a way he is. Spending your days with one foot in the grave is not much like living." He blew a thin stream of smoke into the air. "You said sometimes he seems okay. Do you have any idea why?"

I glanced at the closed door, uncertain how I should answer. Connie's smiling face flashed through my thoughts.

"He has a friend," I offered, "a woman."

I winced realizing I had no trouble telling the truth when it concerned someone other than me. Hanley sat up and jerked the cigarette holder from between his teeth.

"How did I miss that?" he said to himself.

"I think they keep it hidden," I added. "I don't know why."

"That's helpful, Dun. I need to think about this for a while. I won't say anything to him or Fie. It's best that he doesn't know you told me. If they ask, tell them I needed your advice about a young patient, someone about your age."

He stood and ushered me out the door as if we'd been discussing the weather. My head hurt with all I'd heard. Stepping past him, I realized with dismay I had gained yet another secret.

That afternoon I slumped into a weathered deck chair and watched scattered clouds drift overhead like wind-starved ships. Their peach and blue-gray forms reflected off the bay's calm surface with mirror-like precision. I studied the intricate shapes, at once ethereal yet solid, like the future I once imagined for myself.

Gibson emerged from the houseboat and started across the deck, Onward beside him. We had come to check on his progress in authenticating the manuscript. He pulled several cans of beer from an ice chest and then eased into a chair. Onward perched on the bench opposite me.

"Dun, did you know a whole company of black soldiers lost their jobs and pensions back in 1906?" He shook his round head side to side. "That was down in Brownsville, on the border with Mexico. They got blamed for shooting up the town but Gibson here says there's plenty of evidence they didn't do it."

"I'm working on a story for one of the national magazines," he explained. "I figured Onward would be interested so we've been going over my research."

"I thought you were retired."

"When I want to be," he replied. He motioned toward the bay. "With a view like this, who needs work? On the other hand, there are stories that need telling."

My dream of becoming a freelance writer, once fervid, had long since faded. Gibson sipped his beer and studied me.

"Onward mentioned," he finally said, "that you're a journalist."

"I have a degree," I muttered, ashamed to have so little to show for it. "That's about all I can claim."

"I could use a researcher. Interested?"

I stared at him, shocked into speechlessness. He sat back with a knowing look.

"I realize that digging through old books and reams of paper is far from glamorous, not to mention beneath your abilities. But research is the most important part of the process. That's where the truth hides. Our job is to ferret out the facts that separate the real story from myth and propaganda."

"It sounds glamorous when you put it like that."

"Well, it can be. Ever hear of Poggio Bracciolini?"

I gave my head a shake.

"He risked persecution and torture to find a book that had been as good as lost for a thousand years, found it in a remote monastery. Some believe the message it held changed the world. Now, that's some good research."

"You're talking about On the Nature of Things. I saw it on your shelf"

"Good guess," he nodded. "Onward gave it to me."

I turned to him, making no effort to hide my surprise.

"Don't you give me that look, Dun Osay," he scoffed. "You know I like books. Besides, I understand lost and almost forgotten better than most."

I shifted my gaze back to the mirror-like bay, trying to resist the lure of Gibson's offer. I had long ago reconciled myself to the reality of my life. The thought of resurrecting a lost dream only added to my worries.

Thirteen

On my way out Gibson had pressed a scrap of paper into my palm. The note held the name and address of a handwriting expert, a Professor Bernard Mertz. He cautioned me to take great care in ensuring that the manuscript's existence remained hidden from everyone outside our small circle, even the professor. Anything less could prove disastrous.

Bernie Mertz had taught physics at the university for nearly thirty years. He was well-known for developing a procedure to decipher hidden patterns in complex systems, systems involving subatomic particles such as electrons, neutrons and protons. Coincidentally but no doubt related, he also had a preternatural ability to recognize patterns, a talent useful in handwriting analysis. Over the years he had consulted with law enforcement and the courts, even the FBI on occasion.

Bernie had asked me to meet him at his home, a compact bungalow on a tree-shaded street only blocks from the university. With a steep roof sloping from peak to eave, the house looked as if it might have been plucked straight from the streets of an Alpine village. Leaded stained-glass windows completed the effect.

I was about to knock when a voice called from the street. I turned to find a man on a battered bicycle tracing figure eights across the pavement. He waved at me between turns. In his free hand was a dripping ice cream cone. He bumped up the driveway, motioned me to follow and disappeared inside the house. Moments later we were sitting opposite each other in his book-cluttered study.

Heeding Gibson's advice, I had concocted an elaborate cover story involving a trove of letters found in the basement of a Victorian mansion outside Hannibal, Missouri. Plumbers fixing a leak had stumbled upon a water-damaged steamer trunk hidden behind a bricked-up wall and marked with the initials SLC. Inside were stacks of ribbon-tied letters.

I claimed I had brought him a page from one of the letters because I suspected they were written by none other than Mark Twain. When he heard the name his watery eyes lit up like miniature suns. I told him I had also brought along Onward's book of Twain letters for comparison.

I handed over the yellowed page and waited, trying to gauge his reaction. His hands shook as he held it to the light. He studied one side and the other before setting it on the table between us and switching on a nearby lamp. He bent over the slanted scrawl, his nose nearly touching the paper, and I wondered if the stale smell told him something important, something hidden from the rest of us.

For a full minute the only sound was his rasping breath. Now and then he flipped through Onward's book, mumbled something inaudible and returned to the letter. At one point he jumped up and grabbed a magnifying glass, scrutinizing a word as if it held a special meaning. Finally, he sat back and eyed me.

"You have more letters?"

"Dozens, I'd say."

"So, this page is from a letter?"

"Isn't that obvious?"

"Not so obvious as at first glance."

"Meaning..."

"The phrasing is letter-like, yet not quite."

"Our question is whether there is a handwriting match." I could see he wanted to know more and hoped to get it out of me without saying so, just as Gibson had warned. "Phrasing is irrelevant."

"Is it? The page reads like a story."

"Why wouldn't a letter written by a novelist read like a story?"

"Why wouldn't a story by a novelist read like a letter?"

"Are you saying this is in Twain's hand?"

107

"You brought only a single page," he pressed. "Why?"

"Are you going to give me an answer or not?"

"Is there a reason?"

"We were told a single page would suffice." I decided then to call his bluff. "Maybe I should go elsewhere for an opinion."

"No, no, please… the page was enough."

"Then you know the answer." I reached for the paper. "That longhand is Twain's, isn't it?"

He sighed and slid it across the table.

"I'd stake my reputation on it."

I nodded and grabbed the page. We had our answer.

I went straight to the store, hoping to catch Onward still there. I had to tell him the news. But when I pulled up to the small parking lot behind the building, his truck was nowhere in sight.

I was about to leave when the shop door flew open and he stumbled out, a walnut rocking chair in his arms. He began an unsteady path toward the panel truck, stopping every few steps to catch his breath. I wondered what could be so important he felt compelled to attempt a delivery on his own.

By the time I reached him he was nearly to the truck. Moments later we had it secured inside. He tossed me the keys and started for the passenger door.

"Good thing you showed up when you did," he said between breaths. He motioned me behind the steering wheel with a brisk wave. "I don't believe I could've got that big chair into Elvin Poteau's house without breaking something."

"Why not wait for help?"

"Griggs is tied up with a customer and I promised Elvin I'd get the chair over to him by today. He's got the lumbago and thinks a rocking chair is the only way to get over it. He won't go to a doctor and has no use for medicine other than the voodoo potions his sister in Lafayette sends him."

I told him about the manuscript's authenticity during the drive there but he seemed to only half-listen and had little to say about it. I had expected excitement out of him, or at least relief. Instead I got ho-hum. His thoughts remained elsewhere the entire ride. I had little idea what to make of it. Whatever the cause, I found his preoccupation disappointing, not to mention a considerable annoyance.

Elvin Poteau lived southeast of downtown in an area hit hard by the Nineteen Hundred Storm, the worst hurricane in island history. Over six thousand people lost their lives in the storm, most drowning in a massive tidal surge that inundated the entire town. Those who remained witnessed the raising of the island's interior by six meters, an astounding feat of engineering.

The blue and white bungalow Onward pointed me to had been raised an additional eight feet above the street. Green storm shutters flanked the front windows. Towering over the sidewalk, a perilously thin palm tree swayed overhead like a giant metronome.

We retrieved the rocking chair and started toward the house. The staircase leading to the porch was unusually steep and narrow. I tried to imagine Onward carrying the heavy chair up those steps alone. The task was challenge enough for two.

My back to the house, I grabbed the front of the chair and started up the stairs. Onward followed behind, grunting with every step. Neither of us could see much more than the other's sweating face. I had nearly reached the top step when I heard a door open.

"That you, Onward?"

"I'm down here somewhere, Elvin. That's Dun up on top doing the hard work. Good thing he's young."

"I can see it's one tough job alright."

"What'd you mean, Elvin? You can't see a thing."

"I see you huffing and puffing like you're about to keel over."

"That's your ears telling you."

"Now you got to know just because a man's blind doesn't mean he can't see, Onward Cates."

"Then you see how you got the steepest stairs in town."

"Sure enough," he chuckled. "My daddy rebuilt them his own self after our last big hurricane took down the old stairway. He wouldn't listen to a damn word of advice from any person rich or poor, smart or dumb. He got to be one stubborn man."

"So everybody said long as I can remember."

We reached the landing and set the chair on the floor, both of us panting. Elvin stood holding the door open, cane in hand. I could see he was trying hard to stifle a laugh.

"Or maybe you just got too old for this job," he quipped.

"All I'm too old for is these stairs."

"I hear that. I feel it my own self when I climb up them." He raised one foot and then the other, grimacing. "Going down's not so bad, but to make it back up I have to imagine that cold beer waiting for me in the ice box."

Onward nodded at the doorway and we lifted the chair once again and stepped through. Elvin called out directions as we wound through the rooms. Within moments we had it in place.

He tested the chair and then disappeared through an adjacent doorway, returning with three glass jars and an unmarked bottle of red wine. Pulling the cork free with his teeth he poured us each a glass. The wine, a nearly opaque crimson, smelled of fresh earth and leather.

Elvin ran a hand across his freckled scalp, hairless save for a single tuft of white in the shape of a widow's peak. His cloudy eyes appeared to wander of their own accord. Dimples the size and color of ripe crabapples transformed his pale cheeks whenever he smiled. He and Onward seemed an unlikely pair.

"You got to know my uncle Michel," he said, raising his glass, "he sure could make himself up some good bootleg."

"Sure enough could, Elvin," Onward agreed. He turned to me. "Elvin's uncle lives on the same street as Aunt Sophie, your great aunt. He used to come visit his uncle every summer. That's how we came to know one another."

"You ever go back, Onward?" he asked.

"I've been only once in twenty years, for my father's funeral."

"Most of my family still lives in Lafayette so I get over there when I can. After Michel passed on I didn't care much about seeing Mississippi again. Maybe I don't much like to be reminded how they treated us."

"Uh-huh," Onward nodded.

"Nobody took much notice of Onward and me when we were children," he said in my direction. "We'd spend the whole day roaming the streets or fishing or stealing peaches and they just say to themselves those little boys they don't know any different. Soon as we grow up a little, everybody took notice, and I mean it seemed like the whole damn town some days. Cajun boy from Louisiana supposed to spend time with his own, not somebody different from him.

"Now it was the same story back home but I didn't know anybody like Onward there. Besides which, I couldn't see how he was different from me, at least not in any way that mattered worth a damn. But the sad old world follows a different set of rules, leastwise in that part of the world."

"Just got to make your way as best you can," Onward replied, "and not worry about what people might think."

He glanced at his watch and then looked again, jumping to his feet.

111

"Elvin, I got to go! I got to go or I'm in big trouble."

"What you got on that makes you jump like that?" he chuckled and pointed toward the door. "Sure, I can see plain as day. You got yourself a lady waiting. Well, go on then."

Surprised, I looked up at him. Giving me a quick nod, he grabbed my arm and we were out the door in seconds.

Fourteen

I dropped Onward at his house and pondered over how little I knew of him despite seeing him every day. I was so caught up in my own romantic concerns I'd been blind to his. It was a shameful realization.

I had only just arrived home when Moon burst through the back door, waving his arms like a mad man. I paused midway up the stairs. For an instant I thought Ronny had gone on another tirade. But even from a distance I could see Moon's concern was for me rather than himself.

"Quick, Dun," he whispered from the foot of the stairs, "you must make yourself scarce. The police have already been here once."

"The police have been here?" I met him at the gate. "But why?"

"They're looking for your friend."

"What do they want with Onward?"

"They were their usual closed-mouth selves but I overheard a little. I believe it must have something to do with stolen property."

A pit opened in my gut. Did they somehow find out about the silver box? Moon leaned past the gate, checking the alley in both directions.

"You'd better go warn him before they return."

I started for my car but stopped when a police cruiser turned into the alley. Moments later two officers climbed out, one thick-necked and ruddy, the other ghostly pale. I felt Moon move next to me.

"We're looking for a Dun Osay," the thick-necked officer announced. "You wouldn't happen to be him, would you?"

I nodded.

"Do you know where we can find an Onward Cates?"

"Who?" I stalled.

"A black man by the name Onward Cates."

"I haven't seen him," I answered, nearly choking on the lie, "for must be a day or two."

I fought the urge to run. The pale officer took a step closer. His nametag read Sergeant Hicks.

"We understand that you are a close friend of Mr. Cates. Is that an accurate description of your relationship?"

"Who told you that?"

"Just answer the question, sir."

"We just work together." I tried to sound convincing. "You know how it is."

"That's the problem with this country nowadays," the thick-necked officer said beneath his teeth, "you end up having to work with all kinds, like it or not. You know what I mean?"

"Well, I…"

"The feds give them rights and they start to thinking they're equal to us, people like you and me. Am I right?"

I gave my head a slight nod, taken aback by his bald-faced bigotry.

"You don't seem so sure," he added, cutting his eyes.

"I'm sure," I mumbled.

The words seemed to come from another place, someone else's mouth, someone else's words. A wave of shame passed through me.

"Sure of…" he said, leaning closer.

"I don't think they're equal," I muttered.

"Oh, Dun," Moon groaned.

Sergeant Hicks nudged his partner aside.

"And you haven't seen him?"

"I've seen him," Ronny's voice called from the yard. "I've seen the both of them. They act like they're lovers or something. It's disgusting."

I glanced at him and he flashed a hateful grin. The thick-necked officer eyed me while Sergeant Hicks stood waiting for an answer. I shook my head, afraid to speak.

"If you do see Mr. Cates," he said, handing me a card, "I'd appreciate a call."

The radio on his hip crackled and he lifted it to his ear. Then he motioned his companion to the car.

"I do hope," Moon sighed as the car disappeared in a cloud of dust, "that you know what you're doing."

A half hour later I stepped into Carmelo Puglia's café, hoping I might find Onward there. I had already checked his house. A woman I had never seen before peered at me from behind the counter.

"You're Onward Cates friend," she announced, her tone accusatory.

Every faced in the room turned my way. Or so it seemed.

"Why would you think that?" I replied, still rattled by the officers' questions.

She eyed me with suspicion.

"You're not his friend?"

I could barely contain my racing thoughts. I gave my head a quick shake.

"It's just that the police were here and…"

I pivoted and rushed out the door, unable to listen any more. An old black woman standing in the shade of the café turned at my approach. Her cloudy eyes flickered with recognition.

"You're that friend of Onward's."

"No, I… I…" I stammered, unable to move. "I don't know him."

"But I saw you at the furniture store," she insisted, stepping closer and peering into my eyes, "you and him together. I'm sure it was you."

I suddenly recognized her as Mrs. King, the old woman he was helping when I discovered the box missing. Her face wavered before me, surreal and dreamlike.

"It wasn't me you saw," I mumbled. "I'm not the man's friend. You must have me confused with someone else."

"I was shopping for a new chair."

"I have to go now," I muttered, stumbling off.

"I've decided which one I want," she called after me.

Unsure what else to do, I decided to go see Isabel. I needed to find out what the police knew about the silver box.

When I reached the house I mounted the broad porch and paused to take a breath, trying to clear my head. Then I gave the door a light tap and once again prayed that Isabel would answer. Instead, Mrs. Langdon's scowling face appeared in the doorway.

Without the turban her tinted hair shone a metallic copper in the harsh sunlight. Her eyes flashed with disgust. She raised a half-filled tumbler to her lips, squinting at me through the brown liquid.

"You have a lot of nerve," she sneered, "coming here after you brought a thief into my house, a colored one at that."

"What are you saying, Mrs. Langdon?" I acted as if I knew nothing.

"Are you trying to tell me the fourteen-carat gold and pearl necklace I had hidden in my dresser, an heirloom worth thousands, just happened to walk off the same day you and he delivered the desk? I've never heard such nonsense."

"Did you say a necklace?"

"That necklace has been in the family since before the Civil War. My grandmother's initials, VSH, are engraved on the clasp. Such unique heirlooms can be easily traced. It is only a matter of time before your colored friend is apprehended."

"Onward's no thief," I said, finally finding the will to defend him. "Our being here around the time it went missing is purely circumstantial. You have no proof he stole it."

"Do you imagine yourself some sort of junior attorney, Mr. Osay?"

"You just assume that since he's black, he must be guilty."

"I do believe," she replied coolly, "that you're beginning to understand."

"I understand people like you, backward-thinking and hateful. I've been surrounded by them my whole life. People like you are why I left this island in the first place."

"If I have my way," she sneered, "this time you'll leave in chains. I've little doubt you're involved too."

She slammed the door in my face.

I wandered the backstreets aimlessly until finally I found myself parked in front of Tarp's vine-draped house. Why I could not say. I sat unmoving in the windless twilight. An anvil-shaped storm loomed over the horizon, blood red and ominous.

Forcing myself out of the car, I made my way to the house and rapped my knuckles against the bowed-out coffin lid, trying not to think of its original purpose. The door swung open. Tarp eyed me before waving me inside.

"You got something to tell me," he announced, "something that's got to be told."

"Onward is in trouble," I replied tentatively.

"I mean you got something else to say, something about you yourself."

I flinched at the thought. Some hidden part of me must have known all along. I peered into his plum-colored face.

"I did it," I whispered, astonished by the realization. "I denied him three times."

Shame settled over me with brutal clarity. I had no excuses. Fear had undone my supposed belief in friendship and loyalty. I didn't want to think what sort of man I had become.

"Lord knows you got to be feeling pretty low just now," he said as if reading my mind. He ushered me into the kitchen. "You got to be feeling like Saint Peter himself after denying Jesus."

I nodded, unable to speak.

"But look where he got to," he added. He put a hand on my shoulder. "You got some time yet, truth be told."

I suddenly realized why I was there. I had to find Onward.

"Have you seen him, Tarp? Do you know where he is?"

"Sit yourself down." He pointed me to the table. "I got something for you to see."

He disappeared through the doorway, returning moments later with a large Bible, the sort used to record births and deaths. Setting it on the tabletop, he flipped to the middle and lifted out a tattered photograph. He sat down beside me and held the faded image to the light.

Three young men stood at the edge of a tree-shaded porch. Facing the camera, they smirked as if someone had shared a joke, or perhaps a secret. A young woman stood behind them, her hand on a half-open door, one foot on the threshold. Her face held a wistful mix of longing and resignation.

"Your aunt Fie took this picture. This here is your uncle Whit, and this is August." Tarp slid his finger from face to face, letting it rest on the last figure. "And this here is your daddy."

I peered at the image of my father, younger than I'd ever seen him. As I looked closer, I noticed he seemed to be glancing back at the young woman.

"Who is she?" I pointed.

"That's Onward's mother, Viola." He raised the photo for a better view. "She was a good-looking girl, and sweet as buttermilk."

I studied her face. Slim and pretty, she had one downturned eye, giving her a sad but reflective look nearly identical to Onward's.

"Then this is Mississippi," I guessed.

"Same town I grew up in, same town your family came from. The Osay boys visited for a week or two every summer, your father the most out of the three."

"He looks so young."

"We didn't know it at the time," he replied, shaking his head side to side, "but that was the last visit he ever made. War came along and changed everything."

I stared at the image, mesmerized by the young faces, and by how little of my father I understood.

"No one ever told me," I finally said, "that he and Onward's mother knew each other."

"Her mother cooked for your great aunt Sophie, so Viola was around all the time."

"Then they were close?"

I sensed he knew more than he was willing to tell. He pursed his lips and tapped the photo with his finger.

"Now, I showed you this here picture for a reason. I had me a vision, a vision of you, you and us. You got to remember our families are close with one another, always been so. Onward will understand what happened, how you denied him."

"He knows, doesn't he?"

"Don't forget what I told you," he replied, nodding, "when you see him."

"You know where he is," I blurted, my thoughts returning to the reason for my visit. "I need to know, Tarp."

"He said to tell you he's holed up at Gibson's."

I realized at once there was no better place for him than the hidden dock where Gibson moored his houseboat. Tarp waved toward the door.

"You go on, now."

I angled my car behind a thick stand of salt cedar adjacent to Gibson's dock. I meant to keep it hidden if I could. A swirling wind whipped through the bushes, rattling the branches like bones.

119

I hustled across the vacant lot and through the mass of vines, slowing as I descended the steps. I hoped Onward would still be there. Sheet lightning flashed along the horizon, occasionally lighting my way. When I reached the waterside, I spotted the houseboat still moored at the far end, a gray form beneath the starless sky. I sighed with relief.

I had just slipped onto the boat when a figure moved behind the shadows, stopping me in mid-step. Fearing the police had set a trap, I stood listening. I could make out little other than wind and lapping water. Then the boat shifted slightly.

"Dun, is that you?" Onward's voice whispered from the blackness.

"Where are you?"

Saying nothing, he emerged from the shadows, knelt beside the gunwale and untied the bow line. I did the same at the stern. Seconds later, the engine rumbled beneath the deck and the boat lurched from the dockside, moving into the narrow inlet.

I climbed a set of metal steps to the upstairs cabin and found Onward at the helm, the dim glow of the controls painting his face an eerie green. I told him about the necklace as quickly as I could. Without comment, he pointed his chin at the bow.

"Now listen," he said, keeping his eyes on the water. "Go on down and direct me along the channel. I don't want to land us on a sandbar or something worse."

"Where's Gibson? Shouldn't he be up here?"

"Gone to research his article."

"Do you know what you're doing?"

"Sure I do," he said dismissively. "I grew up around boats. Tarp's mother, an uncle and two cousins were all on crews."

"Then why do you need my help?"

"This little inlet here is shallow. Once we get free of it I'll be alright." He motioned to the stairs. "Now, go on before we get ourselves in trouble."

I hustled down the steps and onto the bow. The city glow cast the shoreline in shadow, making the dark water impossible to read. I feared I would be of no help at all.

The remains of a broken piling appeared to my left. I knelt for a closer view. A series of ruffled ovals altogether different from the surrounding surface emerged from the blackness. I realized at once they marked a submerged hazard, likely the remains of an old pier.

I jumped up, frantically waving Onward to the right. The bow swung sharply. I gripped the gunwale, hoping I had seen the hazard in time. Then we slipped past. I watched as the piling faded into the night, finally able to breathe again.

Onward and I repeated our silent dance over and over, dodging one hazard after another. After a trip that seemed endless but was in truth only minutes, and the inlet shoreline fell away and the bay opened before us. A row of red and green lights marking the deeper channel stretched into the distance like a jeweled necklace.

Onward leaned out the window and waved me back upstairs. I lingered in the darkness, knowing that with nothing more to distract us, I would have to face him. The mingled fragrance of salt marsh and seawater swirled about me like an invisible cloak. I breathed in the warm air, hoping Tarp's prediction would prove true.

Moments later, I stepped back into the window-lined cabin. Onward sat at the helm, one hand draped over the wheel, his gaze fixed on the distant shoreline. He motioned me closer.

"You see those yellow lights?" He pointed to a pinpoint cluster on the horizon. "To the left of them is Chocolate Bayou. Past that is Christmas Bay, where we got to cross to get to where we're going."

Troubled by my failure to defend him or even acknowledge knowing him, I heard little of what he said. Would I have gone as far as betraying him? I could not say.

"Onward, I did something, something I'm not proud of. I need to tell you."

"I already heard all I need to," he said without looking at me.

"How'd you hear?"

"Tarp has his ways."

"Are you angry?"

"Angry," he snorted. "Now, why would I be that?"

"But what I did was…"

"After Chocolate Bayou," he continued, "we head down the Intracoastal Waterway for a little bit. Did you know that waterway goes all the way from New York City to Brownsville? I always wanted to make that trip. Start in New York in the fall and stay ahead of the cold weather the whole way. Land in Brownsville about the time the snowbirds get there. Now that would be something. The way time keeps slipping on past, probably won't happen."

"It might."

"Not likely," he muttered. "Now, what was I talking about? I always get to dreaming when I come across the waterway."

"You had us somewhere past Chocolate Bayou."

"Tarp knows a man there, a man who deals heirloom jewelry."

"You intend to find the necklace?"

"Necklace might get us clear of the police."

"How are you going to pay for it?"

"Worry about that when the time comes." He pointed me to the corner. "That cooler over there might have something cold to drink."

I pulled two cans from the small refrigerator, popped the tops and handed him one. Beyond the windows the red and green lights flanking the channel stretched into the distance, converging on the horizon. Pair by pair they drifted past, marking our path across Christmas Bay. Our progress was painfully slow. Every so often Onward would slip into a cove or inlet offering a clear view of the bay and sit watching for any sign of the authorities.

I sat beside him and sipped from the can, saying nothing as the stars winked through the passing clouds, tracing their inevitable path across the sky. The brightest flickered madly before vanishing below the horizon, as if dropping from our view meant death. The image brought to mind Hanley Curtis' description of Whit's condition, imagined or otherwise. That I could make little sense of it only added to my worry.

Onward stirred, bringing me out of my musings. I wondered how much time had passed since we had left Gibson's dock. I suddenly felt exhausted. As if reading my mind, he motioned toward a cushioned bench stretching along the rear wall.

"You go get some rest. I may need you to take over after a while."

"You can't be serious," I complained as I started across the room. "I'm no sailor."

"If you want to stay out of jail, you best learn."

Fie

Our last summer in Mississippi had been a trial of waiting, waiting for the weather to improve, waiting to be freed of old roles and expectations, waiting to learn if Jimmy would go to war. My brothers and I did not know then that we would never again all be there together. Fate had yet to intervene.

My own trials began not long after that final visit. As the oldest of the four children, Whit and I had gone away to college before our brothers. In my senior year I became involved with one of my professors, an intense young man obsessed with making tenure.

Ours was an all-consuming and feverish romance. One afternoon early in the fall term I went to his office. I intended to ask his approval in changing my class project. Late Medieval poetry was, I had found, beyond boring.

He invited me in and closed the door, saying nothing while I attempted to explain my request. I have no idea what I might have said. His blue eyes, deep-set and heavy-lidded, drew me in and held me. Flecks of gold seemed to swim about them like fish. All the while he leaned closer and closer. I could not look away.

Before I realized what had happened we were locked in a breathless clutch. He lifted me onto the desk, scattering papers and sending a clay fertility goddess crashing to the floor. Seconds later I melted into a rush of sensations.

The year passed in a blur of passion, briefly interrupted now and then by the intrusions of work and school. Time apart receded into unimportance while time together seemed to fill all available space. My studies no longer mattered. By the time spring arrived I had decided marriage was in our future, even going so far as to tell Whit.

One evening towards the end of term my assumed fiancé called and asked me to meet him at a lakeside park where we'd often gone. He sounded a little off but I thought nothing of it. For professors the end of finals always meant a frantic rush to grade exams and complete paperwork.

I staked out our usual bench, keeping watch over the path he would likely take. The low sun hovered above the horizon as if postponing night. Swallows crisscrossed the lake in shallow arcs.

Our earlier conversation drifted through my thoughts and it occurred to me that his clipped words and odd tone might be due to something other than the stress of work. His voice had sounded fretful rather than tired, worried even. I suddenly realized his nervousness might signal his intention to propose. After all, the setting was perfect.

I had soon convinced myself I was right. I even went so far as to practice how I would accept. A vision of him kneeling before me flashed through my thoughts and I had to laugh. He was far too proud to be so biddable.

The image vanished as I spotted him on the footpath. Head down, a sheaf of papers under one arm, he shuffled along in a halting stride as if he might turn tail and run at any moment. Nevertheless, I pictured him rehearsing under his breath what he wanted to say, determined to find the perfect word, the ideal phrase. When it came to language he could tolerate nothing less.

He was about to pass me by so I reached out and gave his arm a light touch. He paused in mid-step, turned and peered at me as if I was someone he once knew and hoped never to see again. A shiver ran up my spine.

Taking a breath, I pulled him onto the bench and eased the papers from under his arm. I hoped my presence would snap him out of his strange mood. For a brief moment I thought I glimpsed the man I knew. Then his cold gaze returned.

Grabbing the papers from my hands, he jumped up and to my horror confessed that not only had he just been denied tenure, he was in fact married. I sat unmoving, struck speechless as tears spilled down my cheeks. By the time I could see again he was gone. He left town early the following morning.

Needless to say I was devastated, not to mention humiliated, and could not face the shame of telling my family the truth. Instead, I concocted a farfetched story that I had eloped with a fellow student who then died trying to save a drowning boy. Without intending to I suddenly became a widow. Adding to my shame I swore Whit to secrecy. Only a twin would have agreed to such deception.

I found a job at the university so I could remain away from home and avoid difficult questions, but after mother died I decided it was time to venture back. I missed the place and the rest of my family more than I could say. My sister-in-law's difficult pregnancy gave me another reason to return. Dun came into this world only a month later.

Widowed in truth, Whit returned shortly after. The irony did not escape me. But I was grateful for his help in caring for the boy. Dun needed a man in his life, the more so as time went on.

Growing up, he had the usual bouts of mischief-making and unruliness but nothing untoward. On the contrary, there were times I wished for more trouble out of him. He was entirely too serious. Losing both parents in short order can have that effect, I suppose.

Eventually I came to realize that he felt somehow responsible for their deaths, that if he had been better, more worthy of affection, they would not have left him alone in the world at such a young age. On the surface it makes little sense, I know. He never knew either of them. Nonetheless, from the time he was old enough to feel such things the guilt pained him like a poorly healed wound, vague and elusive. I heard it in his self-doubt, witnessed it in his indecisiveness, in all he held back.

By the time he started high school the old doubts and fears seemed to have lessened a bit, or so I gathered from what little a teenager offers in the way of conversation. For the most part I was forced to read between the lines and guess at the rest. All in all I was encouraged even though I could see he still had a considerable way yet to go.

His cousin Griggs was an influence, some good and some not. He and Dun had always held a friendly but intense rivalry in sports and school, but when girls entered the picture there was no contest. Griggs was naturally predisposed to the fairer sex and they all seemed to know it. Dun on the other hand was awkwardness itself.

Then in the fall of his junior year he managed to find a steady girlfriend, Kim Holland. His abrupt change in attitude was impossible to miss. It seemed as if he had gone to sleep and woken up somebody else altogether. The old self-doubt had been replaced by a self-assured cockiness, especially when Griggs happened to be in the room.

I sometimes wonder what would have happened had Kim remained in the picture. A part of me believes he would have ended up a different man. But it was not to be. Three months after their first date her father was transferred overseas. She was gone within the week.

Dun slid into a deep and inconsolable sadness. At first I assumed he would snap out of it in a few days, a week at most. But by the time three weeks had passed with no change I was beside myself with worry. Nothing I said or did seemed to make the slightest bit of difference. A recent spate of drug overdoses by distraught teens only added to my concern. I even browbeat Whit into having a man-to-man talk with him but to no effect.

A pattern soon emerged. Each day after school instead of making his usual beeline to the refrigerator Dun retreated to his room without so much as a hello. He refused phone calls and visitors, even including Griggs and most surprising of all, Onward. I was at my wits' end.

Then one afternoon an idea occurred to me. Before Kim had arrived on the scene Dun had been jilted repeatedly, typically after one date. The revolving door of

127

girlfriends came and went so quickly I could scarcely remember their names, much less their faces. But amid the continual change the one constant was Marti Finch, his friend since kindergarten.

An hour later I ushered her through the door and down the hall to his room. Blonde and freckled, in cut-off shorts and a tee shirt, she was the quintessential tomboy. When she turned to me with a puzzled look her blue eyes shone like twin pools. But I saw something more in them, something substantial.

Without a word of explanation, I rapped the door with my fist, waited a moment and then ushered her inside. I had already decided the best chance for getting through to him was to proceed without asking permission. He would either see her or send her away.

An hour later I returned with a tray of brownies. Music drifted from the stereo. Marti sat cross-legged on the floor. Dun was opposite her, sprawled across his beanbag chair. They scarcely noticed me setting the tray between them. I tiptoed back down the hall, resisting the urge to hope all was now well.

Fifteen

I bolted upright, awoken by the low roar of a straining engine. The cabin windows rattled with a jumbled mix of metal and glass. I sensed the rhythmic vibration of water racing beneath us.

I jumped from the bench and hurried to the helm. Onward stood erect and vigilant, his eyes fixed on the channel markers. From time to time he glanced over his shoulder toward the eastern horizon.

I followed his gaze. Though still night, a hint of dawn rose above the bay. At first I could see nothing other than the dark water and lightening sky. Then a pair of flashing lights emerged from behind a mile marker.

"Are they after us?"

"Hard to know for sure but I don't want to find out."

"Who do you think it is?"

"Could be a sheriff's deputy or game warden. Coast Guard's the one most likely to be out this far."

"What do we do?"

He jutted his chin at a row of posts barely visible in the early light. The markers veered from the main channel in a crooked row, leading to a narrow break in the shoreline.

"That's what I'm looking for," he nodded.

"You're going in there?"

He swung the boat into the shallower channel without answering and eased the throttle back, cutting our speed in half. The bow dipped and rose as the wake swept beneath us. I peered through the window into the brightening east, finally spotting the flashing lights, now much closer.

Cutting the running lights, he inched up the throttle. I surveyed the approaching shore, a mass of salt grass and mangrove. A scattering of small trees peppered the otherwise featureless thicket. Shorebirds stirred in their low branches.

Within minutes we had reached a shallow break between two points of land, the narrow opening Onward had pointed out earlier. A winding waterway stretched away from us, lime-green beneath the growing light, mysterious and beckoning. We pressed on.

Stands of scrub oak edged the bank, partially shielding us from the bay. Onward pulled the boat up to one of the taller stands and cut the engine. The cabin windows stood even with the treetops.

I followed him onto a gangway running alongside the upstairs windows and helped secure the boat to an upper limb. Only the occasional cry of a seagull broke the quiet. He turned to me and held a hand to his ear, pointing toward the bay. The whine of an approaching boat drifted past us.

I peered through the mass of branches. A Coast Guard scouting boat sporting a front-mounted machine gun came into view, carving a deep wake into the deeper water of the channel. A white-clad sailor stood on the aft deck scanning the horizon with oversized field glasses.

I watched his every move, searching for any clue to his intent. Our waiting seemed to have no end. My stomach tightened as the boat drew even with the smaller channel and slowed to a crawl. Then to my surprise the sailor pivoted, slipped inside the wheelhouse and the engine roared. Within minutes the boat had disappeared from sight.

A sudden breeze swirled through the tangle of branches as if even the trees sighed with relief. I leaned against the gangway railing. Onward moved next to me, let out a low chuckle and clasped my shoulder. Then he slipped through the door.

I lingered by the treetops as the early sun scattered shards of light across the inlet in ever-shifting patterns, jewel-like and mesmerizing. Baitfish skittered over the surface and vanished. In their wake a web of tiny ripples spread until fading from sight.

I glanced through the cabin windows. Onward lay stretched out on the bench, his eyes closed. I cringed to think of how I had failed him and, even worse, that he had heard about it. I hoped Tarp had been right in predicting he would understand.

I wandered downstairs and retrieved the Lucretius text from the bookshelf. Easing into Gibson's overstuffed chair, I flipped idly through the pages. A short passage caught my attention, a line about throwing off the fear of death and embracing life.

I thought of Whit again and the change I noticed when Connie had joined us in the bar. Clearly, he cared for her. So why keep their relationship secret? And, equally important, what was the cause of his fatalistic view of life? I could not even hazard a guess.

I leaned back and sank into the deep cushions, falling into a restless sleep filled with vague images, gossamer-like and fleeting. Whit and Fie appeared first, then Connie, then Isabel, and finally Marti. Unlike the others, she lingered, her face luminous and sharp with detail.

She drew near. Her hair smelled of fresh earth and sea salt, organic and sensual. Taking my hand, she pressed herself close. I felt the heat of her skin move through me.

She pulled back and peered into my face, looking as if she had some terrible secret, a secret she had no choice but to tell. Tears welled in her eyes. She reached up, put her hand on my shoulder, and then she burst into flames.

I bolted upright and sat blinking into the over-bright room. A low sun streamed through the windows, casting the cabin in a garish yellow. I blinked again, trying to rid myself of the nightmare. The aroma of coffee and bacon drifted past.

"I sure didn't mean to give you a start," Onward called from the kitchen. "But supper is just about ready."

"You woke me?"

"Gave you a little shake," he chuckled. "You must've been having yourself some kind of dream, moving and shaking and making all kind of noise."

"Did you say supper?" I asked as I climbed out of the chair. I wanted to avoid talk of the dream. "I slept that long?"

"Might as well. With the Coast Guard around we got to stay here until dark."

I joined him at a small dining table wedged between the kitchen and outside door. A brisk wind whistled through the screens. He lifted a platter of scrambled eggs and bacon from the counter and set it between us.

"You cooked us breakfast," I complained, frowning at the plate, "when the sun is about to set?"

"All Gibson had in the icebox is on the table. Besides which, you just woke up." He scraped a pile of eggs onto his plate. "But if you don't want it, I believe I can finish it all."

"That's real thoughtful of you," I quipped, grabbing the platter.

A half-hour later I finished cleaning up and wandered to the bow. The sun sat perched on the horizon like a blood orange. I found Onward leaning on the gunwale, staring into the distance. I sat opposite him.

Lost to his thoughts, he took no notice. I had intended to ask him about Tarp's friend, the man we were going to see, but the look on his face stopped me.

"You ever come close to getting married, Dun?" he finally said.

Surprised by the question, I sat for a moment not knowing how to answer.

"That's a strange thing to ask."

"Well, have you?"

"Why do you want to know?"

"I had it on my mind and got to wondering."

132

Spotting the same troubled look I had seen before, I realized he had something to tell me, something important. Whatever it was, I wanted him to continue.

"No, Onward, I've never come close, nowhere near," I replied honestly, hoping to encourage him. "What's this about?"

"How about children?"

"You mean have a child of my own?"

"Ever want to?"

I shook my head in answer.

"Ever wonder why I came here so young?"

His strange questions, one after the other, worried me. I soon found myself hoping whatever he had to tell me was something mundane, even ordinary.

"Our families have known each other a long time," I replied, "so Whit offered you a job. I figured that was the reason."

"Whit took me in but that's not all of it."

"What do you mean, not all of it?"

"My mamma sent me away, Dun, couldn't stand the look of me."

"Your own mother threw you out?"

"She sure enough did."

"But why, Onward?"

"I made a mistake, got a girl pregnant."

"That's not reason enough to banish your own son."

"Mamma was a church-going woman, three times a week, every week. I had shamed her and sinned against the Lord. That's how she put it. She said she had to send me away to save my soul from evil."

"I always wondered why you didn't go back for her funeral."

"How could I go when I knew for a fact she didn't want me there? Truth is it was always like that between us. Long as I can remember, she acted ashamed of me. I never could understand what I did to deserve it, but her scorn was there all along. Getting that girl pregnant just gave her something real to latch on to."

"What happened to the girl?"

"Her family sent her away too. I tried to find out where but I was too late."

I heard a change in his tone and realized he meant recently.

"That's why you disappeared after your father's funeral. You went looking for her."

"Partly it is."

"What happened to her?"

"Like I said, I was too late. She passed on a few years back."

"You never saw her again?"

"I contacted the family more than once asking for her address so I could write her, but they wouldn't tell me, said she had enough troubles already."

"What about the child?"

"Don't know much of anything about her."

"You have a daughter?"

"She's back over in Mississippi somewhere. I tried to find her but didn't do any good."

"I never knew, Onward," I muttered, shocked by his confession.

"Haven't ever told anybody before now."

An awkward silence fell over us. I had no idea what to say and, by the look of him, he had said all he wanted to. His gaze drifted back to the horizon.

I sat watching his profile, wondering why he had decided to tell me, only me, and why now? Could it have to do with the troubled look I'd spotted days earlier? I saw no better explanation.

A mixture of tenderness and affection filled my throat. I'd never known my mother so I had little to go on, but I could scarcely imagine such treatment. Perhaps he thought because I had no mother I'd understand better than most. He stood upright and surveyed the twilight.

134

"Looks like the sun is about done for the day." He pointed his chin down the inlet. "We got to head back to the main channel and cross Christmas Bay to find Tarp's man."

"What do you know about him, Onward?"

"Tarp said to keep my wits about me," he replied, stepping past. "The place where he lives keeps some bad company."

Sixteen

Sheet lightning flashed across the sky, silhouetting the horizon but somehow deepening the night. Other than the occasional channel marker, we moved through utter darkness, no moon or stars to light our way. Shorebirds passed overhead marked only by their pitched calls.

Bothered by Tarp's vague warning, I paced the cabin. Onward sat at the helm and paid me no mind. His steady gaze remained fixed on the line of channel lights ahead. A heavy wind whistled through the window screens, now and then rising to a mournful moan and adding to my troubled thoughts.

Feeling restless, I stepped out the door and onto the catwalk. The deck stretched below me, white against the black water. Now and then a faint glow seemed to rise from beneath the bow as if a sputtering lantern hung somewhere out of sight.

I descended the narrow stairway for a closer look. Grabbing the gunwale rail, I leaned over the side. At first the prow seemed only a dim shape slicing the water.

I waited but saw nothing out of the ordinary. My arms began to cramp. I had almost decided to give up when all at once the water below me exploded in a lime-green flash. The formerly dim wake suddenly morphed into a galaxy of star-like points, all glowing for an instant before fading.

I had heard of phosphorescence but had never seen it up close. I dropped to my stomach and stuck my hand into the water. Glowing light trailed off my fingers like the tails of tiny comets. Mesmerized, I watched my fingertips paint the passing surface in an eerie green light.

The boat swerved to my right and darkness again enveloped us. I jumped to my feet. The channel lights were now receding behind us. A distant cluster of floodlights illuminating a pier and dock appeared above the bow.

I hurried back upstairs, trying to stifle my anxiety over what dangers might await us. Onward slowed the engines and trained a flashlight on the water. The beam moved beneath the surface in wavering shafts, showing the lighter green of the shallows. I knew without asking that running aground would prove disastrous.

He handed me the lamp, motioning me to keep it trained on the way ahead. Our passageway seemed to shrink by the minute. I had begun to think the channel might disappear altogether when a series of closely-spaced poles appeared to our right. Lit by the blazing spotlights of the pier, they marked the rest of our way.

Minutes later we eased alongside a low dock. I wondered if we were being watched. Tying off the boat, we followed the pier to a low bluff and short set of stairs. Fifty yards beyond, a low-slung house stood in near-darkness, its open garage lit by a single hanging bulb. In the doorway a trio of men sat hunched over a table crammed with beer bottles, most of them empty.

I followed Onward along a concrete path that wound through a stand of mesquite trees. The murmur of voices drifted past us, carried on the shifting wind. The men seemed oblivious to our approach.

We reached the pool of light cast by the bulb and Onward paused at the edge, watching as the group swilled beer and slapped the tabletop with playing cards. The soft two-beat rhythm of country music twanged from a nearby radio. Cigar smoke hugged the ceiling.

The man facing us had narrow, tar-black eyes and a rust-colored beard sprinkled with gray. To his left, a younger man in a ball cap and sweat-stained shirt sat squinting at his cards. The third man, bald and wearing a khaki work shirt, leaned his elbows on the table, smirking at the others as if they had missed something important. I figured him for the owner.

Onward motioned me forward and I stepped into the light. I could feel him following close behind. The man facing us glanced up and looked again, jumping from his chair and nearly knocking over the table. Playing cards fluttered to the floor. The other two men followed his gaze to where we stood. They eyed us warily, occasionally glancing toward the far corner where a shotgun leaned against the wall. I knew we had to act quickly.

"We were sent here by Tarp Cates," I called, raising both hands. "He's the granduncle of my partner."

"You're taking chances, darkie," the young man slurred, standing and pointing at finger at Onward, "sneaking up on people like that."

"Just because you're black as night," the bearded man added, "doesn't mean you can go prowling around where you don't belong. A man can get himself hurt that way."

"We figured you saw the boat," I yelled, hoping to avoid a confrontation.

"What boat?" The young man squinted through the haze of cigar smoke. "You and the darkie best not lie to us. We don't tolerate liars around here. Maybe we should just run you prowlers out and…"

"Shut up, Melvin," the man in khaki barked. He grabbed a bentwood cane from the back of his chair, pulled himself up and nodded toward the doorway. "You and Homer can go now."

"Don't send us away on account of them, Tobias," he complained. "We still got us some beers left."

"You've had enough. You can hardly talk right. Now, go on and get." Melvin hesitated, glancing between us and the beer cooler. Tobias glared at him. "Do you need me to show you the way?"

Homer sighed and grabbed him by the arm, ushering him into the darkness. Moments later a truck engine rumbled beyond the trees before fading into the distance. Tobias leaned on his cane and studied us.

"You boys really come here by boat or did you just tell that story to mess with those two nitwits? I admit it's

138

tempting. They may have half a brain between the both of them."

"It's the truth." I gestured toward the water. "The boat's tied up at the end of the pier."

"We can't see the pier from inside here," he replied, squinting into the trees.

We introduced ourselves and then he turned his gaze to Onward.

"How is old Tarp then?"

"He still fishes most every day."

"He always did like his fishing," he chuckled. "You're family?"

"Tarp is my grandfather's brother."

"He's a good man, a rare breed anymore. Those two that were just in here may be dimwitted but they'd just as soon slit your throat as look at you if the price is right. There's a lot of their type around these days.

"Tarp, on the other hand, is one man I always knew I could count on if things got tough. Him and me, we worked together at two shipyards, the first one on Trinity Bay, the other up Chocolate Bayou. That's where I got this here." He tapped the cane against his shin. "Damn owners had no use for me afterwards, gave me the heave-ho without so much as a good-bye.

"Tarp got the same treatment six months later. We were nothing to those rich bastards, no more than bone and muscle. All they cared about was their profit and to hell with the working man. Tarp is the opposite of that. He'd stick by you no matter what."

"That's sure enough true," Onward nodded.

"So, he sent you here to find me?"

"He said you could get us to a man who deals heirloom jewelry. We mean to find a gold and pearl necklace that went missing a day or two back."

"The old lady who owns the necklace claims Onward stole it," I added. "We intend to prove her wrong."

Tobias squinted into the darkness, for a moment lost in thought.

"It's true I know the man, even do business with him now and again. His name is Luca Fort. He's a step above an outright crook, but a small step. The men he deals with are rougher. They can be downright dangerous if they think they're being set up. So, I'll admit I'm reluctant to send you."

"We got to find that necklace, Tobias," Onward replied without hesitation. "We appreciate any help you can give."

He pivoted and motioned us to follow. Moments later we were bumping down a rutted roadway in a rusted-out jeep. The car's rattling din made talk impossible.

Passing through stands of dense brush, the narrow road seemed to parallel the shoreline. Occasional clearings offered glimpses of the moonlit shallows beyond. Lightning flashed over the treetops, silhouetting the clouds into fantastical shapes.

We had travelled no more than a mile when a cluster of cabins appeared beneath a vapor lamp. The small houses shone ghostlike beneath the silver light. Chained to a thick stake, a mongrel raised his head and regarded us with intense but silent interest.

Tobias parked alongside the shell drive, cut the engine and started for the cabins. I did the same. Onward made no move to leave. Instead, he sat staring at the dog as if in a trance. I backtracked and leaned in close.

"You've never seen a dog before?"

"That's a big dog," he muttered.

"I'd say about average as dogs go." I nodded toward the cabins. "We'd better catch up with Tobias before we lose him."

"Looks mean too."

"You're not scared of the mutt, are you?"

"Just careful is all. I've had my trouble with dogs."

"Look at the size of that chain," I countered. "He's not going anywhere."

"Can't tell for sure."

Realizing we had lagged behind, Tobias paused and motioned us to follow. I pointed at the dog. He motioned again with an impatient wave.

"If you want to find that necklace," I said beneath my breath, "we've got to go, dog or not."

"I don't know," he muttered. "I've had my trouble..."

"I'll walk on the side nearest him so he'll get to me first," I added. "Otherwise, you're on your own."

I turned and started down the drive, hoping my ploy would work. Footsteps soon sounded behind me. We joined Tobias beneath the vapor light. The largest of the four cabins stood to our left. Painted camouflage green and tan, it had a tin-roofed porch stretching across the front. Castoff chairs and a dilapidated sofa littered its length.

Using Onward to steady himself, Tobias took his cane in hand and rapped the floorboards repeatedly with the gnarled grip. An echo of scrambling footsteps rumbled behind the walls. Seconds later, the door opened a crack and a face peeked out. Then a bald man in chartreuse coveralls opened the door and stepped onto the threshold. His earlobe held a gold stud.

"I thought I told you to stop that, Tobias," he scowled. "That heavy cane banging on my porch sounds just like gunfire."

"But why stop," he chuckled, "when it's so much fun?"

Luca moved to the porch rail and frowned down at us. Melvin appeared behind him, wide-eyed and breathless.

"Who got shot?"

"Get a grip, Melvin," he snapped. "We have visitors."

Homer ambled through the door and snorted in disgust.

"Them again," he muttered.

Melvin jutted his chin at Onward.

141

"I could've guessed he'd be the one, Luca. His type brings trouble wherever they go."

"Then why didn't you say so, you idiot, instead of running around like a scared rabbit?"

"I see you boys found somebody else to mooch off of," Tobias quipped. "Better hide your beer, Luca."

"Don't mind them." He pointed the two men back inside. "They were just leaving."

"He pilfered our beer," Melvin whined.

Luca glared at him and he slinked through the doorway mumbling to himself. Luca faced us again and ran a hand over his shining scalp.

"Now if you'll please tell me what brings you here, Tobias." He pulled at his earring. "I've been terribly busy since that hurricane hit down south and all sorts of valuables just started appearing out of nowhere."

"My friends here are looking for an heirloom, a gold and pearl necklace. I told them you have knowhow when it comes to such things."

He turned to me with a regretful frown.

"You must understand that my clientele won't appreciate me dealing with certain people." He glanced at Onward. "I'm sure you can understand."

"I understand better than you know," I replied.

"You do, do you?" He looked me up and down. "I don't suppose you'd want to have a drink, just the two of us, so we could, you know… negotiate?"

"Are you going to help us or not?" I grumbled.

"I'll take that as a no," he sighed. "What I meant to say is that I have to consider my bottom line in these sorts of dealings."

He rubbed his hands together as if Christmas dinner had just arrived. I'd about run out of patience.

"Do you have the necklace," I barked, "or not?"

"No need to get yourself in a tizzy." He threw his hands into the air. "I know where you can find it."

"Then tell us… please."

"As I said, dealing with certain people puts me in a delicate position. However, if you gentlemen can offer the right price then perhaps I can manage to, as they say, look the other way."

"You want us to pay you?"

"Valuable information in exchange for remuneration is the business at hand, is it not?"

"That's robbery."

"A fair price for a needed item," he snipped, his hands on his hips, "is anything but robbery."

"How much then?"

"Fifty dollars American is the going price and I never negotiate."

I glanced at Onward and he waved me closer, bending to my ear.

"We got to play him like he's trying to play us," he whispered. "Just follow my lead. When the time comes, don't offer him a cent over twenty dollars."

"Now, I got to speak up," he said, waving a finger in the air, "because I asked Tobias to bring us here and all, and he did because him and my uncle Tarp have been friends a long time. I understand you're a businessman, but I got money to pay for nothing but that pearl necklace. If you won't tell us where to find it then I guess we'll be on our way."

He pointed me toward the drive and I started for the jeep. Luca's footsteps clattered along the porch floorboards.

"Wait!" he called. "Maybe I spoke too soon."

Onward paused in mid-step and turned to face him.

"Well, there could be another way," he said. "If you play it right, the folks who sell us the necklace will pay you something for sending us to them. A good businessman would know how to go about setting that up. But you have to tell us where to find them first."

"You want me to give you the information for nothing? I won't do it. I can't. What if word gets out I'm an easy touch? I'd be ruined."

"Alright, then," he shrugged, "I guess we'll be on our way."

He started along the drive again. I hesitated, waiting to see what Luca would do.

"You must understand," he called to Onward. "I have my reputation to maintain."

Seeing my chance, I hustled back to the porch and moved in close.

"He won't pay you," I said under my breath, "but I will. No one needs to know how much but you and me."

"Forty dollars?" he whispered hopefully.

"I was thinking more like ten."

"Perhaps thirty?"

"Well," I replied, starting for the stairs, "I'll tell him I tried."

"Okay, twenty-five."

I pulled a twenty-dollar bill from my pocket and nodded to where Onward stood waiting.

"You can see he won't pay. Best take this and keep your reputation intact."

With a snort of disgust, he snatched the money from my hand. Then he pointed to the road.

"Elrod Monteux lives on the other side of the peninsula, about a quarter mile from here. Just follow the road. He's been trying to sell a pearl necklace he picked up from some islander, trying a bit too hard if you ask me. So, I took a good look at it and decided to decline his offer."

"Why is that?"

"He thinks he hoodwinked some surfer into selling him a valuable heirloom for cheap, but the truth is the necklace is well-made costume jewelry worth a quarter of what he paid for it. I wouldn't give him more than forty dollars at the most. By the way, that expert advice is free of charge because I'm counting on you to keep our little secret. Now, please leave and don't come back."

He pivoted and disappeared through the door. I hurried to join Onward, my mind racing with all I'd heard. Tobias stood waiting beside the jeep. I repeated Luca's report on the whereabouts of the necklace.

"Will you take us?" I asked.

"Elrod Monteux is as mean as a snake and about as dangerous," he replied with a solemn nod. "Don't underestimate him."

Seventeen

Within minutes we had travelled the short distance across the peninsula. Lightning flashed again somewhere beyond the trees. Tobias parked alongside the road and cut the engine. Through the scattered brush I spotted a corrugated metal building in the middle of a small clearing, 'Monteux Salvage' stretched across one side in red paint.

I surveyed the adjacent yard for sign of Elrod Monteux, finding nothing other than a slew of rusted anchors and marine winches. A pier and dock stood beyond the trees. The restless bay rose and fell below the walkway, scattering shafts of light among the pilings.

I hopped out of the jeep and followed Onward to where Tobias stood lingering in the shadows. He pulled a thin cigar from his shirt pocket, bit off one end and lit the other with a kitchen match. His face flickered in the brief flame, mask-like and impassive.

"I'd better wait here," he said, blowing a thin stream of smoke into the air. "Elrod and I don't exactly get along. I probably shouldn't tell you this, but the last time I saw him he pulled a gun on me. Lucky for me he's a bad shot."

"Any advice on how to handle him?" I asked.

"Be ready to run," he said with a smile.

"One thing I know how to do," Onward chuckled, "is run when I need to."

He turned and started for the clearing. I wanted answers to all the questions crowding my thoughts so I moved alongside him.

"Why would Mrs. Langdon report a stolen heirloom valued in the thousands," I said in hushed tones, "when the necklace was worth a fraction of that?"

"I've been thinking on that too and I keep coming to the same answer."

"She had it insured?"

"Got to be insurance money she's after."

"But that's fraud."

"Maybe so, but might the best thing for us anyhow."

"You're thinking we can get her to drop the charges," I guessed, "if we she realizes we could turn her in."

"Woman like her won't want to go to jail just to lord it over a black man."

"You think the necklace was even taken? Maybe she just said it was stolen so she could claim the money."

"No, I figure she found it gone and saw her chance."

"Then who stole it?"

"Maybe you can ask the man yourself."

He pointed his chin toward the clearing where two figures stood silhouetted by spotlights. I squinted into the glare, wondering if either held a gun. One of them thrust his hand into the air.

"Hold on right where you be standing," he called, "and say what you want to be coming here for."

As far as I could tell, his accent hailed from southwestern Louisiana. Because of the glare, I could make out little of his face. I raised my hand to block the light and they both flinched.

"They sure are nervous," I whispered between my teeth.

"Then you best do the talking," he whispered back, "and be ready to run."

"We're looking for Elrod Monteux," I called out.

"What you'd be wanting with me then?"

"We understand he has a pearl necklace for sale."

"Who's been telling you that there?"

"We went to see Luca Fort. He told us."

He stepped aside and motioned us toward the building. Moments later we entered a high-ceilinged room stacked with blow torches, power tools and the thick rope used in marine salvage. Two underwater diving suits hung on the wall above a row of compressed air tanks.

I wondered if the place was a legitimate business or a front for dealing stolen property, or both. Elrod pointed us

147

to a nearby table and chairs. The other man vanished through an adjacent door and then reappeared, setting a wooden lockbox on the tabletop. Elrod sat opposite us.

Pulling a key from his shirt pocket, he unlocked the box and began sifting through the contents. Though his skin was light and his hair red, his features resembled Onward's in nearly every respect. Based on his appearance and accent, and the fact that he seemed to have no problem with Onward's presence, I guessed he must be of mixed blood, probably Creole.

He rested the lid on the table and pulled out a necklace, holding it to the light. A dozen gold beads separated by a string of pearls ended in a heavy gold clasp. Engraved on one side were the letters 'VSH'. I had no doubt it was Mrs. Langdon's.

"This necklace here is fine as you ever find anywhere, I guarantee," he said as he fingered the gold beads. "Me, I can make you a good price for this one. Maybe you want something else too."

I glanced inside the lockbox and then looked again. Surrounded by jewelry, silverware and crystal, a silver box sat partially covered by a felt cloth. I recognized the gold filigree at once. The box was the one I'd discovered in Mrs. Langdon's desk. I turned my gaze back to the necklace, struggling to hide my surprise.

"You got yourself some kind of look there," he said, squinting at me, "like you got a question to ask Elrod. Go ahead and ask."

I gave my head a shake, too shocked to speak.

"How come you don't talk to me then? You got to think some damn thing about these here pearls, good or bad."

Onward turned to me, clearly puzzled by my speechlessness. I pointed into the lockbox.

"How much," I managed, "for that?"

"You mean that little box? Ah, that there is not much of nothing, just cheap silver. Who wants a little silver box when you can have this fine pearl necklace, gold bead and all?"

"I'm just curious."

"The ladies," he added, dangling the necklace before me, "they like this one here, I guarantee."

"I know someone that likes boxes."

He dropped the necklace on the table and sat back, turning his gaze on Onward. A hint of anger flickered in his gray-green eyes.

"Man like you got nothing to say?"

"I got plenty," he replied, his voice cool, "but my partner drives a hard bargain, so I just sit back and let him do his work."

"A hard bargain is it?" he snorted. "I tell you what. You and your friend here, you buy this necklace and then we see about that there little box."

"I'll give you twenty dollars for it," he offered, "and another twenty for the box."

Elrod burst out with a sneering laugh, glancing back at the man in the corner.

"What do you make of that Maurice? The man, he says his friend drives a hard bargain, so then he goes and drives himself right off the damn cliff and into the sea."

"Man drive that hard," he replied, his voice like gravel, "likely to drown."

"Maybe we just keep this here necklace and that little box there too. What'd you say to that, Maurice?"

"I say if you drive too hard, you get what you get."

Onward shifted in his chair, a slight change, hardly noticeable, yet I knew he was about to make a move. I hoped I could follow his lead. He stood and motioned to the necklace.

"You don't want to sell us your necklace," he said with a shrug, "then we got nothing more to talk about."

"No, no, no," Elrod replied with a nervous wave. "Now you sit yourself back down. I'm just messing with you. We still got us some business to do here."

Onward sat again and tapped his finger on the tabletop.

"Then tell us your price so we can get on with it."

"How much you got?"

"I made my offer already. It's time to hear what you got to say."

Elrod sat back and regarded Onward with a thoughtful grin.

"Where you come from, your people?"

"Mississippi."

"Ha, I knew that there!" he shouted, sitting up. "We come from the same people, you and me."

"Is that right?" Onward replied, nonplussed.

"Sure we do. My great grandmother, she was born on a plantation half mile from the big river himself. Family worked those fields for five generations, day in, day out. We got the same blood in us, you and me, just like I figured."

"My offer's the same anyhow, family or no."

A bitter frown replaced his smile. He leaned across the table and stuck a finger in Onward's face.

"Man, why you want to break my back here? You and me, we got to stick together. Our people got us a hard time making it in this world, you got to know."

"Can't deny it. But we still need to know the asking price."

"You got to cut me some slack here," he complained. "Me, I'm just trying to make a living. You know how it is, brother."

Onward flinched at the word and then glanced at me. I still had little idea what to expect.

"Sounds like we got no more talking to do," he said, standing.

I watched them both, unsure what I should do. Elrod glared up at him.

"If you got to have my offer," he snorted, "then I say show me how much you got and we make us a deal before midnight, I guarantee."

Maurice reached for his pocket and I spotted what looked to be a pistol-shaped bulge. Or so I imagined. Keeping an eye on Onward, I rose from my chair. Elrod smiled up at us and held out his palm.

I raised a hand to show Maurice I was no threat and reached into my pocket, feeling for the only money I had left, two twenty-dollar bills. Unmoving, Onward stood over Elrod, his face without expression.

All at once the roar of a car engine echoed through the doorway, followed by red and blue light flashing across the walls. Elrod jumped from his chair, sending the table careening. The silver box and necklace skittered across the floor.

Maurice raced out the back door, Elrod close behind. Stunned, I stood watching after them. Onward scooped up the box and necklace and grabbed my arm, pointing me to a corner door. In seconds we were through and into the night.

The thicket soon gave way to a low bluff scattered with brush. To our left a creek wound inland, disappearing into a mass of mangroves. Despite the dim light I could see the outgoing tide pulling at the matted roots. Voices called behind us, followed by the jumping flash of spotlights. I guessed we had seconds before they reached us.

Onward hopped onto the narrow beach and I followed, pressing myself to the bluff. The dark void of the bay stretched away from us. He tapped my shoulder and pointed down the shore. A canoe sat beached twenty yards away.

Keeping to a low crouch, he hurried to the boat, slid the bow into the water and gave the end a gentle push before slipping inside. I clambered in after him. We could only hope the canoe's low profile would allow our escape.

I pressed myself to the bottom. The tide hissed along the hull, pulling us into an ever-darker night. Occasional shouts echoed through the darkness. After what seemed hours, he peeked over the side and then pulled himself upright. Putting a finger to his lips, he slipped a paddle from beneath the seat and dipped it into the water. I did the same.

Following the shoreline, we kept close watch for Elrod or the sheriff, using the occasional pier or porch light to guide our path. Now and then a siren wailed in the distance. Otherwise, the dip and pull of our paddles was all that broke the silence.

We rounded a point and the houseboat came into view alongside Tobias' well-lit pier. I pushed my paddle deeper into the water and pulled hard, feeling Onward do the same. We both wanted out of there as soon as possible.

An instant later he jerked upright and thrust a hand backward, signaling me to stop. I peered over his shoulder. A sheriff's deputy stood silhouetted in the open door of Tobias' garage. I could see we would never make it past the brilliant light of the pier. Tobias faced the officer, his hands in his pockets. I wondered if he had seen us.

Seconds later I had my answer. Pointing the deputy away from the bay, he motioned us toward the shoreline with his free hand. I squinted into the near-darkness. Down a narrow path a cabin sat surrounded by dense brush. Unsure what to expect, I steered toward it.

Eighteen

The path to the cabin met the bay at a concrete boat ramp. Passing though the bluff at a low angle, it offered a hidden path through the thicket of mesquite and acacia. I beached the canoe beside the ramp and grabbed the box, slipping the necklace inside. Onward was halfway to the cabin by the time I climbed out.

I reached the narrow porch and crouched next to him. Thunder rolled overhead. Wind whipped the treetops, rattling the branches like bones.

I peered past the corner. Tobias' garage lights glimmered through the trees, offering a slim view of the surrounding area. Neither he nor the deputy was within sight. Having the houseboat so close yet unreachable was torturous but paled next to the threat of jail. We faced enough trouble without also getting caught up in Elrod's illegal schemes.

I had almost convinced myself we should try a run for the pier when a brilliant flash turned the night into day. For an instant, the entire scene stood captured in a blue-green glow. Then an earsplitting crack sliced the air, followed by pounding thunder. The garage and pier went dark, along with houselights scattered down the coast.

I grabbed the box and took Onward's arm, pushing him toward the pier. The pilings stood barely visible against the tossing bay. The pier itself being too risky, I headed for the shadows beneath it. We could follow the pilings to the dock, swim around one end and enter the houseboat on the bayside, out of view. I hoped Onward would follow my lead.

Within seconds we had slipped beneath the pier. I started into the water and then felt his hand on my shoulder. He pulled close to my ear.

"Where're you off to?" he whispered.

"We'll swim to the far side of the boat," I replied impatiently. The last thing I wanted was to waste time explaining. "Then we can get in without being spotted."

"No, no, Dun," he muttered, "we got to go another way."

"What?"

"I can't do that."

"Why not?"

"Just can't."

"Are you telling me you don't know how to swim?"

"Course I know how to swim," he hissed. "I grew up a stone's throw from the Mississippi."

"Then let's go."

"No, you got to find us something else."

"If you can swim then what's the problem?"

He kept his eyes on the water. Frustrated by his evasions, I waited for an answer.

"Sharks," he finally said.

"Sharks?"

"Might be sharks out there in that deep water."

"What deep water? Don't you remember how shallow it was getting here? There aren't any sharks in that water."

"Not true. In East Bay I saw a six-foot black tip take a man's fish right off his line, three feet deep. Fish nearly took a bite out of him too before he left out of there."

"There is no other way, Onward. If we get on that walkway, we'll be spotted for sure."

"Not nothing between you and that shark but those canvas shorts. You want to lose your privates to some old fish?"

"Listen to me, Onward." I pressed my face close to his. "Either you go and turn yourself in to the sheriff right now or we take our chances. I'll go first, so if the big fish gets me you can skedaddle."

"Well, I don't like it."

With that, I started into the bay, feeling my way along the bottom. I held the box over my head. The water had reached my waist when something slimy slipped between my ankles. A shiver jolted my spine. Trying to look unconcerned, I glanced over my shoulder but Onward's gaze was fixed on the water around him. I took another step and felt the passing movement again, so I launched myself into the bay, swimming from one post to the next and trying to keep my feet off the bottom. I could hear Onward splashing behind me. The wind had died and the sound echoed beneath the pier in a watery cascade.

"Try to be quiet," I hissed, "or you'll get us caught for sure."

"We got us too many jellyfish under this pier," he said between breaths. "Don't want to swallow one."

We reached the end of the pier and thunder rolled overhead in a series of chest-rattling thumps. Despite my best effort, I couldn't help but imagine Onward's sharks slicing through the water behind us. Luckily, the dock stood only inches above the bay despite the outgoing tide. I grabbed hold of the floorboards with my free hand and began pulling myself along the edge. The houseboat stood at the far end, rising above the water like a castle, white against the black horizon.

The still air lay heavy on the bay, amplifying all sound. I moved slowly, trying to keep the noise to a minimum. I could feel Onward at my back.

A low roar rose somewhere in the darkness behind me. I stopped to listen. The sound seemed to be moving our way.

"What is that?" I whispered to him.

"Don't know but we best get onboard before it gets here."

Uncaring of what noise I made, I pushed through the water as fast as possible, keeping an ear open to the approaching roar. Thunder rumbled again just as I reached the boat. I grabbed hold of the gunwale, dropped the box in and hoisted myself over the side. An instant later Onward tumbled onto the deck beside me.

All at once the wind returned in a sudden gust, making the roar even louder. I peered into the darkness. A gray veil emerged above the bay, vague and undulating.

Before I had a chance to stand, a wall of rain slammed into the boat, filling the air with a choking mist. For a moment I could hardly breathe. The houseboat tilted toward the dock, straining the moorings.

I managed to stand and stumble across the deck, falling to my knees beside the bow cleat and grabbing the rope. In the rush I caught my hand on a loosened screw, tearing a deep gash in my palm. Somehow I managed to untie the line.

I glimpsed Onward through the deluge, doing the same at the stern. Fearing the wind would prevent us from leaving I jumped onto the dock and leaned into the gunwale. The boat stayed put.

I felt the engines rumble beneath the deck. I moved closer to the bow and pushed again. Nothing moved. The wind howled around me. I shifted forward as far as I dared.

The gale seemed to ease, if only slightly. Leaning across the water, I gave a final push and fell back onto the dock, but the effort was enough. The prow shifted, clearing the pilings by inches and edging into the open water.

I jumped up and ran to the stern. I knew if I missed my chance to get aboard I would be stuck. Onward would have no chance of returning in such a wind. I moved to the back edge of the dock and hesitated, reminding myself how close we were to escape. Then I launched myself into the air.

The wind seemed to grab me, pushing me upward over the water. Time seemed to slow. I imagined myself sailing through the darkness, weightless and birdlike, floating briefly before slipping beneath the black water.

Instead, I slammed into the gunwale. The boat's solidity and the pain in my chest shocked me back to reality. Sheets of rain peppered my face. I gripped the railing despite my throbbing hand, hanging on and trying to regain my breath. Then the boat shifted toward the channel and away from the wind, allowing me to clamber over the side.

Knowing the deluge would make navigating the narrow passage a near-impossibility, I wrapped my hand in my handkerchief, hurried to the bow and dropped to my stomach. The closely-spaced poles we had passed earlier emerged from the darkness. Squinting into the storm, I pointed Onward left or right as we crept along. I could only hope he would see my signals through the downpour.

After what seemed hours, the lights of the main channel appeared in the distance. I pushed myself up and peered at the hopeful sign. A shiver passed over me.

Though the worst of the rain had moved on, a veil-like mist swirled over the black water in an eerie and graceful dance. I felt a strange elation at the sight, as if beauty in the face of near-disaster held a special meaning, of what exactly I could not say. Still, I was moved by the image.

A faint knocking sounded behind me. I turned over and looked up to find Onward at the upstairs window, one hand on the helm, the other waving me inside. I guessed we had reached the deeper water of the bay.

I rose stiffly, retrieved the box and climbed the stairs. Keeping his eyes on the way ahead, he motioned to a nearby cabinet without saying a word. Inside, I found a bottle of cognac and half a dozen tumblers. I poured us each a quarter glass, handed him one and then downed mine in one swallow.

By the time I had stopped shivering we were well into the bay. I went downstairs and rifled through Gibson's closet, finding a pair of Army surplus shorts and a denim shirt. The well-worn clothes were oversized but blissfully dry. Seeing that he had taken most of his wardrobe with him, I grabbed what little was left before heading back upstairs.

I took over the helm and handed Onward what I'd found, a Hawaiian shirt and orange pants that I could easily imagine on Moon. He held the clothes at arm's length, frowning like I'd given him a filthy rag. Then he dumped them in my hands and nudged me aside.

"Aren't you going to change?" I said, keeping hold of the wheel.

"I believe these clothes here," he replied, fingering his wet shirt, "will have to do."

"But you're still dripping. Look at the puddle you left."

He glanced down and then pointed his chin at the clothes.

"You got to do better than that, Dun."

"Gibson took most everything with him."

"He sure did," he snorted. "Those got to belong to somebody else. Pimp's the only man wears orange pants."

"But we're in the middle of nowhere. Who's going to know what you're wearing way out here?"

"Me, I'll know."

"Come on, Onward, be sensible."

"That's what I'm talking about." He shook his wet sleeve. "This right here is what you call sensible clothes."

"You're going to make yourself sick."

"Least I won't look like a pimp."

He shivered and pulled a damp handkerchief from his pocket, running it under his nose.

"See what I mean?"

"I'll... be... alright," he said between sneezes.

I pushed the clothes at him and he took them with considerable reluctance, disappearing downstairs. He returned minutes later. His face held a mixture of humiliation and defeat. I stepped aside as he reassumed the helm.

"You don't look too bad," I said, trying not to laugh, "for a pimp."

"Got to stay between us, Dun," he muttered, glaring at me. "Don't you tell anybody, Griggs most of all. I'd never hear the end of it."

I nodded my agreement and leaned back in the captain's chair, watching the channel lights drift over the bow in crooked lines, the blackness beyond deep and featureless. Having decided I would approach Isabel about the truth of the necklace, using her as a go-between with her grandmother, I wondered if there might be a way to return the silver box without Mrs. Langdon ever knowing. After I'd seen Isabel, I would go find Griggs. Since he'd lost the heirloom, I figured he should have a hand in its return.

Fie

Whit was recently widowed and living in the city when father asked him to come home and help with the family business. To say that he had little choice in the matter would be a grand understatement. A request from our father held only one answer.

In any event, Whit was in no condition to resist. Jimmy's death had hit him especially hard. As oldest of the three boys, he felt he had an obligation to protect his youngest brother and he had failed. That he also had been passed over by the draft only compounded his sense of guilt.

Six months after his return I could see he was in a state. He flitted from one project to the next, unable to concentrate on any one thing long enough to do any good whatsoever. He brought to mind a caged bird. Mistakes were all but guaranteed, and from a business standpoint he was a disaster. Father spared no words in pointing out his inadequacies.

He might have gone on like that forever if not for a single harrowing night. Father had just finished dessert when he and Augie got into a horrible argument, the final disagreement that sent my brother off to start his own furniture store. The row started at the dinner table and then moved to the porch.

Father had the habit of smoking a single cigar after dinner, and in warm weather he would move to the veranda. That night Augie followed him out, never ceasing his tirade. The quarrel had to do with Augie's habit of making decisions without checking with the others beforehand, as if the store belonged to him and him alone.

Whit usually steered clear of their arguments but something in Augie's tone that night drew him onto the porch. Knowing he and Augie would someday share in decision-making might have had something to do with his *interest, but he had been worrying over our father's health for some weeks prior. I could not blame him. Father's usual robustness had seemed to abandon him overnight.*

I busied myself with the dishes, trying not to listen. I'd heard enough of my brother's anger and dissatisfaction. But when the talking turned to shouting I rushed outside.

By the time I reached the porch Whit and Augie were faced off like boxers. Red-faced and wheezing, our father stood between them.

"What do you know, anyway?" Augie turned to our father and jabbed the air with his finger. "You're nothing but a used up old man."

"Don't talk to him like that!" Whit snapped.

"He never listens to me."

"Maybe he has good reason."

"Being older doesn't make you the expert."

"You need to show some respect."

"He treats me like a child."

"If you want to be treated like an adult," Father broke in, waving the cigar at him, "then stop your whining and act like one."

Augie began pacing the floor, muttering to himself.

"I could make the store work if you'd let me."

"The store is fine as is."

"I'd call it mediocre, at best."

"You think a college degree has taught you everything you need to know." He blew a thin stream of smoke into the air. "Well, you're wrong. Experience and prudence, not just knowledge, are the marks of a good businessman."

"You can't be serious."

"I've been at this a lot longer than you."

"You're behind the times, a dinosaur of the furniture world. We could be making three times what we are now if we attracted more than old ladies and poor people."

"Our store has provided for the needs of this island, this entire island, for over thirty years. We're part of the community. They count on us."

161

"When's the last time you checked the books?"

"I have no intention of risking our standing in the community merely for profit." He motioned toward the stairs. "If you can't understand that then perhaps you should try your luck elsewhere."

I gasped. He had never spoken so coldly to any of us. Augie looked as if he'd been slapped in the face. Whit gave the doorway a wistful glance, no doubt wishing he had been given the choice of staying or leaving. Augie turned his hateful glare on father.

"It's no surprise mother died before her time," he sneered, starting for the door. "She could've been living in style, but because of you she had to scrimp and save and work herself sick to make ends meet."

"Augie!" I yelled.

I stared at him in disbelief, stunned by his cruelty. I turned as the cigar hit the floor in a cloud of sparks and father slumped onto the bench, pale and breathless. Whit rushed to his side. When I looked again Augie was gone.

From that moment on Whit treated the store as if its continued existence depended on him alone. Arriving before sunrise six days a week, he often worked long into the night. I pitched in where I could.

Father, on the other hand, never got over the effect of that night. His regretful words weighed on him, adding to his rapid decline. He was dead within the month. Whether Augie felt any responsibility for father's passing I could not guess, but I knew for certain Whit would never forgive him.

Nineteen

The Twain manuscript lurked in some dark recess of my mind, as disturbing as it was unforgettable. I had just finished it. Jim's marriage to a woman of mixed heritage, pale-skinned despite her Choctaw blood, had proved difficult, the town's prejudice against them palpable and then disastrous. Returning from the fort late one evening, he finds her brutalized and near death. She dies in his arms.

The military convenes a routine inquest. Grief-stricken, Jim sleepwalks through a week of waiting. Initially sympathetic to his plight, they instead decide to charge him with her murder. He sees little hope of a fair trial. Dishonorable discharge and prison are likely.

Believing he can intervene yet again, Huck races to town. But he is too late. Jim has hung himself in his jail cell. The book ends with Huck, alone and jaded, returning to a life of aimless wandering. The prejudice and bigotry of the time had overwhelmed them both. In Onward's view, the dark tale came out of the death of Twain's daughter a year earlier. I could see why he chose not to publish.

Hoping to rid my mind of the story, I left Onward asleep on the bench and slipped out. The sun had just cleared the horizon. I'd been unable to get much rest, my thoughts bouncing between the manuscript and all I had yet to do. I mounted the dockside stairway, pushed through the wall of vines and returned to my car. It seemed as if an entire month had passed since I sat behind the wheel.

My plan was to catch Isabel just as she left for work. On my way there, I stopped in at the home of a longtime friend of Whit's, a semi-retired jeweler named Morris Markowitz. I'd known Morris my entire life. I hoped he was still the early-riser I recalled from my childhood.

I pulled into the narrow driveway that ran alongside his small bungalow. A few years before selling his jewelry shop, Morris had attached a tiny workspace to his garage. That's where I found him.

He sat bent over a low table, a diamond ring held by a miniature vise before him. At my approach he looked up and blinked at me through the magnified lenses of his jeweler's glasses. His watery eyes glistened like gray lagoons. He leaned on the table and peered over the glasses.

"Is that Dun Osay I see before me," he said in an old man's hoarse tenor, "a grown man and no more a teenager?"

"I see you still like an early start, Mr. Markowitz."

"Work is what keeps me going, that and a few glasses of wine at dinner, sometimes even port if the weather is cold."

He pulled off the heavy glasses and looked past me.

"Whit is not with you today?"

"No," I replied, feeling a tinge of guilt for my neglect. "It's just me this time."

"But..." he said with obvious concern, "how is he, Dun?"

"Not well. To tell the truth, he worries me."

"Yes, I thought as much." He nodded solemnly. "The old man's fear has hold of him."

"The old man's fear?"

"The fear that life is passing him by and he has little to show for it, that he will vanish from the earth without leaving a trace."

"But he took over the store and kept it running all this time." I said, trying to reconcile his words with Hanley's perplexing assessment. "People come from all over because they trust him and value his work. And he took me in and raised me when he could have looked the other way."

"You know that. I know that. But all he can see is what he didn't do, the choices he didn't make when he had the chance. Such a belief leads to a very dark place."

164

"What can I do?"

"Ah, well," he sighed, "this is no easy thing. He must believe he still has a life ahead of him, a life worth living."

"But how do I convince him?"

"Who can say?" he shrugged. "Something will come to you. In the meantime, you have other reasons for coming to see me?"

"I do." I reached into my pocket and pulled out the necklace. "I have something I'd like you to appraise."

He studied the pearls through the thick lenses and then moved to the gold beads, humming to himself. He was finished in less than a minute.

"This jewelry," he said, slipping off the glasses, "it has a story?"

"I'd rather not say if you don't mind."

"Fine, fine," he said, dismissing my answer with a wave, "but please don't tell me you paid a big price."

"Not at all."

"I'm relieved to hear it. Oh, don't misunderstand me. The necklace is well-made for costume jewelry. But I rarely get a request to appraise such items, and when I do it usually means disappointment for the owner."

"So someone could pass it off as a valuable piece?"

"Absolutely, and it happens more often than you might think."

Knowing I had little time to spare, I thanked him and hurried out. Whit's welfare still weighed on my thoughts. I sped through the backstreets, reaching Mrs. Langdon's yellow Victorian in minutes.

Isabel's blue sedan sat parked well beyond the wall of bushes separating her grandmother's house from the next yard. I had just cut the engine when she rounded the hedge. I hurried across the street, reaching the car just as she opened the door, but before I had a chance to speak she pivoted, wide-eyed, and pressed herself to the fender.

"Lord Almighty, Dun," she yelled, "you scared the life right out me!"

"I'm sorry Isabel," I whispered, hoping to avoid Mrs. Langdon's notice. "I don't want your grandmother to know I'm here."

"You better hope she doesn't see you. She'll call the police."

"I had no choice. I need your help."

"You want my help?" She stared at me like I'd lost my mind. "Dun, she says you and Onward stole from her. How do you expect me to help you when I know that?"

"Onward didn't steal anything," I replied, pulling the necklace from my pocket, "and here's your proof."

"You're telling me you stole it?"

"Of course not," I huffed. "I don't know who stole it. But I do know that Onward got it back."

I explained the entire ordeal as quickly as I could. Then I handed her the necklace. She fingered the pearls and eyed me.

"You're sure this is nothing more than costume jewelry?"

"I took it to a jeweler I've know my whole life just to be sure."

"I had a feeling she was up to something. She's been talking non-stop about the insurance payout."

"Now will you help me?"

"What do you want me to do?"

"Tell her we know the necklace is a fake. If she'll drop the charges, we won't tell anyone."

"She won't like it."

"Remind her that insurance companies don't take kindly to fraud."

"I have to go now," she said, slipping inside the car.

I leaned in the window, suddenly wishing I could turn back the clock to that moment beside the oleanders, her lips against mine. She nodded at my blood-stained bandage.

"What did you do to yourself this time?"

Her voice held no sympathy. Ignoring the question, I leaned closer. She turned away.

"Can I see you later?" I ventured. "We could make another try at Leroy's Bar."

"Dun, with all this to deal with," she answered coolly, "I'm hardly in the mood for a party."

She started the engine and pulled away without even a goodbye. Disappointed, I watched her disappear from sight. My thoughts again turned to Whit, so I decided to check on him before tracking down Griggs.

I sensed something amiss as soon as I pulled to the curb. The front door and the screen door stood open and neither Fie nor Whit were anywhere in sight. With growing apprehension I checked the back yard, finding nothing. I was rounding the front porch when Fie appeared at the top of the stairs.

"Dun, I'm so glad you're here," she called, her voice tense. "Whit has been asking and asking for you."

I'd never seen her so worked up. Fie's no-nonsense presence under the worst circumstances had been family lore as long as I could remember. When Whit was cursing everything in sight and I was paralyzed with indecision, she would always remain in complete control.

Motioning me to follow, she disappeared inside. I hurried up the stairs, across the porch and through the door, following the murmur of voices. Even from a distance her clipped words held more than their usual terseness. I paused outside Whit's bedroom, worried what I might find inside. Then I took a breath and pushed through.

Fie paced the floor, muttering under her breath. He was propped at the head of the bed. His face held a gray pallor that concerned me more than I could say. She moved beside him, erect and imposing in her high-collared dress.

"I will not hear any more such talk, Whit Osay." She pointed a finger in his face. "I just won't hear it."

"Well, I can't see the point of living," he muttered, "if there's no enjoyment left in it. What about that is so hard to understand?"

"Dun, you must talk some sense to him," she said, turning to me. "Your uncle doesn't know what he's saying."

He frowned and waved me over. I stepped past her and moved alongside the bed.

"Tell her you and I need to talk in private," he said under his breath.

"You want me to tell her to leave?" I whispered.

He motioned me closer.

"What do you think talk in private means?"

My relief at his familiar prickliness quickly gave way to concern over what he meant to tell me. Had Hanley Curtis finally found a physical cause for his illness? Or might he have actually decided to take his own life? A host of grim possibilities crowded my thoughts as I ushered Fie toward the doorway.

"I won't go," she protested. "Whatever he needs to say, he can say it with me right here."

"This is man talk, Fiona," he barked, "a private matter between Dun and me."

"A likely excuse if I've ever heard one. But you men could certainly stand to talk more, so I'll let you have your time." She started for the door. "Besides, I could use some tea to settle my stomach. I find your manly stubbornness irksome."

"Make mine whiskey," he called after her.

"Whit, what's this about?" I said, returning bedside.

"A man needs part of his life to be his and his alone."

"What part are you talking about?"

A bitter smile crossed his lips. My mind filled with Morris Markowitz's advice. I needed to help him see his life was worth living. But I had no idea how to begin. The one thing I knew for certain was that he worried me.

"Tell me what you meant about not seeing the point in living," I ventured.

"I meant just what I said. Quality is everything. When that's gone there's no sense in going through the motions. That's not what I call living."

"You're not thinking about killing yourself?"

"Why in the hell would I do that?"

"It happens."

"I won't say I never think about it. In fact, not too long ago I… is that what has Fie all worked up?"

"Of course it is, Whit. Listen to yourself."

"The truth is I got some bad news."

"The doctors found out what's wrong with you?"

"Are you kidding?" he said with a smirk. "They don't have a clue. Maybe if I kick the bucket they can cut me open and find out."

"Then what bad news?"

"Connie's been transferred to Sydney, Australia, of all places. You won't believe how long it takes to fly there, not to mention the cost. And now that her responsibilities are limited to the southern hemisphere, she'll have no excuse for coming through here. I'm not sure if I'll ever see her again."

The look on his face, defeat mixed with resignation, startled me. Whit had never been one to give up. But I could see the critical difference her move made. Rather than die by his own hand, would he simply decide to stop living, just as Hanley Curtis feared?

I peered out the window and searched my mind for some words of hope or encouragement, finding nothing but empty platitudes. The reality was inescapable. She was halfway around the world and he would see her rarely, if at all. Long-distance relationships were notoriously hard to keep. I was about to resort to some meaningless cliché when the bedside phone rang.

"That'll be Connie calling before she turns in," he said as he reached for the receiver. "I was trying to find you

169

because I want you to go to the store and check on Griggs. Lately, he's been way too upbeat. I think he must be up to no good."

On my way out, I found Fie waiting at the end of the hall. Taking my arm, she led me into the living room and pushed me into a chair. She sat opposite me and frowned at my wrapped palm.

"Dun, you've hurt yourself. Let me fix you a proper dressing."

She reached for my hand but I pulled away. I suspected she wanted to know what Whit had told me.

"Is there something you needed?"

"I need your help," she answered. "I'm worried about Onward."

"Onward?" I said, surprised. "Don't you mean Whit?"

"Well, he does concern me, but I've seen him like this before. I did my bit of acting back there in the hope seeing you might snap him out of his self-pity. I'm sure you can understand, knowing the situation."

"I don't recall any situation," I replied evasively. "Why should he feel sorry for himself?"

"Dun," she said, eyeing me. "Don't play stupid with your aunt. I'm not blind. I know about his clandestine meetings with that woman."

She made no effort to hide her disapproval. I could see there was no point in trying to sidestep the truth.

"I thought he wanted to keep their meetings private."

"Yes, he likes it all very dramatic and hush-hush," she snorted. "Men remain boys in so many ways."

"Then what about Onward?"

"It's so unlike him to skip out on work. Do you know what happened?"

"We ran into an unexpected problem, a problem that couldn't wait."

"What sort of problem?"

"Fie, it's not my place to say. You should ask him."

170

"Dun, you must tell me if he is in serious trouble."
She peered at me for a long moment. "You know how important he is to this family."

I nodded but her tone was unlike any I'd ever heard from her. Try as I might, I could make no sense of it.

"Onward just hasn't been himself lately," she added, mostly to herself. "I can't imagine why."

I had no answer for her. All he'd confided in me failed to fully explain his troubled demeanor. Or so it seemed. In any event, I still needed to find Griggs. Leaving her to her thoughts, I slipped out.

I entered the store through the back door and followed the short hallway to the main floor space. Yet to open for the day, the room stood empty and quiet. I found him in the kitchen bent over a pile of foil-wrapped tacos. He looked up at my approach.

"Where the hell have you been, Dun?" he frowned. "Onward didn't show yesterday. I'm not surprised as unreliable as he is, as they all are. Lazy spooks have no regard for the clock."

"I told you not to talk about him like that, Griggs," I barked. "You sound like your father."

"Don't compare me to him," he bristled.

"Besides, Onward's more reliable than any of us."

"If you say so," he grumbled. "But that doesn't change the fact I had to handle the entire place by myself. What happened to you?"

"Something came up," I replied vaguely.

I had no intention of telling him any more than I had to. In typical fashion his frown vanished and he sat back, grinning.

"I'll bet you finally made it with that babe from the old lady's place, didn't you?"

"No," I muttered.

After our awkward parting, the last thing I wanted was to discuss Isabel. His face filled with mock concern.

"You mean you still haven't… you know, done the wild thing?"

"Is that all you think about, Griggs?"

"I think about food." He pointed to the tabletop. "I got these egg and chorizo tacos for helping the girl that sells them change her flat tire," he said between bites. "Help yourself, cousin."

I sat opposite him. Seeing Whit in such a state had left me with little appetite. Griggs stuffed the last of tortilla in his mouth and motioned to the table again.

"Aren't you going to have any? After all, they're free."

I shook my head in answer. He grabbed another taco.

"Although I have a feeling," he added, winking, "that woman wants more out of me than a tire change. So, I might just have to oblige her. She's not bad look…"

"I have the silver box," I interrupted.

I'd heard enough of his boasting. He paused in mid-bite.

"You mean the silver box that got stolen?"

"I want you to help me find a way to return it."

"How did you find it?"

"Never mind that."

"But we've been through this. Don't you want to sell it?"

"I'm going to return it with or without you. But I think you owe me the help."

He stared at me for a moment. I could see his mind was working.

"You're right," he finally said. "I should help and I will. Besides, life is about more than money."

"That," I snorted, "does not sound like the Griggs I know."

"I've been doing a lot of thinking since I came back, Dun." He gestured around the room. "This place has a way of growing on you sort of slow and quiet. Then all of a sudden, you realize that selling furniture is important work."

"Come on, Griggs," I complained. I was feeling more than a little protective of Whit. "Don't make fun of the store. You might not like working here, but the business holds a special place in our family."

"Dun, I'm not making fun." He sounded surprisingly sincere. "Because of my father, I never wanted to have anything to do with any kind of business, especially this kind. But I enjoyed being on my own yesterday. Not because I could slack off - I was way too busy for that - but because I liked the work. I think I finally get it.

"Picking out furniture is very personal. The decisions buyers make involve how they see themselves, how they want to live their lives, how they want other people to see them. And I help them make those decisions. Think about that, Dun. I play a role in someone's evolution, helping them decide who they want to be. How amazing is that?"

Once again Griggs had surprised me with his insight and candor. His ease in reading people was both impressive and confounding. And just when I'd decided he would betray his own mother to get what he wanted, he confides something heartfelt.

Twenty

Leaving Griggs to open the store, I started for Gibson's dock. I was not due back at work until two. I knew Onward would need to lay low until Mrs. Langdon actually dropped the charges, so I decided to stop off for groceries.

On my way, I dropped by my apartment for a change of clothes. I was heading down the stairs when Moon called from his back stoop. Moments later I stood beneath the bright lights of his kitchen. The warm air was thick with aromas.

"You sit yourself down there," he said, motioning to the table, "and prepare for some heavenly fare, one of my new recipes. I hope you brought along your appetite because I made enough to feed an army."

I wondered to myself when I'd last eaten and my growling stomach answered back. I sat watching as he scurried around the kitchen, shaking bottles and stirring pots like a mad scientist. Setting aside his spoons and spices, he pulled an armful of porcelain serving dishes from the cabinet and set them on the table. Moments later a steaming bowl appeared before me. He hovered at the end of the counter, watching.

I spooned out a mouthful of the reddish stew and was immediately startled by the taste, an intense mix of flavors backed by a powerful spiciness. Once I'd started I could not stop. Moon paced the floor, huffing and sighing and casting me an occasional glance. Finally, he rounded the table and peered down at me.

"Dun," he said, exasperated, "at least come up for air long enough to tell me what you think."

"First," I said between bites, "tell me what you call this."

"Have you been starving yourself for some strange reason?" he complained. "If you must know, the dish is called jambalaya. But do you like it?"

I nodded and set the spoon in the empty bowl. He sat opposite me, his face filled with worry.

"Do you really like it, Dun?" he whispered. "You're not just saying so to be nice?"

"Moon, you're an artist. Where did you learn to cook like this?"

"Don't you remember me telling you? Aunt Francine taught me when I was a youngster."

"Well, you learned well. It should come in handy for all those parties you keep having."

"But that's only part of it, Dun," he said, breathless. "I've decided to open a restaurant and I'm beside myself with excitement."

"I thought you didn't need to work anymore."

"Not having to worry about money is a fine and good, but having something that's your own doing, that you created yourself, is even better. I finally have a reason for getting up in the morning, Dun, a real purpose beyond my boring day to day life. And I have you to thank for it."

I sat back, puzzled.

"Why would you thank me?"

"You told me to find something I enjoyed and spend my time doing it," he answered, grinning. "So, that's what I've done."

I left him puttering among his steaming pots and resumed my quest for groceries. Moon's happiness was both uplifting and dismaying. I still had little idea what I would do with myself, or even if my future held anything close to the satisfaction he had found.

I chose a tiny market on a short, seldom-used street. I still had reason enough to avoid unnecessary notice. The Tran family had bought the dilapidated house after fleeing the war in Vietnam. They had opened the store initially to serve other refugees, but it quickly became popular with college students, eventually gaining recognition as a neighborhood icon.

I pushed through the screen door and past the front counter. His back to me, Mr. Tran stood on a stepstool dusting shelves packed with dried seaweed, gingerroot and ginseng. Despite the creaking floors and rusted screens, the place was immaculate.

I slipped down the central aisle, grabbing whatever caught my eye. Whit had long held an open account with the Tran family. Though the aisles were always crowded with unopened cartons and crates of produce, making progress slow, I cared little. The market held an undeniable charm.

At the end of one aisle a huge stack of boxes partially blocked the way, leaving only a narrow passage to one side. The uneven tower looked ready to fall. Watching that I not upset the pile, I started to ease past. Then I realized someone was doing the same from the opposite direction. Already committed, I had no escape.

I pressed myself to the shelves, thinking I would soon be face to face with a foul-breathed drunk or a grizzled deckhand just off a boat. Or so it imagined. Keeping my eyes to the floor, I waited for them to pass.

Instead of grimy shoes, a pair of sandaled feet appeared below me, the bare legs above them tanned and shapely. Scarcely an inch stood between us. The scent of fresh earth and sea salt wafted past me, stirring first my memory and then my pulse. Startled, I looked up and found myself face to face with Marti Finch.

"Dun Osay," she said, grinning. "Are you stalking me?"

I stood transfixed by her blue-gray eyes. Her closeness, her smell, was almost more than I could tolerate. Almost but not quite. I made no attempt to move. She looked to her left and right.

"Sort of a tight squeeze, isn't it?"

176

I nodded, unable to speak.

"Funny how we keep running into each other, don't you think?" She moved closer. "It's sort of like fate, if you believe in that sort of thing."

"Whatever it is," I finally managed, "I wish it happened more."

A blush spread across her face, making her even prettier, though I could not say how. She seemed near perfection as she was. I felt a sudden and surprising pride that I could have such an effect on a beautiful woman. I should've known better. My pride got me into trouble more often than not.

She turned her eyes. She was, after all, involved with someone. An awkward silence enveloped us. Then she noticed my bandage. Lifting my wrist, she examined the grimy wrap, gently squeezing my palm and fingers. When she finally looked up, she kept her hand around mine.

"Will you let me take a look at this?" She nodded toward the doorway. "I live right around the corner."

I left my groceries with Mr. Tran and followed Marti the block and a half to her home, a beige and green bungalow tucked midway along a tree-shaded avenue. Maroon storm shutters flanked the front windows. The yard's single palm drifted in the breeze.

She led me through a sparsely furnished living room and into a small kitchen, pointing me to a chair and then vanishing through the doorway without a word. Seconds later, she reappeared with a canvas case and a bottle of disinfectant. Sitting opposite me, she lifted my hand and cut through the cloth with surgical scissors.

I watched as she removed the bandage and examined the cut, probing the ragged edge, her fingers confident yet gentle. She pulled a square of gauze from the kit, soaking the pad with disinfectant and then dabbing the wound. I scarcely felt the pain.

Instead, my gaze drifted to her profile, the gossamer hair along her temple, the wisps of curl behind her ear, the slight imperfection of her nose. The blemish, if it could be called that, only made her more human, more appealing, flawed yet beautiful. I took a breath, realizing I had to get a grip on myself.

As if reading my thoughts, she turned to face me. I realized with a start, her lips were only inches from mine. I leaned closer. Kissing her would have been so easy.

Instead, I hesitated. In that instant, her eyes flew open and she pulled away. I felt like I had been caught cheating. She sat back in her chair and scrutinized me, her surprise fading into a wistful sadness.

"The night you walked me home from the party," she finally said, "the night my dorm mother locked me out, why didn't you try to kiss me?"

"Well, I… I…" I stammered, taken aback by her frankness, "did you want me to?"

"And after the concert," she continued, "why not then?"

"With your sisters right there?"

"I wouldn't have cared and neither would they."

"Marti, what's this about?"

"Are you going to answer me?"

I stared into her blue-gray eyes, realizing I had always considered her off-limits. We were friends, good friends, for most of our growing up. As a result I was unable or unwilling to think of her as anything else, as if some unwritten rule bound us to our roles. Or so I thought.

But the intervening years had broken that taboo. Too much had happened; too much had changed. I was no longer the person I had been then and, clearly, neither was she.

"I was afraid to try," I muttered.

I tried to hide my surprise at the confession even though I knew how she brought out the truth in me. She peered into my face with a pained expression.

"But why, Dun?"

"Our friendship was too important to risk ruining."

I turned my eyes, realizing the depth of my mistake. She sighed and nodded her understanding.

"I sometimes wonder how different things might've turned out if you had tried."

I couldn't help but hear the finality in her tone. As if to underscore the point, she turned her attention back to my hand. She took less than a minute to finish.

She stood and gathered her things, pausing to frown at the pile of dirty dishes filling the sink.

"Three of us share the house," she complained, "but only one of us likes to keep it clean."

"Marti," I started, hoping to continue the conversation, "could we…"

The shrill beep of her pager stopped me. She groaned and snatched it from the table.

"Not again…" she muttered. "I have to go."

Grabbing her purse, she vanished through the doorway. I sat staring at the white bandage, dazed by her abrupt departure and even more by her questions. Whether I'd been wrong to tell her the truth I could not say.

Twenty-one

Gibson stood waiting outside the cabin when I reached the dock stairs. Even from a distance his expression told me right away something was wrong. He motioned me to follow and disappeared inside.

I stepped into the cramped cabin expecting to find Onward with him. Instead, he sat alone at the kitchen table. In his hand was a folded piece of paper.

"You'd better take a look at this," he said, handing it to me.

I set the groceries on the counter and unfolded the paper, recognizing it at once as an arrest warrant. Onward's name was typed across the top. I stared at the form in disbelief. I had thought we would have more time.

"They took him?"

"They were called about a suspicious vehicle hidden behind some bushes. When they traced to license plate to you, they knew they'd find him somewhere nearby."

"I thought I was being so smart," I muttered, disgusted with myself, "and now look at what I've done."

"I offered to stall them so he could slip away but he refused. He said you would know what to do." He pointed to the paper. "What's this about? He didn't have a chance to tell me."

"I'll explain later," I replied, starting for the door. I had no time to waste.

I sped towards Mrs. Langdon's house, my thoughts plagued by my earlier encounter with the police. I didn't want to think what might happen to Onward while he was in their custody. At that moment his innocence meant nothing.

I hurried up the porch steps and banged my fist on the door of the tall Victorian, expecting an argument from the old lady. Instead, Isabel answered the door. She frowned and glanced into the house.

"What are you doing here, Dun?" she whispered. "I told you she'll call the police if she sees you."

"I have no choice, Isabel. Onward was arrested."

I was counting on the interest in him I'd seen from her at Carmelo Puglia's cafe. She sighed and stepped onto the porch.

"I was afraid something like this would happen. That's why I'm here. I took an early lunch to convince her to drop the charges, but she's resisting."

"Either she tells them," I said, biting back my anger, "or I will. Tell her that."

Suddenly, the door flew open and Mrs. Langdon appeared on the threshold, her face crimson. Isabel pressed herself to the wall.

"Grandmother, there's something I need to…"

"Shut up, Isabel," she barked. She turned and glared at me. "You think you're so smart, that you can change the world and make things different than they are. But you're wrong. There is a natural order to society. People must stay in their place. Trying to convince them otherwise is simpleminded and just plain wrong."

"You're awfully sure of yourself. But I'm not here to argue. We both know what the necklace is really worth. I want the charges dropped now."

"I won't do it. If your friend didn't steal it, he surely made off with something else of mine. You know how they are."

Out of patience, I turned to Isabel.

"You can do it. You can tell the police you found the necklace. Please, Isabel. If not for me, do it for Onward."

Her grandmother stepped between us.

"Isabel," she warned, "you will not listen to him."

Isabel stared at me for a moment and then answered with a reluctant shake of her head. The old woman pointed a finger in my face.

"You think this is over," she sneered, "but I assure you it is not."

Pulling Isabel behind her, she disappeared inside. The door slammed with a shudder.

Minutes later, I stood outside Whit's bedroom. I had decided Onward's best chance at freedom was with him. He'd had dealings with nearly everyone on the island at one time or the other. Despite whatever ailed him, he would just have to find the strength to do his part.

I found him just as I had last seen him, propped against the headboard. His listless gaze followed me across the room. Any other time I would have been gone easy with him but my concern over Onward overruled all else.

"Get up," I barked, "you're coming with me."

"What are you talking about?" he replied listlessly.

"Onward is in jail. We have to get him out."

"Onward..." he said, suddenly alert, "is in jail? What on earth for?"

He clambered out of bed and hurried into the closet without waiting for an answer, reemerging moments later fully dressed, his face flushed, his eyes shining. Motioning me to follow, he vanished through the door. I had no idea what to make of the change.

I was still explaining all that had happened when we pulled up to the police station. We pushed through the doors and stopped before a low counter. The woman behind it eyed Whit knowingly.

"I wondered how long it would be before you'd show up," she drawled.

Though her face held no malice, her expression was far from friendly. Her eyes had a hard look to them, like she'd seen too much. I found myself feeling guilty just standing before her. Of what exactly I could not say.

Behind her a hall scattered with benches ended at a locked gate. An officer beside it sat thumbing through a newspaper. A row of cells stood just beyond. Arms dangled from the doors as if disembodied. Whit pressed his palms to the counter and leaned in close.

"I believe you get better looking every year, Liz," he said beneath his breath. "How do you do it?"

She smoothed back her hair. Pulled into a tight knot, it shone bluish-purple beneath the fluorescent lights.

"Don't you waste your smooth talk on me, Whit Osay," she snorted. "I know better."

"But, Liz, we went to the prom together."

"Now there was my first in a long list of mistakes."

"Oh, so that's how it is."

"Is and has been long as I can remember."

"But you're going to tell me where I can find Leon anyway."

"Of course I am. I never could say no to you, Whit. You ought to know that by now." She nodded toward the corridor. "He's expecting you."

He managed to get a pen and notepad from her before we left. I followed him along the narrow hallway. Ringing telephones, overloud voices and slamming doors echoed off the bare walls. A man in a beige raincoat lay curled on a bench, a dingy cap covering his face.

Whit paused midway down the passage and put a hand to my chest, checking in both directions.

"When we get to Leon's office," he whispered, "let me do the talking. No matter what I say, just go along with it and try not to look surprised. As far as anyone is concerned, you write for some snooty East Coast magazine."

He handed me the pen and pad. Confused, I held them at arm's length.

"I'm a journalist?"

"It's a ploy, Dun," he said as if I was a ten-year-old, "our leverage to get Onward out of here. Understand?"

Without waiting for an answer he continued down the hall. We stopped in the doorway of a cramped office. Plaques and certificates scattered the paint-chipped stucco. Opposite us a red-faced man in shirt sleeves sat hunched

183

over a desk crowded with papers. A wrinkled tie hung loose from his collar. He looked up, frowning.

"So, you're not dead yet," he said, eyeing Whit.

"You'd be one to know," he snorted. "You've seen enough dead people."

They shook hands and Whit nodded in my direction.

"Leon, you remember my nephew, Dun."

He gave my hand a firm squeeze and motioned us to sit.

"Now, Leon," Whit began, "to get right to the…"

"Before you start to going," he interrupted, "let me have my say. I know why you're here, Whit, and I can tell you right now there's not a thing I can do about it. Old Mrs. Langdon may be new in town but she knows people, influential people, people you don't want to cross if you can help it. Policing is more politics that you might think. There are complications on all sides and I have to consider every one. And if I don't watch my step, I'll step right in it."

"Are you through?"

"Well, through enough I guess."

"Leon, I'm going to tell you something you don't want to hear." He gestured toward me. "I brought Dun along for a reason. You know those big-time magazines up east, the ones you see in all the stores? Sure, you know the ones. Well, Dun is a journalist and he's working on a story about racism in law enforcement."

"Now hold on, Whit. What are you getting at?"

"I believe you know the answer, Leon."

"You're saying we're keeping an innocent man behind bars because he's colored?"

"I'm saying he's no guiltier of stealing that necklace than you or me."

"I can't just let him go free without proof."

"No, maybe not," he replied, standing. "But you can release him to my custody."

"Are you out of your mind?" he barked. "Think how it would look. I already explained my situation is difficult."

"Your situation is worse than you think, Leon. If you refuse to release an innocent man to a trusted member of the community, Dun will have to include the entire episode in his article. Think how that will look.

"A story this good could get made into a book, maybe even a movie." He leaned in. "Which good-looking actor do you think they'll cast in my place?"

"You're supposed to be my friend, Whit," he grumbled.

"I am your friend, Leon, and I'm doing my best to protect you from making a colossal mistake. What are the odds of staying chief if your name is broadcast all over the country as a racist lawman?"

He sighed and leaned his elbows on the desk, his face a mix of frustration and defeat.

"What am I supposed to tell Mrs. Langdon?"

"Don't tell her anything. We'll keep a low profile until we can clear things up."

"Don't you let me down, Whit," he muttered, "or there'll be hell to pay."

Twenty-two

The sun had nearly set by the time Onward and I dropped Whit at the house. His release had seemed to drag on forever as it wound through the city bureaucracy. He had said nothing since leaving the jail. I sensed he had no wish to speak of his ordeal.

The store had already closed for the day, so I knew the only place I might find Griggs was his house. While awaiting Onward's release, I had spent a restless afternoon ruminating over how I might return the silver box. I felt it something I must finish despite Mrs. Langdon's hostility. Doing otherwise would be lowering myself to her level. But she could not know. In truth, I found a grim satisfaction imagining her at the desk, ignorant of the heirloom in its hidden compartment only inches away.

My plan was to have Griggs distract her while I slipped in. With his considerable charm I felt we had a fair chance of success. If all else failed I could abort the plan and send an anonymous note explaining where to find the box. I had to be rid of it.

I parked next to Griggs' tiny bungalow, leaving Onward to his silence. I was anxious to get on with my plan. Reaching the landing, I pounded my fist on the door and stepped back. To my surprise, the rusted latch gave way.

I watched as the door slowly swung open. A shaft of twilight fell across the floor, followed by a frantic mix of rustling fabric and hushed voices. I peered into the dim interior. For a moment I could make out nothing. Then Isabel's face emerged from the darkness, a twist of bedclothes clutched to her throat. Griggs sat next to her.

For a moment my mind refused to accept what my eyes could see. The two of them in the same room, much less in the same bed, fell beyond belief, beyond understanding. A wave of disappointment, anger and humiliation passed over me. I wanted to yell, shout, break something.

Instead, I stood unmoving, my mouth open yet silent. The image of them beneath the bedclothes, wide-eyed and startled, blotted out all else. I don't want to think what I might have done given more time. But suddenly Onward's hand gripped my shoulder, pulling me away, leading me stumbling back to the car. I recall little else.

When I came to my senses I was sitting in a low-ceilinged room lit by a scattering of neon beer signs and little else. He sat opposite me. On the table between us a phalanx of beer bottles stood empty. Looking exhausted, his elbows on his knees, he stared at the floor. I could not imagine myself in his place.

I blinked into the reddish glow of the dim bar trying to clear my mind of a beer-induced fog. A half-dozen mismatched tables and chairs crowded the room. Across a tiny dance floor, four men sat hunched over a poker table, cigar smoke hovering above them in a blue cloud.

Along the far wall a bar stacked with unmarked bottles, some clear, some tawny, stood between the door and a single boarded-up window. A bald man in a stained apron lurked behind the counter. His scalp shone in the red neon like an oversized Christmas ornament.

I faced Onward again. He seemed to study me with his downturned, thoughtful gaze. Although bleary-eyed as I felt, I couldn't be sure of much.

"You're about back to your old self," he said in a kindly tone. "I can see it in your eyes, sure enough."

"I don't know how," I slurred. "My eyes aren't working so well."

"You're young. You'll sober up in a minute or two."

"Who says I want to?"

"Hmm..." he said with the hint of a smile, "sounds like you got your spark back too."

"These are all empty," I muttered, rummaging through the bottles.

"You had yourself some kind of surprise, you did," he continued. "I don't know when I've heard so many curse words strung in a row."

"I don't remember. Anyway, I don't want to talk about it."

"Alright then," he nodded, "probably best to let it go."

"Where are we?" I asked, hoping to change the subject. I surveyed the room again, my vision slightly clearer. "Looks like a dive."

"This here is Clancy's Hideout and that's what we're doing, hiding out. Sure beats working."

He leaned back and clasped his hands behind his head, looking annoyingly relaxed. Sitting around doing nothing was the last thing I wanted right then.

"I'm not done with my plan. Let's you and me go get…"

The door flew open, slamming against the wall and stopping me in mid-sentence. Two men stumbled through, one clay-colored and short, the other thin and dark as Tarp. The bartender fixed them with a tense stare. They started for the bar but, seeing me, the short man veered toward us with an unsteady determination. I could see Onward go calm the way he did when sensing trouble.

"You got some nerve bringing him in here," the man grumbled, stopping feet away. "This bar is not for him and his breed."

His companion loitered in the shadows. The beer and all that had happened combined to forge an angry foolishness in me. I clasped Onward's shoulder and leaned close.

"What kind of breed am I," I said, grinning, "mongrel or purebred?"

He gave his head a quick shake, warning me off.

"We're just having us a few beers," he said to the man. "Been a long day for both of us."

The man took a step closer and waved a finger at me.

"He best watch his mouth. This here is our place. Either you get on your way or we put you out our own selves."

Onward looked to his right and left.

"More than enough room for everybody. I believe we'll just sit here and mind our own business."

"I know you heard what I said," he said between clinched teeth.

"Don't listen to him, Onward," I barked. "I'm not leaving. In fact, I'm going for another beer."

I stood and he jerked me back down onto the chair.

"Time's past for that."

I leaned inches from his face.

"Don't tell me you're going to let him tell you what to do."

He ignored me and instead studied the other man, his face still in shadow.

"Now I got to wonder," he finally said, "if your mamma knows where you are, Marcus Kane."

"What?" The man went rigid and glanced at the door as if he expected his mother to walk in at any second. "How do you know…"

"You telling me you don't remember your old baseball coach, boy?"

He hesitated and then stepped from the shadows.

"Lordy, Mr. Cates," he said, thrusting his hands in his pants pockets. "I didn't recognize you."

"You're taller, Marcus, but you're still skinny," he chuckled. "Tell her she's not feeding you enough."

"I don't live at home anymore, Mr. Cates," he replied, shifting from foot to foot, "not for a long time."

"But you still get a meal anytime you show up."

"I can't deny that," he said with an sheepish grin.

"You tell her I'll get over to see her sometime real soon."

"Sure thing, Mr. Cates, I'll be sure and tell her." He grabbed his companion's arm, jerking him backward.

"Now, we got some important business to discuss, so we better get going."

"You take care of yourself, Marcus," Onward called as they retreated to a distant table.

"I'm not leaving because of them," I complained.

"Weren't you just saying how you had something you had to…"

"My plan!" I yelled, jumping up. "I have to finish."

Somewhere beneath my clouded thoughts, I felt compelled to complete what I had started, to correct the mess I'd set in motion. At that moment I wanted to be rid of the silver box more than anything. The heirloom represented all my failings, all I wanted to forget, all I hoped to leave behind. I could think of little else.

I hurried out the door and across the parking lot, Onward close behind, but just as I reached the car he snatched the keys from my hand.

"You got to sober up some more before you drive anywhere."

"I'm sober as a church deacon," I replied, grabbing at them. "Now give those to me."

"No sir. I'll drive you home."

"I can't go home, Onward. I have to finish my plan."

"What is this plan you keep going on about?"

"I'll tell you when we get there."

I hustled around to the passenger door, hoping I could come up with a new strategy by the time we got to Mrs. Langdon's house. Replacing the box without Griggs' help would be difficult at best. Still, I was determined to find a way.

I pointed Onward to a vacant lot midway down the block, well away but with a clear view of the house. Isabel's blue sedan was nowhere in sight. I felt a mix of relief and disappointment despite the circumstances.

Putting such thoughts aside, I peered through the windshield at the two-story Victorian, old but still imposing. I had managed to cobble together a makeshift plan on the way there. I figured it gave us a chance of success, just not much of one.

The house stood dark other than a single porch light. At such a late hour, a heavy drinker like Mrs. Langdon would likely be asleep. Or so I hoped. We watched and waited in silence. After a half hour had passed with no change, I decided there was no sense in postponing any longer.

I pulled the silver box from behind the seat and set it on my lap, lifting the lid. The manuscript fluttered in the night breeze. In my beer-induced haze, I had convinced myself I must be rid of both the box and book in order to put an end to my torment. I started to close it when Onward thrust his hand inside.

"What plan you have for these papers, Dun?" His skin stood dark against the yellowed page. "You know the book has got to stay with us."

"I need to put it back, Onward, all of it, the box and the manuscript. It's the only way I can make things right."

"What do you think that old lady will do soon as reads even a little of this book? She'll burn it, that's what, sure as the sun rises. Person like her never will let this story see the light of day."

"The book doesn't belong to me any more than the box does."

"You don't know what you're saying, Dun." He slipped free his hand and grasped my shoulder. "This story belongs to the world. The world needs this story. Mark Twain told it because he had to, because it needed to be told. Now the time is right for it to be heard."

"But I have to be done with this," I muttered, suddenly exhausted.

His words settled over me like a great weight. A part of me wanted to crawl onto the rear seat and sleep forever. The rest wanted to turn back the clock and start again. I ran my fingers across the string-bound book, unsure what to do.

"Return the box to where you found it," he said, quietly. "The story belongs to all of us. That's how you set things right."

"The story belongs to all of us," I repeated. I wondered if he was right.

An image came to me of Twain standing before the box and then hesitating, manuscript in hand, convincing himself that the world was not ready, could not tolerate such a story, that it could make things worse for people like Jim and Huck. Despite grieving over the death of his daughter, he hid the book away. At that moment he must have realized the story was lost to him forever, though possibly not to the rest of us.

The image slowly faded as my eyes refocused on the manuscript. The hard reality of my decision was as unavoidable as it was clear. In a moment of self-pity, I had pushed from my mind the fact that the box and the book never belonged to me, that I had stumbled on them by accident. In truth, they were one and the same. I had no right to keep either. I took a breath and locked eyes with him.

"I have to return the book, Onward. I'll never be able to live with myself otherwise. If she burns the manuscript, then so be it. I should've never had it, never even known about it in the first place. Besides, I don't believe she'll ever find it."

He peered at me with that strange mix of affection and disquiet I had come to know well. Then he closed the lid and placed my hand over it. Without another word, he climbed out of the car. Within minutes, I was down the alley and through Mrs. Langdon's back gate. I paused in the side yard, spotting him beneath the shadow of the tall hedge separating one yard from the other. He would act as look out.

The weakest part of my strategy was the assumption that she would have a spare key hidden somewhere on the back stoop. If I was wrong, the plan fell apart. I checked beneath the doormat. Nothing. Then I tried the flowerpots, finding only a layer of windblown sand. I ran my fingers along the top of the doorway with the same result.

I had run out of places to check when I noticed a patch of loose mortar in the brick skirting. I knelt and set the box on the floor. Then I eased out the broken wedge. The key lay just inside.

Within seconds I was in the kitchen. I paused for a moment and held my breath, listening for any sign of movement. The house stood silent. Light from the street streaked the hallway floor, guiding me along. That the curtains would be open at such a late hour struck me as odd but I let the thought pass as I concentrated on my destination.

Easing along the wall, I kept one eye on the stairs. To my left, the study stood in near darkness. I stepped across the threshold and peered into the dim light, trying to locate the desk. What I spotted instead took my breath. For a moment I could not move. There beneath the shadows sat Mrs. Langdon, slumped across the desktop.

I could see right away she was dead. Still, I eased up next to her and watched as if she might wake any second. She stayed still as a fencepost. I checked for a pulse and found nothing. Her skin lay cool beneath my fingers despite the over-warm room.

I set the box on the desk and hurried to the front door, switching off the porch light and waving Onward inside. Then I waited in the study doorway. I had never before seen a dead person.

I thought of my long-dead parents, my memories of them built on faded photographs and often-told stories, and of Fie holding my mother's hand as she took her last breath. What must it be like to watch someone you love die. I could not imagine.

Onward's footsteps pulled me from my dark thoughts. I knew by his ragged breath he was as rattled by the sight

193

as I had been moments earlier. He moved next to me and peered into the room.

"She's been gone for long?"

"Looks that way."

"I don't much like being in the room with a dead body, no matter that she was a mean old crow. I guess you had yourself a shock coming on her like that."

"I thought being done with this would make things better," I muttered, "but now I don't know what to think."

"Time for thinking is later." He glanced up and down the hallway. "We best finish up before that girl decides to come home."

I retrieved the box and motioned him to move the chair so I could reach the hidden compartment. He took Mrs. Langdon by the arms to keep her from toppling onto the floor and pulled the chair aside. I removed the drawers and then hesitated, unsure if I should keep the manuscript after all.

A bright flash of headlights jerked me from my indecision as Isabel's car passed the living room windows, heading for the garage. As quickly as I could I slid the box back into place. Then I stood and we slipped out the door and back into the night, its darkness strangely comforting.

Twenty-three

Barely able to keep my eyes open, I turned into the alley behind my apartment. On the way there I had dropped Onward at his house. I kept imagining how good it would feel to fall into bed. Then my headlights fell across two figures midway down the block. Partially shielded by a black sedan, they appeared to be moving around each other in some sort of dance. I switched off the lights and cut the engine. Muffled screams and grunts drifted through my window.

Suddenly awake, I slipped out the door and hurried toward what I could now see were two men. With their attention focused elsewhere, they had not noticed my car. As I drew nearer I realized they were directly outside my gate.

I paused beneath the shadows and stood puzzling over the scene. Two men I'd never seen before were dancing outside my apartment despite the late hour. Or so it seemed. The sedan still blocked most of my view.

My first thought was that this is just the sort of mischief I might expect from Moon. An image of him pirouetting in my living room and striking his wallflower pose flashed through my thoughts. Then all at once I realized what was actually happening. Without thinking I ran toward them, shouting as I went.

They looked up. Even from that distance I could see the hatred on their faces. They started toward me and then froze as the windows of a neighboring house lit up, throwing bars of yellow light across the alley. A figure moved behind the shades. Giving me one last look they pivoted and hustled into the sedan, speeding off in a cloud of exhaust.

I peered into the dim shadows below my apartment. Where the car had been, Moon lay sprawled on the ground, his face to the dirt, one arm pinned beneath him. He did not move. For an instant I stood frozen, fearing he was dead. Then I heard a low groan.

I rushed to his side and tried to turn him but he cried out, covering his face with his free hand. I leaned close to his ear.

"Moon," I whispered, "it's me, Dun."

"Dun," he gasped. "Watch out… two men…"

"You don't need to worry about them." I bent and slipped my arm under his shoulder. "I'm going to turn you over now."

Trying to avoid hurting him any more than necessary, I eased him onto his back. He lay back blinking into the darkness. Above his right eye, a jagged cut had oozed blood down his cheek. Other than a split lip, I could find no additional injuries.

"Okay, let's get you up."

I lifted and he sat up, wincing.

"Dun, it hurts to breathe," he gasped. "I think it's my ribs."

"I'm calling an ambulance," I said, standing.

He grabbed my ankle with a groan and squinted up at me, the pain clear in his eyes.

"No, Dun, please," he pleaded between breaths, "please don't. I can't go to the hospital."

"You could be hurt bad, Moon." I knelt again. "You have to see a doctor."

"You don't understand. The police will be there. They'll have questions, questions I don't want to answer. They are not friendly toward people like me. Trust me, I know."

"You have to see a doctor."

"Take me to a doctor then."

"Where other than an emergency room am I going to find a doctor in the middle of the night? Besides, moving you is risky."

"I'll take my chances. Will you help me, Dun?"

His face shone a ghostly white beneath the scattered streetlight. I had no idea what to do but knew I had to do something. Then an idea came to me.

By the time I had him stretched out on the back seat, I was drenched with sweat. My plan, if you could call it that, hinged on one question I had no answer for. I could only hope Marti would be at home.

I passed Tran's market and turned left fearing I would not recognize her street, much less her house. Needless to say, my thoughts had been elsewhere during my first visit. To make matters worse, Moon rattled on incessantly, apologizing over and over. I had begun to wonder if his injuries included more than just his ribs. He had been hit in the head after all. Then a house appeared beneath the streetlight glow that seemed familiar. I pulled to the curb.

Leaving him in the car, I made my way up the shell walkway. The muted grays of night gradually gained color, showing the storm shutters flanking the front windows to be maroon just as I remembered them. Despite exhaustion, my memory still seemed to be working.

I reached the door and was about to knock when I spotted the faint glow of a lamp through the curtains of the far window. Someone was awake despite the late hour. In a houseful of women, the chance that the room belonged to Marti was so-so at best. Nevertheless, I decided that disturbing one roommate beat waking the entire house.

I treaded across the lawn and into the flowerbed. The yard's lone palm fluttered above me in the warm breeze. Leaning past the bushes, I knocked on the window frame and stepped back. Muted footsteps sounded inside and then a woman's face appeared between the curtains. I recognized her at once as Marti's friend, the one I had met at Leroy's bar, the one who, watching us, flashed me a knowing smile. I wondered what she must be thinking now.

Instead of annoyance at the late-night interruption, she smiled and pointed to the door. By the time I reached the porch Marti was standing in the doorway. Her hair hung past her shoulders in a damp mass. She looked like she hadn't slept in days. Even so, I couldn't take my eyes off her.

"I just got out of the shower," she said as if my late appearance was nothing out of the ordinary. She ran her hands across her face. "I had to work late again."

"You look great anyway," I replied. "But you always do."

A warm blush moved up her neck and into her cheeks. She locked eyes with me for an instant and then glanced past me.

"There's someone in your car," she said, pointing to the street. "What's he doing?"

I followed her gaze. Moon had somehow managed to open the door and was inching along on his back.

"No," I muttered, "he shouldn't be doing that. I think his ribs are broken."

By the time I reached the car, his feet were nearly to the ground. He still lay prone on the seat.

"Moon, stop," I shouted, motioning him to stay put. "You're going to make things worse. Then I'll have no choice but to take you to the hospital."

Marti appeared at my side. I expected her to be angry at the intrusion considering she had only just left work. Instead she glanced at me with a mix of understanding and approval, and then leaned through the door.

"Okay if I take a look?"

Moon raised his head and locked eyes with me.

"You must promise you won't make me go to the hospital."

I nodded and he waved her inside. She squeezed herself between the seats, knelt and gave his arm a gentle squeeze. Easing back, he draped a hand over his forehead.

"Oh, if only I hadn't been so upset over breaking up with Ronnie," he moaned, "I don't believe any of this mess would ever have happened."

"I'd like to hear about it," she said as she began probing his chest, "if you want to tell me."

I could that see she meant to distract him from the pain by getting him to talk, a foolproof plan in Moon's case.

"I'll relate the sad tale but only if I'm not made an object of pity... or of folly, for that matter."

"Of course."

"Well, I decided to drown my sorrows at Mary's, my favorite bar, when I met two college types. They were so nice, not to mention good-looking, that I almost started feeling alive again. When it came time to leave they offered to give me a ride home. You see, Mary's is only a few blocks away so I walked over.

"I suppose, looking back, I should have sensed something awry. The two of them were overly friendly, and they kept plying me with drinks. What would two youngsters want with an old thing like me, anyway? But I was feeling sorry for myself. So, I tossed good sense aside and obliged wholeheartedly.

"When we got near the house they continued on to the alley. They claimed it would be safer for me to go in the back door. I still suspected nothing.

"Once we were out of the car, they started calling me all sorts of names, getting themselves in all worked up and shouting threats at me and people like me, words I will not repeat here. The next thing I knew I was on the ground and they were kicking at me with a fury. I did everything I could do to protect my face, so the rest of me took the worst of it."

"That sounds awful," she said as she checked the cut over his eye. "They had planned it all along, targeting you in some sort of sick game."

"The cruelty of people toward those who are different is beyond understanding. But I've already resolved to glean what wisdom I can from my mistake and forget the rest. Life is simply too short to do otherwise, don't you think?"

"I do." She pulled herself up. "Now I'm going to get my bag. You'll feel better once I have you taped up."

She winked at me and started for the house. I waited by the car, relieved to know he would recover.

"I'll bring you some pain pills too," she called over her shoulder.

"Did she say pills for the pain, Dun?" He gasped. "Oh my, she'll be my friend for life if she brings me pills."

A half-hour later, he lay stretched out on the seat, snoring. I followed Marti back inside the house and she pointed me to a threadbare couch before vanishing down the hallway.

All at once, I felt exhausted. The events of the day had finally caught up with me. I slumped onto the over-soft cushions and laid my head against the seatback, meaning only to rest my eyes for a moment. I was asleep in seconds.

Twain's manuscript appeared in my hands, the yellowed paper rough against my fingertips. The dark story flashed before me. His newfound freedom lost to prejudice and racism, another sort of bondage, Jim takes his own life. Huck can only watch, powerless in the face of larger forces. How much had much changed since? I could not say.

I looked up as thunder rolled overhead. A sudden wind coursed through the trees, crackling the leaves like burning parchment. I struggled to stay upright amid the gusts. When I looked down the manuscript was flying from my hands, the pages rising into the air like yellow birds. Helpless, I watched as they vanished into the night.

I woke to a dark room. Marti sat on the edge of the couch peering down at me. All she had on was an oversized tee shirt. Saying nothing, she took my hand and pulled me to my feet, leading me down the hall and into one of the three rooms. A bed and dresser filled the cramped space.

I was suddenly awake. I started to speak but she put a finger to my lips. Kneeling, she untied my shoes and

200

slipped them off. Feeling awkward just standing there, I began unbuttoning my shirt but she stopped me and instead climbed into the bed, pulling me in beside her.

I eased back onto the pillows and tried to fathom her intentions. I was still fully dressed. I had no idea what to do next. As if reading my mind, she drew closer, laid her head on my chest and closed her eyes. Within seconds she was asleep.

Despite my excitement, the soft rhythm of her breathing, the heat of her body, moved through me like a drug. The bed seemed to float on a warm sea. An image of her stretched out beside me, moonlight in her hair, a salt-laced breeze wafting past us, filled my mind with a strange mix of mystery and desire. I would hold onto that feeling, I vowed, and make sure it never slipped away. Or so I hoped.

Twenty-four

When I awoke Marti was gone. I found a note on the dresser saying she'd left for school but nothing more. The house stood silent around me. Our night together seemed more dreamlike than ever.

When I reached the car Moon sat up, groaning. The bruise over his eye had turned a purplish-yellow but his color was much improved overall. He squinted into the mid-morning sunlight and motioned me into the driver's seat.

"Hurry up, Dun," he complained. "I'm in dire need of one of Francine's gin and tonics. Despite begging like one of mamma's Pekinese mutts, Marti declined my request for more pain pills."

"If you're feeling well enough to complain," I chuckled, "maybe you don't need them after all."

"Oh Dun, I don't mean to sound ungrateful. Marti is a peach. I owe both of you a dinner for saving me. Once the café is up and running, just name a date."

"A date," I mused wistfully.

Her image again filled my mind, and I wondered when or even if I would see her again. The meaning of our silent, late night encounter remained a mystery. Was it a beginning or merely her gentle way of telling me goodbye? I could not say.

Leaving Moon to a tall glass of Francine's special concoction, I headed out the back door. I had parked on the street to avoid a return to the scene of his beating but I needed to stop by my apartment and change clothes before going to the store.

The mere thought of work depressed me. After all that had happened, I dreaded seeing Griggs. But there was no way around it. A swirl of images filled my head, he and Isabel in bed together, Mrs. Langdon slumped over her desk, the silver box and manuscript, even the pearl necklace. The secrets and lies had no end.

I reached the stairs and started up but then stopped in mid-step. Griggs sat perched on the third step, his elbows on his knees, his sun-streaked hair tossed by the morning breeze. Rather than his usual carefree indifference, his face held a mix of shame and disappointment.

"Isabel left," he said in a listless monotone.

"She's gone?"

I stared up at him as my mind raced with possible explanations. He stood and ambled down the steps.

"She found her grandmother dead late last night. A heart attack, they said. The old lady wanted to be buried back in Missouri, so Isabel went to make the arrangements."

Despite my resentment at getting jilted, I felt sorry for her.

"She won't be back will she?"

He shook his head in answer.

"Dun," he started, "I didn't mean to…"

"You never do," I snapped, cutting him off.

An apology would only add to my humiliation. Seeing I would hear no more, he took a breath and stood.

"Before she left she talked to the police about Onward."

"You know about the necklace?"

He nodded.

"And she agreed to drop the charges?"

"I had no problem convincing her."

"I'm not surprised," I muttered.

Knowing his way with women, I imagined she would have done just about anything for him. The mere idea irked me. Seeing my consternation, he put a reassuring hand on my shoulder. I wasted no time in shaking it off.

"You're not understanding, cousin."

"I understand all too well, Griggs."

"I told her I took the necklace."

"Sure you did."

"That's right, I did."

"Why would she believe you?"

"Because it's true."

I squinted at him, wondering what sort of game he was playing.

"What are you saying, Griggs?"

"After we returned the desk and you were doing business with the old lady, I slipped in through the back door and snatched it off her dresser. It took less than a minute."

"But why, Griggs?" I was barely able to contain my frustration. "Do you realize how much trouble you caused?"

"Old as she was, I didn't think she'd even realize it was missing." He shrugged. "How could I know she'd blame Onward?"

"Don't tell me you needed the money."

"She sure as hell didn't need it."

"That's no excuse." I looked at him askance. "Did you admit to taking the necklace or did Isabel just figure it out?"

"I told her about the box too."

"You did what?" I yelled, exasperated.

"I confessed."

"You don't really expect me to believe any of this."

"Why not when it's all true?"

"The Griggs I know never cared much about the truth."

"I've changed my ways, Dun. That's why I told her. I know I'm a disappointment to you and her and nearly everyone else. But I'm determined to do better. Like I said, working at the store is part of that. Besides, I felt for Isabel. She had just lost her grandmother."

"And I'll bet she thanked you for your honesty," I sneered, unable to put aside my resentment.

"I even offered to return the box," he continued, "but she wants nothing to do with her grandmother's belongings."

"I get it," I scoffed. "All she wants is you."

"She never wants to see me again. She plans to sell the house, so she has no reason to come back... ever."

"Then you get what you deserve for chasing after her."

He gave his head a slow shake.

"Dun, you have it backwards. She came to me, not the other way around."

"She did what?"

"She showed up at my place out of the blue and asked to come in."

"Spare me the details," I muttered.

"What was I supposed to do, send her away?"

"I don't want to talk about it."

I suddenly realized that of the two of us, he had always been more honest. If not entirely truthful, he was himself at all times, good, bad or indifferent. I on the other hand hedged my answers whenever possible by hiding behind half-truths and misdirection, never letting anyone get close enough for a clear view, anyone but Marti. That habit had likely spelled the end of any chance I might have had with her as well. The mere thought depressed me.

"You have to believe I never meant to…"

"Enough, Griggs," I barked. "I mean it."

"Okay, you win," he sighed. "The truth is I didn't come here to tell you all that."

"Great," I grumbled. "What is it, then?"

"Onward sent me. He said Gibson needs to see you right away."

"Why?"

"He didn't say but I overheard something about a lost book."

I brushed past him and hurried up the stairs without another word. My return of the Twain manuscript had dogged my thoughts despite all the distractions. How would I tell Gibson what I'd done? I had little idea.

Within minutes, I was back at the vine-draped entrance to his dock. I slipped through and followed the stairs to the waterside landing, spotting him on the upper deck, his feet up on the rail, a notebook in his lap. He motioned me onboard with a quick wave and returned to his notes.

Once upstairs, I followed the gangway toward the stern as I ran through possible explanations for my loss of the manuscript. Perhaps he would understand my decision. Doubts crowded my mind.

At the rear of the cabin an extension to the gangway formed a deck with just enough room for a bench and two chairs. He still sat hunched over the notebook, his ruddy face deep in thought. White hair floated about his head in an ever-shifting cloud. I sat on the bench and waited, forcing myself to be patient.

I let my gaze follow the inlet to the wide expanse of the bay. Clouds drifted over the water, their intricate folds reflected off the surface in pastels of blue-gray and cream. The image, so real yet nothing more than an illusion, reminded me of my growing list of lies and deceptions. I had to look away.

The mangroves below us sighed before a light breeze. Shorebirds stalked the shallows with patient precision. Occasional puffs of wind skipped over the inlet, leaving corduroy ripples that spread outward in widening arcs.

Gibson set the notebook aside and looked up, wide-eyed and blinking, as if surprised to find me there. Without a word he motioned me off the bench and lifted the lid, fishing two beers from a sea of ice. He popped off the tops and handed me one.

"They've decided to make a book out of it," he announced cryptically, "full length, with notes and bibliography, the whole works."

I sipped the beer and tried to decipher his meaning. The manuscript was complete. Besides that, what need would a novel have for notes and bibliography?

"They want all that?"

"I'm too busy for a project this size," he continued. "Are you willing to take it on?"

"You're asking me?"

"Of course I am, Dun. That's why I got you out here." He motioned at the notepad. "I'll let you have what I've collected so far, and I'll assist as much as I'm able, less now, more later."

"Well, I…" I stalled, having no idea what he was talking about.

"I imagine you're feeling out of practice, but I told the publisher you're the right person and…"

"You told a publisher that?"

"Don't look so surprised. I read the pieces you wrote for the university paper and I was impressed. Hell, I was jealous."

"I can't believe you found them," I said, flabbergasted.

"I do research for a living, remember?" he smirked. "Now, I realize Brownsville is not an easy place to get to."

I nodded as if I understood. Finally, the suspense proved too much.

"Wait, wait, wait!" I blurted. "What does the manuscript have to do with Brownsville?"

He stared at me like I'd just slapped him.

"You mean the Twain manuscript?"

I gave my head a quick nod and waited for the questions to start. Instead, he began collecting his papers.

"I'm talking about the Brownsville riot," he continued, "the travesty foisted on a regiment of black soldiers in 1906. When you were last here we discussed the project. The difference is that now I'm asking you to handle most of it. So, what do you say?"

I was so relieved I could barely think, much less speak. I nodded, hoping it would be enough. He glanced at his watch and stood.

"I'm still waiting for the magazine's green light, so nothing's certain. I'll be out of town until next week. In the meantime, think it over. I'll need a firm commitment when the time comes."

Fie

Six years passed before I could return to Mississippi and honor my silent promise to Onward. In all that time he had rarely mentioned his family or even the town. Though I had long since given up on prodding him to tell me why he left home, my affection for him demanded that I do what I could to understand.

Crossing into Mississippi at Vicksburg, I headed south and arrived at my Aunt Sophie's a little before noon. She was her usual cheerful self although I could see that age was catching up with her. After lunch and a long visit, I left her napping and ventured across town to see Viola.

When I had called earlier I noticed an unmistakable terseness to her tone but thought little of it. After all, over twenty years had passed since I'd last seen her. But she made no effort to open the screen door as I waited on the porch and instead pursed her lips into a polite but unfriendly smile. She went on to say she had no intention of talking to me about her family. After an awkward standoff I left, having decided to take an alternative route in my quest.

Minutes later I stood before the modest frame house owned by her aunt, Opal. Sophie had told me that Opal's husband had been killed in an accident at the paper mill a year earlier and since then she had lived alone except for three stray cats she had taken in. Cats were constantly showing up at her back porch. She still made and sold butter so fresh milk was always on hand.

She gave a quick greeting and ushered me into the kitchen. She was grayer than I remembered and a bit plumper, but she still had a curious but unconcerned air about her, as if she saw the world as too capricious to be bothered by for long. She pointed me to a chair and I watched as she busied herself about the room.

A butter churn sat idle in the far corner. She lifted the lid and reached inside. For a moment I thought she meant to put me to work again. Instead, she pulled out a bottle of bourbon and set two teacups on the table, quickly filling them. Then she slipped the bottle back into its hiding place.

"Now if anybody asks, you and I are having afternoon tea. You never know who might see themselves in unannounced."

I recalled my only other visit to her home, years earlier, when an older woman had done just that.

"Do you remember when Viola and I came here with her mother?" I ventured.

"God blessed me with a good memory," she nodded and then reconsidered. "Though some days remembering seems more like a curse. There's plenty in my past I'd rather forget."

"A woman in a purple dress and sequined hat showed up that day."

"Uh-huh," she chuckled, "and waltzed right in like she owned the place."

"She seemed to recognize me," I shrugged.

"That was Audra Castleberry coming around to do her gossiping. She always managed to hear things before anybody else."

"I had the feeling she disapproved of me for some reason."

"Oh, she had her reasons."

I waited, having no idea what she meant. Seeing my puzzlement, she leaned across the table

"Her family came from slaves close around here," she nodded. "Now do you understand?"

I gave my head a quick shake.

"Lord Almighty, don't you know your family owned a plantation just down the road?"

"Well, yes," I replied, still confused, "but I never gave it much thought."

"And they owned slaves," she nodded.

210

"What does that have to do with me? Lots of other people around here had slaves."

"But not from Audra's family. So when she walked in and recognized you…"

All at once I got her meaning.

"You're saying her family and my family…" I gasped, nearly choking on the words, "that they were our… that we…"

"Sure enough!" She slapped her palm on the tabletop, jostling the cups. "They worked your family's land for generations."

"But I didn't have any part in all that."

"Don't imagine that makes one whit of a difference around here. A family that owned slaves may forget their past but it's not so easy when your family was the slaves." She eyed me for a moment. "But that's not what brought you here, is it?"

"No…" I hesitated, suddenly unsure whether I had a right to pry into Onward's life. "I'm afraid I made a mistake in coming."

"You meant to ask me about someone?"

I nodded.

"Well you're here so you might as well go ahead and ask."

"I'm not sure it's my place to nose about in someone else's business."

"Let me decide that." She patted my arm. "I won't answer anything I don't think is right."

"Even if it has to do with Onward leaving home?"

She sipped her whiskey and studied me as if deciding how much she was willing to say. Her critical gaze did nothing to bolster my confidence in asking.

"Why do you want to know about that boy leaving here?"

"He's seemed troubled ever since he came to us. I want to understand why."

"Why not just ask him?"

"I've tried every way I know."

"Well, if he wants to keep his business private then I won't go against him."

"I understand," I sighed. "A part of me always knew that would be the answer."

She turned to the window and sat for a long moment lost in thought.

"Sure seems a shame to make such a long trip just to turn around and leave without anything to show for it," she said, facing me. She refilled our cups. "Do you know the real reason seeing you got under Audra Castleberry's skin?"

"There's more?"

"Then your brother never told you?"

"Whit knows?"

"No, I mean the one with the temper."

"Augie."

"He was snooping around outside your Aunt Sophie's kitchen and heard Audra talking to Viola's mother. That was the day before he fought with your younger brother."

"Jimmy."

An image of that day knotted in my chest. Viola and I had just returned home from grocery shopping with her mother. The moment I stepped out of the car I knew something was wrong. Muted shouts and a terrible pounding came from inside the house. An instant later Jimmy and Augie burst through the back door, taking it off its hinges, and tumbled down the stairs in a grunting, swearing heap. Punches landed with gut-wrenching thumps. Viola looked on in horror.

Without thinking, I threw myself between them. Someone's fist caught me just below the eye. The next thing I knew I was sprawled on the ground. My cheek throbbed but the pain was worth stopping them. By the time Jimmy helped me sit up, Augie had disappeared.

"I'd never seen them fight like that," I whispered.

212

"Mostly there's no accounting for what young men get up to, but I have an idea about this one."

She raised her cup and motioned me to do the same.

"To facing the truth," she toasted.

Our teacups clinked dully. I tipped mine back and drank as much as I could stand. A rush of warmth moved up my neck and over my scalp. Though I felt less than sure I wanted to hear more, I had to ask. For a long moment she regarded me with a mixture of sympathy and amusement.

"You and Audra are related," she finally said as if commenting on the weather.

I stared at her, dumbstruck.

"What could you possibly mean?"

"Your mother's great grandfather had a girl child by a former slave. The baby was fair with auburn hair and, they say, looked just like him. To avoid a scandal he browbeat one of their married daughters into taking in the baby and claiming it as her own. That little red-haired girl was your great grandmother."

"And you're saying Augie knows?"

"Right after Audra told us that story I happened to need something from the dining room and when I stepped through the doorway I nearly tripped over him. I saw right away he'd been listening and wasn't happy about what he'd heard.

"Your brother Jimmy was always polite and respectful to me, Bea and Viola, and to the other working folks that had reason to come around to your aunt's house. He treated everyone the same and would help out when a hand was needed no matter who you might be. But Augie always looked down on my sister and me, treating us like we had no place in that house.

"After he overheard Audra he went to stomping around, slamming doors and muttering all manner of curse words just loud enough to hear. Audra got so upset she had to leave. Then the next day he gets into a fight with his brother."

"He never said a word about it."

"Of course he didn't. He imagined himself better than folks like us. Then he learned that he's not so different after all, that he has the same blood, comes from the same people. A man like him can't face that truth."

Though stunned by what I'd heard, I wasn't entirely surprised. Such stories were not exactly rare in that part of the world. But suddenly I saw Augie in a new light. His overweening pride in the Old South, his prejudice and bigotry, his flying of the Confederate flag and, above all, his anger finally made sense. He despised himself for what he had learned, for what he was, and had turned his anger on the rest of the world, and most of all on Griggs.

Despite the shock, I had to laugh at myself and my folly. I had traveled there to better understand Onward's family and instead learned the truth of my own. I scarcely knew what to make of it. All I knew for certain was I would do my best to help the next generation avoid repeating our mistakes.

Twenty-five

I looked out over the store and could almost believe all that had happened was little more than one long and strange dream. Griggs wandered the showroom floor like he had nothing better to do. Onward was in the shop putting the final touches on a mahogany sideboard. Whit had returned home. His recovery had lasted just long enough to secure Onward's release.

Yet despite the calm and routine, I'd been on an endless roller coaster of excitement and dread ever since leaving Gibson's houseboat. I wanted the writing job more than I could say. But I had little confidence I was up to the task. It had been years since I had written anything substantial. Whether I could do so now was anyone's guess. I had no choice but to await his return, an experience both pleasant and painful, much like life itself.

Leaving Griggs to close up, I wandered back down the hall. Onward needed a ride. He had loaned Tarp his pickup. I found him at the back of the shop, draping the sideboard with a protective cover.

Minutes later we stood before Tarp's whitewashed cottage. The morning glories had closed for the day. Their twisted petals gave no hint of the soul-stirring blue that would arrive come morning.

I followed him to the stoop and he pounded on the strange bowed-out door scrawled with the Feldman's name. As we waited, I found myself wondering if he had drowned at sea. Such a fate would have been poetic considering the way he had landed on Tarp's doorstep.

"I figure he was a sailor," I announced, "who was lost overboard during a great hurricane, maybe even the Nineteen Hundred Storm."

I ran my fingers over the letters to emphasize the point. Onward gave me a disapproving glare.

"Just because a man's coffin gets washed up in a storm doesn't mean he met the same end. He could've burned up in a fire just as likely."

"No, I figure water had to be involved in some way or other. Maybe he perished in a big flood."

"Or maybe," he snorted, "he just slipped in the bath. Only takes two inches of water to drown."

"Still has to do with water," I countered.

"You got some imagination, Dun. I guess that's the writer in you. Someday you're going to be a famous…"

"That you prowling round again, Feldman?" Tarp's voice boomed through the coffin lid. "Sounds like you and me got to tangle some more."

Onward glanced at me and leaned close to the door.

"Tarp, you open this door," he yelled.

"I told you to stop coming round here, Feldman."

"Tarp, it's me, Onward."

"You got no reason to be spooking round my house. Now you go on back where you came from and leave an old man in peace."

"Feldman's long dead and gone."

"You can't fool me, Feldman. I know you too well by now. Now you go on and skedaddle."

"Uncle!" he shouted.

"You give in? Is that what you're saying?"

Onward turned to me and put a finger to his lips.

"Yes, I give," he called. "I'll be on my way then."

He motioned me to step aside and then joined me. We pressed our backs to the house. Seconds later the latch clicked and Tarp's face appeared in the slim opening. Then Onward stepped out onto the stoop, showing himself.

"Is that Onward?" Tarp called as he swung open the door. "You got to have seen him, Onward. Where'd he go?"

"Tarp, it's been only me and Dun out here all this time. Now you got to stop all this nonsense."

"No nonsense to it," he grumbled. "I know what I know and that's the truth of it."

"All right, Tarp." Onward raised both hands. "I didn't come here to argue with you."

"That's what I like to hear." He turned and motioned us inside. "Now y'all come on in. I got something for you."

We followed him to the kitchen sink where a mountain of boiled crabs sat cooling. He waved his hand over the orange and white pile.

"Take what you want. That there's more than I can ever eat."

Onward pulled a bowl from beneath the counter and began loading it with the spiked crustaceans.

"Tarp has crab traps all over the bay," he explained as he picked through the pile. "He needed to borrow my truck to trade out the old traps for new ones."

"We got us a king tide out there," he said, turning to face me. "King tide is the highest tide of all. I don't believe I ever saw the tide flow so hard and deep as today. Man could drown in that water. Tide like that can take a boat under if it gets in the wrong spot."

He peered at me, his watery eyes shining, and ran a thumb under his jaw. The look on his face sent a shiver up my spine.

"That king tide just now recalled me a vision that came yesterday or day before," he continued. "I saw you standing there just like you are now, truth be told, with floodwater flowing and churning all around you."

"Now Tarp, don't you start in on Dun again. He's heard enough of your prophesying."

"Dun needs to know about this vision here. This vision has got to be different."

"You'll give him the fantods, sure enough."

"You know about Jonah," he said, pointing at me, "and how he got swallowed by the big fish?"

I searched my memory for the Old Testament tale.

217

"Being swallowed kept him from drowning if I remember right."

"Old Jonah turned from God," he nodded, "so God sent a storm and Jonah ended up in the sea. He might've drowned but God sent the fish to swallow him. Big fish got his attention too."

"Was that your vision?"

"No, but I was reminded of Jonah when I had my vision of you and that rough sea." He ran his thumb under his jaw again and studied me. "That tide today was just like the Mississippi on the rise. I remember watching the river as a boy. When you see those whirlpools and the water all boiling up, you know there's something evil just beneath, something that can pull you under and hold you.

"That old sea can be just the same. You got to beware of those big tides, tides like I saw today. Riptide can take you under lickety-split."

"Come on now, Tarp," Onward scolded. "Dun knows better that to get himself into a riptide."

He set the overfilled bowl on the counter and covered it with a dishtowel. Tarp leaned close to my ear.

"You watch out for yourself anyway," he said under his breath. "No fish big enough around here to save anybody."

Rattled by his speech, I could only nod. Onward grabbed his keys from the countertop and started for the door.

"You get those crabs on ice before they spoil, uncle," he called over his shoulder.

I followed him through the narrow backstreets toward his house. He said he had something to show me. I could tell by the gleam in his eye he was up to some sort of mischief.

On my way there Tarp's strange and unsettling vision had been replaced by my doubts over the fate of Twain's manuscript. Isabel's untimely arrival the night of her grandmother's death had given me no chance to reconsider my decision. Had I been the right in returning it after all? I could not say.

Hoping to set my misgivings aside, I pulled to the curb outside Onward's house. Surrounded by a thick stand of palmetto, oleander and orange trees, the home stood midway along a dead-end road of crushed oyster shell. To either side, weathered buildings in various states of disrepair marked a once-busy warehouse row. Yet standing on his porch, I invariably felt immersed in a tropical paradise.

Built before the Civil War, the house had originally served as an office for a horse-drawn carriage company. A stable stood nearby. He had converted the barnlike building into a woodworking shop not long after moving in. He harbored hopes of one day making custom furniture for a living.

At that time of evening, the porch light cast knife-like shadows across the road. I climbed out of the car and made my way up the gravel walkway. He had already disappeared inside.

I stood in the shadows and recalled the many times I had visited as a child. Onward would pull several books from the shelves and hand them to me before heading for his woodshop. Surrounded by the fragrance of orange blossoms, I stretched out on the wood floor and passed the afternoon with the likes of Charles Dickens and Harper Lee.

I mounted the stairs and stepped into the living room. The sweet and sour smell of books, of frayed covers, brittle paper and cracking glue mixed with the acrid odor of fresh varnish. Other than the familiar floor-to-ceiling bookshelves, the room was crowded with new furniture, some made of birds-eye maple or mahogany, others of tiger oak or walnut, and a few of varieties I'd never seen before. I knew without asking he had made them all. His deceptively simple style had an unusual look, a subtle asymmetry that gave each piece its own personality.

He ran his palm along the top of a rectangular table too small for dining but larger than a typical accent piece. The center panel held a single drawer. I let my gaze drift over the warm tones of cherry, one of my favorite woods, reddish-brown and luminous beneath the satin-like finish.

"You know what this is?"

He rapped his knuckles on the corner and gave me a quizzical look that held a tinge of mischief. I knelt for a better view. Long-limbed and sleek, the graceful design had a weightless quality, as if the legs hovered just above the floorboards. I guessed I could pick it up with one hand.

"It's a desk," I replied, shrugging.

"Dun, you got to do better than that."

I sighed and rubbed my forehead, still rattled by Tarp's strange vision.

"Onward," I griped, in no mood for a furniture quiz, "why are you asking me when I can see you already know?"

"You got to be almost as cranky as Tarp," he snorted, "once you're tired out."

He moved around the table and tested the drawer. The runners slid silently along the wooden grooves. I found myself wondering why he wanted to show me that particular piece. I guessed he was especially proud of the work, not that he didn't have reason enough. But I sensed another purpose.

"Now you must be wondering what I'm up to," he announced.

"A little."

"Then why don't you go ahead and ask?"

"All right, I'll bite. What's this all about?"

"I decided to take an old design from around eighteen fifty-seven or so and make it new, like it belongs to this day instead of back then."

220

Confounded by his response, I squinted at the desk as if an answer lay hidden somewhere in the finish.

"I can see it's a nice piece but I'm not following you."

He turned to me and I saw in his eyes that same mix of affection and consternation I'd seen since my return to the island. I scarcely knew what to make of it. He again ran his hand over the table.

"This is a writing table, Dun," he finally said. "You got to take up Gibson's offer and get back to your journalism."

Stunned, I looked from him to the table. I was touched by the thoughtfulness of the gift but even more so by the confidence he had in me.

"Onward, I can't," I said, fingering the smooth wood. "This table must be worth hundreds. You shouldn't just give it away."

"Sure I should. I have more furniture orders than I can keep up with." He bent over the desk as if penning in an imaginary script. "Think of it, Dun. Could be Mark Twain used one like it to write one of his books."

An image of Twain at the desk came to me and I felt the hope of writing again grip my throat.

"I don't know what to say," I managed.

"No need to say a thing. Just get to work."

Table in hand, he started for the door when the ringing phone stopped him. He set the desk aside and vanished down the hall. Moments later he reappeared, grabbed his keys and made for the door, motioning me to follow.

"Trouble with your uncle," was all he said.

Twenty-six

When we arrived at Augie's house Fie was waiting on the doorstep, her jaw set, her coal-black eyes revealing little. Yet her crossed arms and erect stance said volumes. I was sure she and her oldest brother had locked horns again. She was never one to turn away from trouble when she believed she was right.

She waved us to follow and disappeared inside. Onward hesitated at the threshold, giving his head a quick shake but saying nothing. He and Augie had a long history, none of it good.

The living room held the same tense silence I recalled from my last visit. Whit stood in the far corner like a boxer between rounds. Riley sat behind him, forehead to his knees, pressing himself to the wall. A red hand-shaped mark covered his left cheek. Augie was nowhere in sight.

Fie appeared beside me and nodded toward the back door. I spotted Griggs through the window, pacing the dock and talking to himself. Now and then he paused long enough to wipe blood from beneath his nose.

"This time my no-good brother has gone too far," she said under her breath. "He and Whit nearly came to blows, something that hasn't happened since they were young men. You can see for yourself what he did to Riley. Babs and Sheila are in the bedroom, both in tears."

I sighed and turned my gaze to Riley. I had no trouble imagining Griggs in his place.

"Augie was holding forth on the admirable nature of the Confederacy," she continued, "when Riley asked what was so admirable about owning slaves."

"That was all?"

"You know how proud Augie is of our family history."

"Ashamed is what he ought to be."

"It's your heritage too, Dun."

"I want nothing to do with that past."

"Dun, your past doesn't just disappear because you want it to. There are good people mixed in with the bad in our family."

She was probably right but I said nothing. She needed more from me than argument just then. I shifted my gaze to the dock.

"What about Griggs?"

"When Augie slapped Riley, he jumped between them. I could see that he didn't want to fight his father, but Augie punched him and the next thing I knew they were on the floor and going at it like rabid dogs. It was all Whit could do to break them up. But never mind all that now."

She took hold of my hand and squeezed it.

"Dun, ever since you were a teenager I've counted on you to be the voice of reason in this family. Griggs said things today he'll likely regret for a long time to come. At least I hope so. To be honest, some of his ranting scared me. Please try to talk to him. Onward can stay here in case Augie shows his face again."

I left them to manage the troubled scene and headed to the dock. Griggs had retreated into the boathouse. I wandered through the doorway but found no sign of him. A faint thumping drifted through the far door, so I followed the sound to an outside landing where the family's twenty-two foot sloop, an older sailboat with a cramped cabin and fixed keel, stood moored. I could hear him inside rifling through the cabinets.

At my approach he jutted his head through the cockpit door as if expecting trouble. His face no longer had the relaxed indifference I'd come to expect. Instead, his eyes shone with a feverish intent.

He waved me onboard and ducked back inside, emerging moments later with a bottle of tequila and a six pack. Setting aside the beer, he put the bottle to his lips and tilted it back. A thin line of the amber liquid dribbled down his chin, staining his shirt.

Sucking in a long breath to cool the fire in his throat, he followed with a swig of beer before tossing me the bottle. He sat perched on the bench like a bird ready to fly. I did not like what I saw in his face. The tequila had seemed only to deepen his determination, to what end I could not guess.

"Fie called you?" he said without looking up.

"She told me what happened," I nodded. "Are you okay?"

"Take a wild guess," he snapped.

Elbows on his knees, he rocked back and forth in an agitated rhythm. I sat opposite him and struggled to imagine myself in his place. What would I want to hear, if anything? For what seemed a long moment neither of us spoke.

The wind hummed through the rigging in plaintive moans, only deepening our silence. Sheet lightning flashed across the northern sky. I had little idea what to do but felt compelled to speak.

"Griggs, listen to me," I finally said. "You can't let him get to you."

I could only hope Fie's confidence in me was not misplaced. He looked up, tossed the empty can aside and popped open another without taking his eyes off me. His anger was palpable.

"I can't let him get to me?" He stood and glowered at me. "What am I supposed to do when he backhands a twelve-year-old kid, his own grandson for Christ's sake?"

"I just meant…"

"What would you know about living in a screwed up family, anyway? Your mother didn't leave home and never bother to write, much less pick up the phone. Your father didn't treat you like dirt. You had Fie. You had Whit. How many times did he hit you, Dun? Tell me that?"

I had no answer for him. There was no point in reminding him my parents were long dead. And I could see that anything else I might say would only make matters worse.

"He said he's disowned me," he continued, "this time for good. I hope he rots in hell or, better yet, Sheila divorces him and takes Riley with her. Whatever happens, I'm not waiting around to find out."

His reckless talk had worried me but I liked the sound of that even less.

"What do you mean, Griggs? You're not going to do something rash, are you?"

"Like…?"

"Like hurt yourself."

"Hell no," he scoffed. "I'm sailing to Mexico."

My brief sense of relief was tempered by a slow realization that he meant what he said. I stared at him in disbelief.

"You can't be serious."

"Just watch me."

"Griggs, Mexico is over four hundred miles from here."

"Not far enough by a long shot but it's a start."

"What about Riley?"

I knew my mistake the moment the words left my mouth. Tears filled his eyes and he jumped onto the cockpit, untying the forward moorings and raising the jib. The small sail snapped in the swirling wind. I stood and watched as he untied the stern. He grabbed a line to keep the boat from drifting into the channel and pointed me to the dock.

"Get off, Dun," he said, wiping his eyes with the back of his hand.

"But Griggs…"

"Get off now."

"Stay and talk to me."

"Don't make me throw you overboard."

Onward suddenly appeared on the opposite landing. The cavernous entrance to the boathouse stood between us like an open mouth. He had yet to spot us but even in the thin twilight I could see the worry on his face. Griggs flung his empty can into the cockpit.

"I don't want him around here," he muttered. "He's the cause of this mess, him and his kind."

"You don't mean that, Griggs," I hissed. "Onward isn't the reason for what happened in there and you know it."

"What I know is that you're going for a swim as soon as I…"

"Dun, you got to come quick!" Onward's voice drifted past us.

I turned to face him. He pointed toward the house.

"Fie needs your help," he shouted. "Whit's had a spell. Ambulance is on the way."

He disappeared around the corner. I clambered onto the dock, no longer thinking of Griggs or his misplaced anger. The jib snapped taut behind me, signaling his departure.

The boathouse stood deep in shadow as I stepped back inside. I could barely see my feet, much less the gangway. Keeping one hand on the wall to steady myself, I hurried along the weathered planks as best I could. I had gone only a short way when a voice echoed through the high-ceilinged room, stopping me.

"He hates me, doesn't he?"

The voice belonged to Augie. I peered into the dim interior, seeing little until he stepped from the shadows. He held a half-empty bottle in one hand, a glass in the other. I glanced toward the dock.

"How much did you hear?"

"Bits and pieces, but enough… or too much."

A bitter grin twisted his lips, a smile of self-hatred and regret. Unable to stop thinking about Whit, I kept moving. Augie swirled the ice in his glass and drained it.

"Sheila's left me," he muttered.

226

That news was enough to stop me. I pointed toward the house.

"Augie, something's happened…"

"And my grandson thinks I'm a monster." He refilled the glass and drank. "He's right."

I felt sorry for him but only for an instant. I needed to keep moving.

"Didn't you hear what Onward said? I need to…"

"He knows better than to show his face in my house," he interrupted. "The damn coloreds are always causing me trouble."

He spit into the dark water below us. Despite his confession, I could see he cared little for anyone but himself.

"I have to go," I said, making no effort to hide my disgust.

"Wait, Dun," he shouted, motioning me to stop. He pointed toward the dock. "He'll listen to you. You're like a brother to him, the brother he never had."

"Fie needs me inside."

"Please, Dun," he pleaded. "Go to talk to him. Make him see that I really do love him."

"You're too late."

"No, there's still time. I know what I did was wrong," he gasped, wiping his eyes. "Make him see in spite of the way I acted. We're family, you and me. You're obliged to help."

I paused in the doorway, resisting the impulse to pity him. His forced smile returned.

"So, you'll talk to him?"

"He left, Augie," I said coolly. "He's gone."

"Gone where?"

I stepped through without answering, reaching the house in seconds. Fie pointed me to the foyer. Whit lay on the tile floor just inside the door, his legs splayed, his right eye swollen shut. Onward was bent over him.

"You got to wake up now, Whit," he said, gently slapping his cheek. "Time for sleeping's past."

I pulled Fie aside. She would not take her eyes off her twin brother.

"Tell me what happened," I said beneath my breath.

"Sheila left to stay with Babs and Riley until she can find a place of her own. When I returned from seeing them off I found him like that."

I knelt beside him. His face had an ashen hue that nearly took my breath. I leaned close to his ear as sirens wailed in the distance.

"We're going to get you through this," I whispered. "Don't even think about leaving us."

He stirred and opened his good eye, taking hold of my arm.

"Dun, listen," he said between breaths, "keep watch… your cousin…"

His eyes rolled back and he sank onto the floor. Fearing he had died, I could not move. Onward pushed me aside and put his ear to Whit's chest. Seconds later the paramedics burst through the door.

Twenty-seven

Framed by spotlights, the hospital stood white against the night sky. Lightning flashed overhead. The freshening wind smelled of the ocean, not two blocks away, and for a brief moment I imagined Griggs alone in the sloop. A storm could mean trouble for a boat that size.

I followed Onward through a winding corridor to the emergency room. Knots of people crowded the waiting area, talking in hushed voices. The harsh, over-bright lights only heightened the reality of our presence there.

Midway down the hall, Fie stood talking with Hanley Curtis. I'd never seen her look so drawn. I was suddenly struck by the realization that she and Whit had spent nearly their entire lives together, most of it in the same house. As his twin, the thought of being separated from him after so long must be terrifying.

"Waiting's got to be harder than most anything," Onward muttered to himself, "except for bad news."

He wandered off. I paced the hallway vowing I would not allow any image of Whit incapacitated, much less dead, into my mind. Instead the Twain manuscript filled my thoughts, unbidden and unwanted. Doubts about my decision knotted in my chest.

I looked up as the automatic doors to the emergency room opened with a rush of cold air. To my surprise, Marti stood in the opening. Spotting me, she hurried over.

"The moment I saw the name," she said breathless, "I knew he must be your uncle."

I searched her face for some sign, good or bad.

"Marti is… is he…" I stammered. "Will he…"

"He passed out because of something called vasovagal syncope," she replied. "It's a sudden drop in blood pressure caused by a stressful event, like the sight of blood or a close call. The bigger problem is that the fall left him with a concussion or maybe worse. We're waiting on the test results."

The news left me speechless. She took my hand and drew close.

"Try not to worry, Dun," she whispered. "It's too soon to know anything for certain."

I studied her face and wondered again about our night together. I might have asked but she gave my hand a squeeze and then abruptly dropped it. I turned to find Onward beside me, Fie next to him. She eyed Marti with interest.

Marti's cheeks flushed crimson, and I felt my own face burn.

"I'm sorry I can't stay any longer." She straightened herself and nodded at the doorway. "With a storm on the way, we're expecting a busy night. There are reports that a building collapsed north of here due to high winds."

"Did I hear you say," Onward said, glancing at me, "the wind took down a whole building?"

"The storm will be here any minute," she called before slipping back through the doorway.

"Griggs…" I whispered.

We turned to the windows. Sheet lightning flashed beyond the rain-splattered panes, silhouetting a line of wind-thrashed palms. Their fronds all pointed seaward. I felt the thump of distant thunder in my chest. Tarp's enigmatic warning came back to me, and all I could think was that Griggs was somewhere out there.

Within minutes we were racing across West Bay in Gibson's houseboat. Onward had figured the gale would push Griggs south, past Chocolate Bayou and on toward San Luis Pass. Leading to the open ocean, the pass was notorious for hidden shoals and dangerous currents. Considering the state he was in when I last spoke to him, Griggs would never see them.

Windblown rain crossed the bow in sheets. Channel markers vanished in the deluge and then reappeared moments later, passing uncomfortably close to our port side. Onward gripped the wheel and peered into the darkness. The gale was having its way with the boat, but rather than slow down, he bumped the throttle higher.

The yellow glow of the Chocolate Bay shipyards appeared to our right, signaling our turn. San Luis Pass lay to the south. The narrow gap marked the western tip of the island and, more important, a major point of tidal flow.

The rain eased so I slipped on an anorak and moved onto the gangway. Despite the channel's wind-tossed surface, I could see the water surging past the markers in swirling eddies. The tide was outgoing.

Within moments the bridge lights emerged from the darkness, rising above the pass in a soaring arc. The curving shore stretched away from us. Onward switched on the spotlight. The tide, higher than I'd ever seen it, had all but covered the scattered mangroves.

The window behind me boomed under Onward's fist. I turned to find him pointing down the channel, past the spotlight glow, to a dim shape floating just above the surface. I recognized it at once as the hull of a boat, a hull painted the same sky blue as Griggs' sloop.

Struggling to stay upright in the coursing wind, I staggered downstairs for a closer view. The sky opened again. Quarter-size raindrops stung my cheeks. I grabbed hold of the gunwale to steady myself and squinted into the downpour. Water swirled past the overturned boat like a rising river. Midway along the side I spotted a hand. I motioned Onward forward.

The engines roared beneath me as the houseboat slowed despite the raging current. He opened the cabin window and called above the gale, pointing me rearward. I realized he needed the anchor to control our position before getting any closer.

I scrambled to the stern, grabbing the fluted end and tossing it over the side. The chain flew off the deck in a violent rattle. I eased the winch counterclockwise, letting out cable to increase our distance. We could only hope the anchor would hold when the time came.

I turned to check our progress. The overturned hull stood twenty yards away. Locking the winch, I motioned to Onward and the engine roar faded beneath the pounding rain. The cable snapped taut.

Suddenly the boat swung left and tilted wildly, throwing me to the deck. Saltwater rushed through the drains and past me. I could see the current slamming against the hull, rising higher with every second. The boat would founder unless I lengthened the line.

I jumped up and jerked on the winch's rain-slick handle. No give whatsoever. Changing my position, I tried again. Nothing. I scrambled to the other side and put my chest to the bar, leaning my full weight into it. With a dull click, the lock released, freeing the line. Moments later the boat swung into place.

The rain had eased again by the time I returned to the bow. Onward was already in the water, a rope tied to his life vest. I motioned him back onboard. My thoughtlessness had gotten Griggs to this point. I should be the one going after him.

Onward dismissed my direction with a wave and pointed to the hull. From where I stood I could see the broken mast angling beneath the surface, likely wedged in the mud bottom. The thin aluminum pole was all that kept the sloop from being swept away.

Water boiled up a few feet past the mast in a broad oval, sending whirlpools spinning off in all directions. Tarp's words came to me again. The boil signaled submerged debris, probably driftwood. The pass was notorious for such hazards. Entire trees regularly wedged themselves beneath the bridge.

"We got to stay clear of that boil," he shouted above the wind. "You let out the rope just enough so I can ease around the stern."

"Let me do it," I called back. "I'm the better swimmer."

"No time to argue." He pushed away from the side. "Start to letting out the line."

The north wind gusted past, shaking the houseboat and sending a shiver through me. The temperature was dropping. Griggs could not hold on for long.

I braced myself on the gunwale, letting out short lengths of line and straining to keep my grip. The tips of my fingers had become numb. Despite his effort, Onward made little progress.

The current surged around him, shifting from side to side, snakelike and unpredictable. I squinted through the blowing mist. All at once I realized my angle was wrong.

Pressing my shoulder to the rail, I slid backward, lengthening the rope as I went. When I reached the cabin, I wedged myself between the wall and the gunwale and began letting out the rope inch by inch. Onward still drifted yards from the hull.

Barely noticeable at first, he began moving across the channel. Within moments he had reached the hull. The current pressed him to the stern, nearly pushing him under. The rope vibrated beneath my grip. Slipping past the corner, he disappeared from view.

Suddenly the line went slack. I hesitated, unsure what to do. Should I pull or hold my place? I had little idea and instead cursed myself and my indecision.

Deciding I could wait no longer, I started to pull when the rope jerked taut, nearly ripping from my hands. An instant later Griggs swung into view, the rope and vest tight around his chest. Seeing him sent a jolt of energy through my aching arms.

I leaned into the rope and pulled hand over hand, making sure he stayed clear of the swirling boil. Within seconds he was alongside the boat. Securing the line, I leaned over the gunwale and held out my hand. He could barely raise his head, much less climb aboard. He mumbled something inaudible.

I prayed I had strength enough to lift him. One hand on the rail, I grabbed hold of him, somehow managing to get him up and over the side. We tumbled onto the deck.

Scrambling to my feet, I dragged him into the cabin and stripped off the vest. He tried to speak between blue-tinged lips. I snatched a blanket from the couch and tossed it across him before turning to leave.

"Dun, wait" he whispered, grabbing hold of my ankle.

I glanced out the door and knelt beside him.

"I didn't mean what I said back at the dock." His glassy eyes searched my face. "I've messed up so much, Dun."

I had no reply. Instead, I pressed my hand to his chest. Then I stood and rushed back out the door.

Untying the line, I swung the life vest high into the air, hoping the wind would carry it toward the sloop. Onward had positioned himself at the stern. The vest hit the current and drifted toward him but at the last moment shifted left, slipping past the hull and out of reach.

I hauled in the line and tried again, aiming further to the right. The vest slipped left again. The possibility it might never reach him flashed through my thoughts.

I was about to try again when the houseboat lurched forward, throwing me to the deck. Out of instinct I turned to the stern. The boat groaned and swung to one side. The cable had snapped. We would be on the sloop in seconds. I scrambled up the stairs and jammed the boat into reverse, thrusting the throttle forward. The engine strained against the surging tide.

But I was too late. The boat's movement had shifted the current. A looping whirlpool surrounded the small sailboat, sending shudders through the mast. I watched as a tree limb twice its size rose from the boil and stood silhouetted black against the gray mist. Then the tree rolled and the limb swung downward in a terrible arc, slamming into the hull. The sloop vanished in seconds.

I rushed out the door and then froze at the sight of Griggs standing on the bow. He had seen it all. A squall swept over us, for a moment rendering him ghostlike and insubstantial. He glanced back at me and despite the rain I could see him smile. Then he grabbed the gunwale and vaulted himself over the side.

I stumbled down the stairway and grabbed a life preserver, hurling it into the water. Too stunned to move, I squinted into the downpour. The channel roiled below me, swift-flowing but empty. They were both gone.

I turned a slow circle. The boat, the rain, the gray sky all stood before me distant and surreal, as if the actual world, all of it that mattered, lay somewhere beyond the spotlight. In an instant it all had slipped away. Or so it seemed.

I might have stood there for hours but a low-pitched roar rose above the rainfall. Turning toward the sound, I peered into the rain. The bridge emerged from the downpour, alarmingly close and drawing nearer by the second. With the tide so high, the boat would be torn apart beneath it.

Rushing back upstairs, I thrust the throttle to full power. My only chance was to run aground. The boat leapt forward and began speeding toward shore. I swung the spotlight across the beach, spotting a small gap between the mangroves. I spun the wheel toward it.

All at once the shoreline rose up before me sharp and well-defined. Strangely, I watched as a fiddler crab scurried for cover. For an instant the boat seemed to hover in place, as if it might manage a smooth landing. Then the hull slammed into the shallows, throwing me into the wall. I slid to the floor. The boat tilted beneath me with a groan.

A numbing ache spread across my cheek and jaw as the cabin walls wavered around me like floating seaweed splashed with red and blue light. I could find no sense to it. Face to the floor, I watched the red and blue fade to gray, then to white, then vanish altogether.

Twenty-eight

Dazed, I stood shivering in my damp clothes. The blanket the deputy had given me did little to cut the chill even in the wind-protected shadow of the hospital. I had refused treatment for the knot under my eye and instead insisted he take me there.

By the time I'd left the pass the Coast Guard had three patrol boats out searching the channel. They had found no sign of Griggs or Onward. Even the sailboat vanished so completely it almost seemed as if it had been no more than a mirage. With a shudder I imagined them all, like Feldman, lost to the sea.

I squinted into the hospital's pitiless glare, dreading the thought of going inside. I had little idea how I would tell Fie the news when I could barely face it myself. The unreality of the entire night held me like a dream. Yet I knew there was no point in delaying. I had to find the words. She was counting on me.

Figures moved behind the second-floor windows in spite of the early hour. Dawn could not be far off. Suddenly Marti stepped into view, putting her hands to the glass and peering out as if expecting someone. I would not let myself believe that someone was me. But seeing her gave me the boost I needed.

Reaching Whit's room, I stopped in the doorway. He was asleep despite the tangle of tubes and wires stretching away from him in all directions. Fie stood before the corner window.

Hearing me she turned. Her quizzical gaze shifted from me to the doorway and back. The worry in her black eyes, so unlike her, knotted in my throat. I moved into the corridor and motioned her to follow.

"You're alone," she whispered as she glanced up and down the hallway. "Where is…"

"Fie, listen to me," I interrupted. "Something's happened."

"Griggs…"

"There was an accident."

She checked the corridor again.

"Where is Onward?"

"When we found the sloop, it had capsized…"

She leaned closer, staring at me as if I made no sense. I had to turn my eyes.

"They tried to save each other," I continued, "but…"

"Dun, what are you saying?"

She grabbed my arm and I faced her.

"They're gone, Fie."

"Gone? That can't be," she replied, shaking her head.

"Fie…"

"I only just saw the both of them."

"Listen to me…"

"Onward was with you. Why isn't he here?"

"He rescued Griggs, but before I could get the lifeline to him the boat went under."

"Onward was…"

"He was with the boat."

"Then Griggs…" she said, her tone hopeful.

"When the boat sank he dove in after Onward."

"You mean they both…"

"The current was too strong, Fie."

She stood unmoving, her face stoic despite her brimming eyes. Then she raised a hand to my cheek and traced the cut under my eye with her shaking fingers.

"I must find some antiseptic," she muttered, "so you won't…"

Her voice trailed off. I led her to a nearby bench. Beyond the windows, the eastern sky was beginning to lighten. She saw none of it. I sat beside her, saying nothing. At that moment words were of little use.

"He was so young when he first came to us," she finally said, her voice just above a whisper, "and terribly sad. He thought he had no one, you see. But he was wrong. I loved him like a son right from the start.

"Fate was less kind to poor Griggs. With a father like Augie he never stood a chance. I'm sure you know that better than anyone."

She wiped her eyes with the back of her hand. Biting back my own tears, I could make no reply. Whit's incoherent mumble drifted through the doorway and she glanced into the room and then turned to me.

"You think we need to tell him," she said, "don't you?"

I nodded. She stood and straightened herself, her black eyes again determined and willful.

"We'll wait until he's stronger." She frowned, pointing to my mud-caked pants. "Now go and get yourself cleaned up."

I woke to a light knocking sound, for a moment unsure where I was. Thin sunlight blinked through the storm shutters. I squinted into the dim room. My mud-caked pants, the result of securing the houseboat's bowline to a clump of mangroves, lay on the floor below me. Seeing them flooded my mind with troubling images.

A louder series of knocks rattled the doorframe, followed by Moon's voice. I pulled myself from beneath the covers, shuffled across the room and swung open the door. He peered at me through the rusted screen.

"Dun, are you hurt?"

"What time is it?" I grumbled.

"How should I know? It must be past two."

I stared at him, my mind still in a fog. All at once I realized too much time had passed since I'd left the pass. I had to go back. I turned and started for my bedroom.

"I know what happened last night," he called after me.

I paused in mid-step and faced him.

"But how did you hear?"

"Gilbert, my new special friend, is a police officer. He phoned when he saw my address on the report." He flicked his finger at the latch. "Now, let me in so I can have a better look at you."

I hurried back to the door, flipped the latch and stepped aside. Taking my arm, he led me to the table, pushed me into a chair and studied my swollen cheek.

"You look almost as bad as I did..." he said, tracing the gash with his finger, "but not quite. Still, you could stand some cleaning up. You'll hold still for me, won't you?"

Without waiting for an answer he disappeared into the bathroom, returning moments later with an armful of supplies. He soaked a cotton swab with antiseptic and began dabbing the wound. As much as I wanted to hear what he had to say, a part of me was afraid to ask. Instead, I tilted back my head, closed my eyes and concentrated on the pain, grateful for the distraction.

"You haven't asked what Gilbert told me," he finally said. "You're not sure you want to know, are you?"

I shrugged. The swab stopped moving.

"Oh, Dun," he sighed, "I don't know if I can say."

I sat up and locked eyes with him.

"Moon, as my friend you have to tell me."

"You are my friend, aren't you?"

Pulling a chair close, he sat and faced me. His sorrowful look knotted in my chest.

"The Coast Guard has called off the search," he whispered. "I'm so sorry, Dun."

His words drifted past me, somehow deprived of meaning. Their terrible finality lay beyond my grasp. Instead my mind filled with a detached emptiness, as if I stood by watching myself.

I rose from the chair without a word and started for my bedroom with little idea what I would do or where I would go. I only knew I could not stay there.

An hour later I stopped before Augie's house. Our last conversation had brought me there. His plea for help might have been self-serving, but it held more than a little honesty. And I had never seen him so distraught. Though I had little idea what I would say, I felt compelled to see him.

I started toward the door when a voice called from the street, stopping me. I turned to find a man standing on the sidewalk, a small dog next to him. The swirling wind briefly lifted his toupee. He wore a pink cardigan over an orange golf shirt and held a half-filled tumbler in one hand.

"He's gone," he called over the wind.

"Any idea when he'll be back?"

"Never is my guess. Packed up and left early this morning. I happened to be out walking Skip here when I ran into him." He swirled the ice in his glass and drained it. "Told me he was selling the place, moving back to the mainland."

"Did he say why?"

"I asked but I could see he was in no mood to visit. The police had just left. Maybe that had something to do with it."

I tried to imagine Augie alone in that big, empty house when he heard the news. I couldn't help but feel bad for him despite his many faults.

"Looks like I'm running on empty," the man said, raising his glass. "I'd better be off."

Depressed by all I'd heard, I started for my car. I had to find an answer, a way to explain all that had happened, all I'd lost. How I could not say.

I once again found myself standing before Tarp's house. Wind pulled at the morning glory vines, rustling through the leaves like whispers. I paused on the stoop and puzzled over why I had arrived there again seemingly without intention.

The strange bowed-out door carrying Feldman's name stood before me, a silent reminder of Tarp's warning. I had to look away. Rapping my knuckles against the dark wood, I stepped back. The house remained quiet. I knocked again, still with no response. I had almost decided to leave but something compelled me onward. The door was unlocked.

Stepping through, I headed for the kitchen. Tarp sat hunched over the table, the old Bible before him, a half-empty bottle beside it. Faint swirls and eddies, nearly invisible, traversed the brown liquid. He looked up and motioned to a chair as if expecting me.

Taking a tumbler from the sideboard, he set it on the table and poured a half inch. He did the same in the glass before him. The acrid aroma of homemade liquor wafted past. I drained my glass in one swallow, hoping the numbing burn would drive away all memory.

He refilled my glass and set the bottle aside. Flipping open the Bible, he thumbed through the crackling pages, turned the book toward me and pointed to a handwritten column. The irregular pattern, clearly by more than one hand, held a list of names.

I scanned the time-blurred lines, unable to decipher much. He had yet to say a word. I glanced up and he pointed me to the lower third of the page. There the ink was darker, the letters clearer.

My gaze drifted to a pair of names written in a cramped longhand. Suddenly it dawned on me that one of them was my father's. The other was illegible. A dotted line stretched between them. From its center a solid line ended in a single name, Onward's. I looked from line to line, name to name, trying to make sense of it all. I could feel Tarp watching me.

"Uh-huh," he finally said, "your eyes see what your head won't."

"I don't understand," I replied, facing him.

"Now that Onward's gone there's something you got to know." He sighed and smoothed the page with his palm.

"This Bible's been with my family since my great, great grandmother's time. She started the family tree.

"This would be me," he said, pointing to a black smear I could make little of, "put in on my baptism day. We got nearly a half-foot of rain that morning."

I nodded as if I understood what he was getting at. I did not.

"And my mother is up here."

He paused and looked away as if some long held memory had hold of him. Questions spread through my mind like spilled ink.

"But what's my father's name doing there?"

I pointed to the line. He slid his finger next to mine, letting it rest on the woman's name.

"You know who this is?"

I gave my head a shake.

"That there is Viola Walker, Onward's mother. Now you understand?"

I shook my head again, unwilling to answer my own question.

"Tell me, Tarp."

"That last summer when your daddy and his brothers came to Mississippi, he and she became friendly." He sat back and took a sip from his glass. "They had grown up together, you see, and had always known each other. But by that summer they were old enough to notice one another in a different way. He was eighteen, she a little younger. You saw her picture. She was a pretty one, truth be told.

"Well, at summer's end he got sent off to college, then to the war. Her daddy sent her to stay with an aunt. Nine months later, she came back."

I sat staring at him, too stunned to speak. He refilled my glass and handed it to me. I scarcely felt the burn in my throat.

"We're brothers," I muttered in disbelief.

"Onward was your half-brother. My nephew, Salmon Cates, married her and gave him our family name."

243

"All those years and he never told me."

"He only just learnt his own self."

Suddenly, everything I'd puzzled over the last few weeks fell into place, his strange looks, his consternation.

"He found out when he went to his father's funeral, didn't he?"

"Same old aunty that took in his mother told him. She thought he had a right to know all along but the family wouldn't allow it. The funeral changed all that.

"After he learnt who his true daddy was, he didn't know what to make of himself, who he was in the world, in his family. If he'd had more time to work it out, he would've come around to telling you."

"Does anyone else know?"

He shook his head. I sighed, realizing I had yet another secret to guard.

"Outside Mississippi, it's just you and me that know the truth of it. That's how the family wanted it so that's how it stayed all these years."

"Until now."

"I believe he would've gotten around to telling your Aunt Fie and Uncle Whit soon as you knew."

"Whit!" I shouted and jumped to my feet. "I have to go."

I sped along the old wharf's narrow shell roads, finally emerging at the edge of downtown. Nearing the store, I slowed at Post Office Street and checked the front door. A handmade sign taped to the glass read 'closed due to family illness'. Fie's doing, no doubt.

I jammed my foot on the accelerator. Just past the corner I happened to glance in the rearview mirror and spotted the inside lights blazing. I slammed on the brakes. As much as I hated a delay, I had to take a closer look.

The showroom stood quiet. I left the door ajar and wound my way through the maze of bed frames and end tables. A low murmur drifted past. The voices seemed to come from behind a wall of china cabinets.

I crept closer and peeked around the end cabinet, hoping for a glimpse of the intruders. I could see nothing unusual at first. Then a pair of shadows fell across the hallway floor. I ducked behind the cabinet.

"Whit Osay," Fie's voice echoed down the passage, "if you were half as sensible as you are stubborn you'd be resting at home now instead of prowling around this drafty old place."

"You don't understand, Fie," he complained. They were drawing nearer. "I have good reason to be here."

I moved from behind the cabinet just as they stepped into the room. Fie nearly jumped out of her skin. Then she fixed me with her cool gaze.

"Dun Osay, where have you been? I've been trying to reach you since early this…"

"Oh, leave him be," Whit barked. "He looks like he's had enough trouble."

He pulled me in front of a mirror. Our bruised faces stared back, garish in the over-bright light.

"We look like a couple of boxers," he said without a trace of humor, "both losers."

A bitter smile crossed his lips. Reminded of my ordeal, I turned my eyes.

"Should you be here?" I asked.

"Don't start nagging me too."

"You just got out of the hospital, Whit."

He sighed and moved to a nearby chair.

"I had to come here, Dun. Onward is… was… inseparable from this place. I came here so I might be near him for a while."

"You could've said so in the first place," Fie grumbled.

"I was supposed to die before him."

"Whit," she groaned, "stop such morbid talk."

"Dun," he continued, "sometimes I find the unfairness of life astounding."

He stood and grasped me by the shoulder, leaning close.

"Dun, listen to me." His face was inches from mine. "Never put off going after what's most important to you. Life is too short. Promise me."

I nodded, moved by his tone. He stepped back and turned a circle, surveying the room as if seeing it for the first time.

"When I was laid up in that hospital I had a revelation."

"Oh dear," Fie muttered. "I don't like that sound of that."

"Pay her no mind," he scoffed. "I've been looking at things all wrong, Dun. For most of my life I considered this store a prison, a place I'd never escape. I never wanted it, you know. I just did what my father expected of me. I thought I had no choice but to take it on, that I owed it to the family to keep the business going. But all that's changed now."

"Whit, you don't know what you're saying." She eyed him worriedly. "I believe that bump on your head has affected you badly."

"On the contrary, twin sister, it reminded me what really matters." He gave her a quick glance. "So, I'm going to sell the place and travel the world."

"Good Lord!" she gasped. "Dun, talk some sense into him. He'll lose his mind without the store to keep him busy."

He locked eyes with me and I saw at once he had made his decision.

"I don't think he will, Fie."

"But Dun…"

"Where will you go?" I asked.

"I don't know." He turned to the window. The street beyond stood awash with light. "Anywhere but here."

"Whit," Fie sighed, "surely you don't mean that. This is your home... our home."

"Well, you never can tell what a person might do," he added, motioning me to follow. "But right now we have more important matters to attend to."

I followed him down the hall, all the while wondering if Fie was right. He paused in the shop doorway, gave me a quick wink and then stepped aside. Mrs. Langdon's desk sat feet away. I brushed past him, knelt and yanked out the drawers as quickly as I could manage. Then I reached in and slipped off the hidden panel. The silver box was still in place.

I set it on the floor, took a breath and lifted the lid. The yellowed manuscript lay just as I had left it. I pressed my palm to the cover and muttered a quick prayer of thanks, grateful for a second chance.

"How?" I said, turning to him.

"I got lucky. Mrs. Langdon's granddaughter wasted no time in arranging to sell off the estate. I decided to stop by the house and an agent happened to be there taking inventory. She was on the phone negotiating with an antiques dealer in New Orleans who wanted to buy the entire lot. So, I made an offer." He nodded at the box. "That's what you wanted, isn't it?"

"But how did you know?"

"Onward told me."

"All of it?"

"Enough."

I pulled out the manuscript and cradled it in my hands, rubbing my thumbs along the rough paper as I made a silent vow. I would not allow the book to slip away a second time. Somehow I would share Twain's story with the world.

Twenty-nine

The following afternoon I parked outside a small church tucked between a palm grove and an abandoned wharf. The chapel's clapboard siding shone brilliant white beneath the cloudless sky. Palm trees stood unmoving in the calm air like an army keeping vigil.

Clusters of people waited outside the church, some smoking, others speaking together in low tones. I spotted Carmelo Puglia scurrying from one group to the next, talking overloud and gesturing wildly. A rotund black man in a clerical collar and dark suit greeted attendees at the door. I wondered if he was the preacher who convinced Tarp he could prophesy.

I caught a glimpse of Whit and Fie slipping through a side door but I lingered well away from the entrance. The thought of going inside held a finality I wanted to avoid. I was not ready to bid Onward farewell.

Within minutes I was the only person left on the lawn. The reverend waved me over before stepping inside himself. Seeing I could procrastinate no longer, I started up the shell walkway and then heard a voice call my name. I turned to find Marti hurrying across the parking lot in a black dress and high heels. I'd never seen her so beautiful.

Taking my hand, she pulled me close and started for the church. She paused at the doorway and faced me, studying me with her blue-gray eyes. With her free hand she gently traced the bruise under my eye.

"Dun, I'm so sorry," she whispered. "Moon came to the hospital to tell me."

Her hand lingered on my cheek. I searched her face, wondering if I saw anything more than pity, love even. I could not guess.

The tremulous notes of a gospel song drifted through the open door. I'd heard Onward hum the tune countless times. Suddenly I was overwhelmed with emotions I could scarcely name, much less understand. Marti turned and pulled me through the entrance, perhaps to spare me from embarrassing myself.

We joined Whit and Fie on the second row. I could barely breathe in the stuffy, camphor-laced room. I had almost convinced myself to bolt when the reverend appeared beside me. He glanced toward the entrance and leaned close.

"You are Mr. Dun Osay," he said under his breath, "are you not?"

I nodded.

"Mightn't you know the whereabouts of Mr. Cates?"

"He's not with you?"

My voice echoed through the hushed room. He winced and put a finger to his lips. I scanned the sanctuary, suddenly aware of Tarp's absence.

"He has not yet arrived and we are past our starting time." He glanced at the crowd and leaned closer. "Sadly, he has no phone so I have no way to reach him."

Whit leaned past Marti and pointed me toward the door.

"Go find him for the Reverend, Dun. We'll keep the crowd in here until you get back."

I needed little convincing. Brushing past the reverend, I headed toward the blinding sunlight of the open door. I could her Marti following close behind.

We were midway down the aisle when a shadow appeared in the entrance. I paused and squinted into the glare, able to see little more than two silhouettes, latecomers I thought. I felt Marti move next to me.

All at once a cloud moved across the sun, dimming the glare. A collective gasp moved through the crowd behind me. Instinctively, I pivoted toward the sound. People shifted in their seats, craning their necks to see past me.

I followed their gaze to where Tarp stood midway down the aisle, his arms spread wide.

"Old Jonah came to me in a dream," he called in a wavering voice, "and he showed me the way."

"Amen," someone shouted.

"Then the sea rose up in a storm and wind," he continued, "and took my grandnephew into the deep. But Jehovah had mercy on him just like he did for Jonah those many years ago. Sent a boat to swallow him instead of a fish, truth be told, but no different, no sir."

I stood unmoving, puzzled by the spectacle. Then he stepped aside and I felt the blood rush from my face. I peered past him, steadying myself on the closest pew, unable or unwilling to believe my eyes. In the middle of the aisle, his head bandaged, Onward stood facing me.

I blinked, doubting my sanity. A wave of tears all but blinded me as the crowd surged forward, rushing past and surrounding him. I stumbled, nearly falling but a hand caught my arm, pulling me onto a pew. When I looked up I found Tarp squinting down at me.

"Uh-huh," he hummed, helping me to my feet, "it's true."

"He's… he's…" I sputtered. "How?"

"When that boat went under," he called over the melee, "he got caught in the rigging and it took him under lickety-split. Next thing he knew he came up in a little pocket of air trapped inside the cabin. With the riptide swirling all around him he saw there was no leaving, so he stayed put and prayed the air would last. Lord was with him that day, just like old Jonah himself.

"Once the current eased he swam out past the broken mast and climbed up onto the hull just before the boat went under for good. By then that wind had pushed him clean past the marker buoys and out into the open water. If not for that life vest you threw him he would've joined old Feldman, yes sir.

"Now," he said, glancing down the aisle, "I got to ask you to keep what I told you about your daddy to yourself. I hadn't said a word about it to Onward. Let him tell you in his own time, when he's good and ready.

"But right this minute," he nodded past me, "I believe you got a pretty lady waiting."

I felt Marti's hand wrap around mine. I turned to her and for an instant thought I saw something different in her gaze, something beyond affection. Drawing her close, I took a breath and pushed back into the crowd.

A week later Onward and I stood outside a plain yellow-brick church fronting the main boulevard. I watched Augie amble toward the entrance, his hands in his pockets, his head down. He had finally gotten around to arranging a memorial service.

I had no intention of going inside. After Griggs had vanished in the storm Augie's animosity toward Onward had only grown. He needed someone to blame and Onward provided an easy target. Besides, we had devised another way to remember Griggs, a way that suited him infinitely more than the dim confines of a church.

Without a word, we climbed into the car and followed the tree-shaded avenue away from town. Neither of us felt like talking. My thoughts again turned to the Twain manuscript, to something I had initially let pass with scant notice but now came back to me in vivid detail.

In the years since he had last seen Jim, Huck had absorbed the casual bigotry and prejudice of the world around him. He had little awareness of the change in himself. He was instead preoccupied with everyday life and had simply come to accept the prevailing view that former slaves were ignorant by choice, untrustworthy and largely deserving of their lesser status.

Crossing paths with Jim again changed all that. Despite his dire circumstances, Jim could barely contain his joy at seeing his young friend. His unassuming affection caught Huck unawares, unintentionally and silently shaming him. Memories of all they'd been through

251

came rushing back and he vowed at that moment to do whatever it took to keep Jim's friendship. He had little idea what that would come to mean.

I glanced at the mahogany box riding between us on the seat. A single carved feather crossed the top. Onward had made the box as a small memorial. Inside, Griggs' collection of arrowheads, antique fishing lures, bird's eggs, shark's teeth, and all the other flotsam he had found over the years jangled like a tiny symphony.

Clouds of blue-gray and indigo drifted overhead as I angled onto a narrow spit of sand wedged between San Luis Pass and the sea. Behind us, the bridge rose in a solemn and elegant arc. It seemed a fitting contrast to Griggs' restless nonconformity.

We climbed from the car and I glanced at Onward, hoping we had chosen right in planning our remembrance at the place we both had last seen him. He popped open the trunk and began passing me the driftwood we had gathered a day earlier. Within minutes we had the wood stacked into a rough pyramid. He wedged the mahogany box on top.

I stepped back as he put a match the pile. An opaque plume rose into the still air and we stood together watching the fire in silence. Beyond the smoke the shoreline stretched away from us in a broad curve, ending at a dilapidated pier. Slate-colored swells zippered beneath the black pilings.

An image of Griggs came to me, the two of us walking the rain-spattered pier, his ease with the fishermen a counterpoint to my reticence. He said he'd brought me there so I would remember who I was and where I'd come from. He had no doubt how to answer those questions for himself.

A flock of pelicans flew past us in an undulating line, up and down and up again, like the lilting notes of a gospel song. I felt Onward's presence visceral and close, knowing the secret that bound us together like an anchor chain. I puzzled over when or even if he would ever tell me what he knew of our shared lineage. Putting myself in his place was beyond imagining.

"He was safe on that boat," he said in a near whisper, "but he jumped in after me. Didn't have to but he did anyway, and to save a black man."

"Griggs was complicated that way. On a given day I was never sure what I'd find in him, good or bad."

He pulled a flask from his pocket and held it up.

"To finding the good in all of us."

He raised the bottle to his lips, tilted it back and then handed it to me. I took a long swallow. My eyes filled with tears, whether from grief or the whiskey I could not say.

A breath of air painted the water in a brushstroke of dark ripples, moving up the shoreline and past us, smearing the sky with smoke. The breeze smelled of salt marsh and mudflat. I breathed deep, grateful for the quiet moment.

Onward stirred and cleared his throat. I turned to face him. His drooping eye peered back at me with the same mix of affection and consternation I'd grown accustomed to, along with something I'd never before seen. I knew then my life was about to change.

"I got a favor to ask," he said, "if you're willing."

Thirty

Sunlight streamed through stands of dense timber, throwing shadows across the blacktop like bars on a cage. The narrow passage felt close and claustrophobic compared to the wide-open sky of the island. I leaned on the armrest and let the warm air rush past my face. Unpainted shacks drifted by, littered with castoff furniture and appliances, their porches dark amidst the honeyed light.

Earlier in the day we had crossed the iron truss bridge spanning the Mississippi River at Natchez. On the eastern shore we stopped to check the river. The fast-flowing current, reportedly at flood stage, swept past the massive pylons in a nerve-rattling roar, throwing off boils and eddies. I had to look away, reminded of the last time I'd seen Griggs.

The trees fell back as we passed a broad pasture bordered by thicket. Grass-covered mounds marking ancient burial sites of the Natchez tribe bulged from the earth like swollen wounds. The air smelled of earth and burning leaves.

Onward pulled into a gravel turnout and cut the engine. Before us stood an oval clearing edged by a wall of brush and towering trees, yellow pine and post oak, magnolia and pecan. A footpath worn to dirt led through the grass, ending at a narrow break in the thicket.

He climbed out and started down the trail. As I followed, I puzzled over his plan. He had yet to say why we had come to Mississippi or confess even a word of our shared parentage. I was tempted to tell him all I knew. Instead I heeded Tarp's counsel to give him time.

We slipped through the narrow opening and paused beneath the shaded confines of the thicket. The still air buzzed with insects, punctuated by tree frogs calling to one another in their high-pitched trill. Rain-dampened leaves dropped earthward like oversized raindrops.

Below us a broad path, rod straight and clear of brush, ran parallel to the tree line. The floor of the odd-looking trail stood four feet below ground level and stretched well into the distance, seemingly without end. We climbed down the short wall and Onward set off at a fast pace. I hurried to catch up, again wondering at our strange pilgrimage. Within moments I was even with him.

"You're sure in a hurry," I said between breaths.

"Got somewhere to see," he replied, making no effort to slow down.

"What is this place?"

That got his attention. He stopped and pointed up and down the trail.

"This here is what's called the Natchez Trace. The path runs over four hundred miles to the north, all the way to Nashville. Buffalo and other animals probably made the trail in the first place but people have used it since, wore it clear down into the ground.

"Back during the Civil War folks came along here trying to get away from the fighting or maybe to catch a steam boat to New Orleans so they could sell off war contraband. In war time a lot of people forget the law and turn plain mean to one another."

"From what I've seen," I muttered, "it doesn't take a war for that to happen."

"You just now figure that out?" he winked.

We continued along the trail until we reached a narrow gap in the wall. An overgrown footpath wound from the opening into the trees. He checked the trail in both directions and then moved onto the path, motioning me to follow.

After a quarter-mile we arrived at a small oval cleared of trees. A stone marker stood in the center. The site was a Confederate memorial. Multicolored leaves littered the ground like confetti, as if the dead had reason to celebrate.

"This is where your great, great grandfather…" he paused and eyed me thoughtfully. "Your great, great grandfather got killed right here just before the war ended. A Union militia not under control of the federal government was marauding all through these woods, killing whoever they found, taking what they wanted and selling it to traders heading downriver. Once they looted what they could, they'd burn the place to the ground.

"Ulysses Grant was burning as he went too, but he decided our little town was so pretty he spared it. Most plantations round about went up in smoke anyway."

"It's hard to accept that my ancestors were fighting to keep slavery."

"Folks fought for a lot of reasons, for honor and pride, to protect their home and, yes, slavery too. But most things are not so simple as we like to make them. Not easy for us to imagine nowadays what it was like for them."

"That's why we made the trip," I guessed, "so I could see for myself where the family came from."

"Partly," he replied as he turned to leave.

A half-hour later the truck bumped onto a tire-rutted road of red dirt. Hundred-foot pines lined the way at even intervals. The forest beyond stood dense and nearly lightless. The anvil-shaped outline of a thunderhead, gilded by a low sun, peeked through the uppermost branches.

Onward followed the winding track up a low rise. The rows of trees moved away from us, merging with the surrounding forest like a retreating army. Lightning flashed in the distance.

He slowed as we crested the hill. Before us a row of fluted columns rose above the remains of a redbrick house. Oddly, the columns were cast in iron. The scene resembled nothing so much as a Greek temple. Past the ruins a brick hut and a scattering of wooden outbuildings stretched to the tree line. A small stream lined with willows meandered down the hill before passing from sight.

A sudden wind swept through the pines in a prolonged hiss, wavelike and eerie, sending a shiver up my spine. Spanish oak saplings bent before the gust, their leaves blood red against the dark underbrush. I had a sense we were not alone.

"This was your family's plantation." He pointed to the iron columns. Bits of white paint still clung to their scrolled tops. "Those are in the Ionic style. They came all the way from Italy, shipped over in pieces and put together here."

We circled the house and approached the outbuildings. The brick hut stood only four feet tall, the wooden roof and door having long since rotted away. The empty doorway gaped at us like an open mouth. From inside came the bell-like sound of running water.

"This was a spring house," I said to myself.

I followed the sound to the rear of the hut. Beneath a mass of grass and ferns, a tiny stream trickled toward the tree line. Onward scooped up a handful of the clear water, raised it to his lips and then froze, his eyes fixed on the thicket.

I followed his gaze. At first I could see nothing out of the ordinary through the mass of tangled branches. Then a shape stirred in the shadow of a gnarled oak. Gradually, the silhouette of a standing figure emerged from the darker hues of brush. Onward took a step forward.

"We don't mean to cause concern," he called out. "We're just having us a look around."

The figure stirred again but gave no reply. Onward took another step.

"Got to be buggy back in there," he continued. "We won't tell anybody you're here. Come on out if you want to."

The shadows wavered and split and came together again, and then a young man, short and painfully thin, emerged from the underbrush. His gaunt face seemed somehow boyish despite the lines creasing his forehead.

His boots and pant legs were splattered with mud. He peered past us to Onward's truck.

"That truck got a radio?"

Onward glanced at the truck and then motioned toward the outbuildings. I could see a makeshift bed piled with blankets through an open doorway.

"Looks like you've been living here."

"You said you wouldn't tell," he snapped. He cut his eyes in both directions. "Did you mean to fool me?"

"I meant what I said," he answered evenly. He nodded at me. "This is Dun Osay. My name is Onward Cates. Will you tell us yours?"

"Why do you want to know?"

"Just trying to be friendly."

The man's face seemed to ease.

"Seth Merrick from Beaufort, North Carolina."

"So, Seth Merrick, you plan on staying here long?"

"I got no plan," he replied, running a hand over his face. "Tomorrow will be two weeks I've been here."

"Two weeks is it?"

Onward tried to hide his surprise. Seth peered past us again, his expression worried.

"You got a radio in there?"

"In my truck?"

"A car radio, shortwave, citizens band, any sort of radio?"

"I never had much use for a radio. What they got on the stations these days is just noise, mostly."

"No, no, it's more, much more. Don't you know the CIA can listen in on you, hear your every word through the signal. Same is true for television, phone. I make sure to steer clear of them all."

"You mean the Central Intelligence Agency up in Washington?"

"They're everywhere. I was hitchhiking to the VA day before yesterday and got picked up by an agent. I spotted him right off. I'd avoid the main roads altogether if I

258

could." He lifted a pant leg to show a plastic and metal prosthesis attached just below his knee. "What's left of my leg got infected, so I had no choice but to go."

"What else do they do for you?"

"The doctors give me medicine, mind control stuff, but I know better than to take it." He stuck a finger in the corner of his mouth and pulled it wide. "I cheek the pill until I'm out of there."

"You don't trust the doctors?"

"Hell no I don't. One of the shrinks has a twin brother, also a shrink. He's plain evil. They're never there at the same time but I can tell which is which. I knew the first time I saw him he worked for the agency. Nowadays if I spot him I'll just turn around and hightail it out of there no matter what needs doing."

He paused and wiped the sweat from his forehead as if the subject alone was exhausting. His wild-eyed look worried me.

"How do you find enough to eat way out here?"

I hoped to shift his focus elsewhere.

"I've made a study of it," he answered, clearly relieved to discuss practical matters, "so I make out all right. The old widow lady down the way gave me a dozen eggs and a laying hen for fixing two leaks in her roof and chopping some firewood. I won't ever eat that chicken. She may be old but she still lays plenty."

"You're living off eggs?" I said in disbelief.

"Of course not," he snorted. He gestured toward the thicket. "I got hickory nuts and pecans, and sometimes even mushrooms. The other day I found some pokeweed down by the swamp. You ever had poke salad?"

I shook my head in answer. Onward turned without a word and started for the truck. I watched after him, puzzled by his abrupt departure. Seth waved a hand before my face.

"Listen up," he continued, his eyes wide. "You got to watch what you eat or else they'll slip something in it."

"You don't really think the government wants to poison you."

"Hell yes I do, and not just me but lots of people, maybe even you." He glanced to either side and leaned closer. "You know what Twinkies are, right? Well, they've put something in them to control your mind. Then they make you do things for them, bad things. You're lucky I'm here to set you straight. You know what I mean, right?"

To my relief Onward reappeared, sparing me from an answer. He held a bulging paper bag to his chest. Setting the bag on the ground, he reached inside and pulled out a small orange and a grease-stained sack.

"You won't find a better orange that this one here," he said, offering the fruit to Seth. "They call them Satsuma oranges. There's two dozen or more in the bag."

Seth eyed the orange with suspicion, hesitated and then reluctantly accepted it.

"You sure this is okay to eat? Somebody might've done something to it."

"No sir, my uncle planted the tree his own self ten or more years ago." He rattled the sack and dropped it in Seth's hands. "He made this salted fish too. Caught it all himself not far from where he lives. Not likely you'll ever know more about what you eat."

Seth opened the bag and sniffed warily.

"I wish I had more to offer but there it is." Onward motioned me toward the truck. "We got to be moving on now, Seth. You take care of yourself."

We retraced our route in silence, lost to our thoughts. Seth was a sad and disturbing reminder of the way a life can come unhinged. I kept thinking of Griggs and whether I had ever allowed myself to see him as he was, good or bad, free of my own prejudices. Sadly, I had no answer.

Thirty-one

The next morning we crossed the narrow bridge spanning Bayou Petrie. The brush-choked waterway wound into the distance, making for the river. Smoke from the nearby paper mill drifted past the treetops in a yellow veil.

A scattering of houses marking the edge of town appeared ahead, most of them small and nondescript. Watching them pass I thought it strange I had never seen the town my father and his siblings visited so often. Why the family had stopped coming I could not guess.

The sun vanished behind a rolling mass of clouds, paling the indigo shadows to pewter. Raindrops slapped the windshield. Thunder thumped in the distance.

The street widened at an intersection flanked by four small churches, one on each corner. Their peeling paint and rotted eaves spoke of the town's slow decline. Farther on, we entered a broad avenue lined with plantation-era homes. An old black man, rail-thin and bent, ambled along the uneven sidewalk pushing a grocery basket filled with what seemed his entire belongings. A hand-painted sign on its side read 'got sick - lost home'. Reminded of the Twain manuscript, I wondered how much had changed since he had written the story, and how little.

I glanced at Onward. He had said nothing since leaving the motel. His face set, he gripped the steering wheel as if it might slip from his grasp at any moment.

Turning off the main avenue, he followed a narrow street past City Hall and the central fire station. The houses grew smaller with every block. At a sharp turn we came upon a wrought-iron gate marking the entrance to a tree-shaded cemetery. Sunlight filtered through moss-draped oaks, painting headstones in pale green.

He drove through, pulled to the side and climbed out. I wondered if the cemetery was the reason for our trip. He had yet to say.

I followed him past a rectangular plot edged by a low iron fence and on to a cluster of gravestones, some weathered and unreadable, others freshly etched with names. We stopped before a gleaming white slab with 'Salmon Cates' carved across the top. The grave next to it read 'Viola Cates'. He stood staring at the headstones for a long moment.

"This here is my parents," he finally said.

We passed another long moment in silence.

"My father was good to me," he continued, "when she let him be. I'm grateful for all he did raising me up. But truth is he wasn't my real daddy."

He turned and scrutinized me with his drooping eye.

"You already heard," he guessed.

I nodded, again reminded I was an easy read.

"Tarp told you?"

"Don't blame him. He believed you were…"

I left the thought unfinished. I wanted to put the memory of that night out of mind if I could. I followed his gaze back to the gravesite, for the first time letting myself fully face the reality of our shared heritage. Somehow, standing there beside him made the connection between us real. It dawned on me that besides sharing the same father, we had both lost our parents early on, figuratively if not literally.

"I know I should've told you before now," he said, still facing the headstones, "but I had a lot of thinking to get through."

"You must've had a shock finding out right after the funeral."

"Sure enough true. Ever since I can remember I thought of myself as more or less the same as my father or Tarp or any other man in the family. They were where I

262

came from, who I belonged to. Then I learnt the truth of who I am.

"Whit and Fie always treated me like family. No man could ask for more. But getting treated like family is not the same as being family. When a man spends his whole life thinking of himself one way and then finds out he's something else altogether, it sets his mind to thinking, to doubting what he knows, who he is. You got to know what I mean."

"I'm still trying to understand it myself. I know so little about my father... our father. The whole story seems unreal."

For a moment I thought that bringing me to the cemetery was his way of revealing his secret, his reason for me asking me along. But the more I thought about it, the less sense I could make of it.

"You could have told me all this at home, Onward. Why are we here?"

"I got somebody for you to meet," he replied, starting toward the truck.

Three blocks from the cemetery we stopped before a small frame house nestled inside a pecan grove. The towering trees stretched away from us in even rows. Stirred by a sudden breeze, yellow leaves fluttered earthward like wounded birds.

I followed him up the porch steps and we paused before the door. He tilted his head close to mine.

"This house belongs to my mamma's aunt, Ophelia," he said under his breath. "I learnt about your daddy and my mamma from her. Old as she is, she can't hear too well so you'll need to speak up with your questions."

"What questions?"

"You'll know when the time comes."

"Is this why we came, to see her?"

He rapped his knuckles on the doorjamb without answering. Footsteps clattered inside. Seconds later the door creaked open and a coffee-colored woman appeared in the opening. Her quick eyes darted between us, sizing me up before settling on Onward.

"Come inside this house, child," she said, swinging open the door.

"Ophelia, I stopped being a child a long time back."

"You're still my little Onward," she replied, smiling. "I've been expecting you."

"You knew I'd come?"

"Of course I did. I've known you your whole life, haven't I?"

She led us through a cramped living room and into a large kitchen. A porcelain stove filled one wall. Motioning us to sit, she lifted the lid off a battered pot and ran a wooden spoon through the steaming contents. A heady mix of spices filled the air.

"Uh-huh," Onward hummed, "something smells good, sure enough."

"I'm just cooking up some gumbo for old Mr. Jackson. He's too old to cook for himself anymore so the ladies close around here share cooking duty."

Moving to the table, she poured iced tea from a glass pitcher and sat opposite us. Lines etched her face like roads on a map. She studied me with her curious gaze.

"I can find your daddy in you though he was still a boy when I last saw him."

"I've been told there's a resemblance."

"What's that you say?"

She tilted her head at me.

"I've seen only photographs," I called out. "You knew him well?"

"I lived in Mobile at the time so I only saw him now and again when I would come for a summertime visit. But I remember what he looked like well enough. He was a handsome boy. It's no wonder Viola took to him."

"He loved her?"

"I believe so."

"What did he do when she got pregnant?"

264

"He never knew."

I stared at her, stunned by the news.

"No one told him?"

"Nobody outside the family ever knew. Her parents sent her to me so I could care for her until her time came. Truth is they were ashamed of her, poor girl. And that shame marked her for life."

"But she eventually came back?"

"Salmon Cates, Tarp's nephew, lived in Mobile then and he started coming around. Before long they got married. He told her he'd take the baby as his own, and he did just what he said he would. He was a good man but he had to put up with a world of trouble from her.

"They moved here when he got a job at the paper mill." She sat back and waved a finger at me. "But that's not why you all are here, is it?"

"I don't know," I said, glancing at Onward, "I've been trying to find out why he asked me along ever since we left home, but he won't say."

"He'll say when he's ready. Now I have a kitchen to tend to." She scribbled something on a note pad and handed it to him. "I believe this is what you're looking for."

"Come on, then." He stood and started for the door. "We got one more stop to make."

Three blocks from the cemetery we passed a columned two-story house, white with green trim. Onward checked the paper Ophelia had given him, slowed and turned a half-circle, parking a safe distance away but with a clear view of the stately home. Honeysuckle drooped from the porch trellis in a green mass, still blooming despite the late season. The heavy fragrance wafted through the passenger window.

Onward stared at the empty street, his hands still gripping the wheel. I could see he needed something from

265

me but I had little idea what it might be. I climbed out and rounded the truck, stopping at his window.

"This is why you asked me along," I said, nodding toward the house. "You know who lives here and you want me to... to…"

I paused, hoping he would finish the thought. His eyes slowly refocused, though he kept his gaze on the street.

"I don't even know what she looks like, Dun, not the color of her eyes, not if she's tall or short, skinny or round."

"She who?"

"Does she like lemon in her tea or milk, like Ophelia?"

"Who do you mean, Onward?"

"I sure do hope she likes books." He gave his round head a slow shake. "If that tide had taken me like it did Griggs, I would've died never knowing."

"Never knowing what?"

I struggled to corral my impatience. He turned to me, his expression a mixture of hope and fear.

"You got to convince them, Dun. I know you can do it."

"Convince who, Onward? What's this about?"

"I need to see my daughter."

I glanced at the house, more mansion than home.

"Your daughter lives here?"

"The house belongs to her grandparents. She's staying with them while she's in college." He pointed me down the street. "You go up there and talk to them."

"Why don't you go?"

"Dun, these are the same folks who kept her mother from me all those years. You think they're going to talk to me now?"

"If they won't talk to you, why would they listen to me?"

"I don't know. You're a writer. Make up some story about why you need to see her. Then I'll be here waiting."

As much as I wanted to help, I wasn't keen on making a fool of myself.

"What sort of story?"

"Think like old Mark Twain. Something will come to you."

"But Onward…"

"Law's bound to show up if we sit here too long."

He waved me toward the house. I figured the girl's grandparents were only trying to protect her. If I could come up with a convincing story they might let me in. But I had to make it right. The odds of getting a second chance were close to zero.

I searched the truck looking for anything that might prove useful. Onward's black suit hung below the rear window, Tarp's family Bible beneath it. I'd puzzled the entire trip over why he'd brought them but every time I asked he managed a vague reply that answered nothing. Suddenly an idea came to me.

I hurried back to the passenger door and grabbed the suit off its hook but before I could even remove the hanger, he snatched it out of my hands. He held the coat to the light and brushed the collar with great ceremony.

"I got this cleaned in case I needed to look good today. I don't want somebody's dirty hands all over before I even get a chance to wear it."

I rubbed my palms on my pant legs and gingerly lifted the Bible.

"Onward, listen to me." I held up the thick book. "If you want to see your daughter I'm going to need to borrow that suit and this Bible."

"What do you want with that old Bible?"

"We're wasting time."

"You got to give me a reason."

"I have a story all worked out just like you asked." I held my thumb and forefinger apart. "See if you can find a strip of white paper about this wide. Write a short note telling your daughter you want to see her."

267

He handed me the suit and I changed into the coat and pants as quickly as I could in the truck's cramped cab. By sheer luck, I had brought along a nice shirt. I finished dressing and he handed me the paper.

Moments later I stepped onto the porch. I slipped the strip into place, trying to calm my racing thoughts. I was about to knock when the door swung open and an older woman appeared on the threshold. Her pale skin matched the honeysuckle blooms. I stared at her, speechless. Onward had forgotten to tell me his daughter's mother was white. The irony was laughable. Still, I could barely manage a smile.

"Good Lord," she gasped. "Reverend, I am sorry! I heard footsteps and thought you were the postman."

As we introduced ourselves I eyed the rolling pin she clutched to her chest. I hoped she meant to use it for cooking and not on me.

"I didn't mean to startle you," I said, pressing my palm to the Bible. "I often take a moment to pray before I make a call."

"You're calling on us? But why? We already belong to a church."

"Then you're familiar with this little book, no doubt."

I held the Bible to the light. She nodded with a mystified expression.

"This Bible is in the old style, meant to record a family's heritage from year to year, generation to generation, ad infinitum." I thumped the wrinkled cover, doing my best to impersonate my grandfather, a sometime revival tent preacher. "And it has done just that in my family for more years than I can recall."

"I see," she replied timidly.

"Young people today need such traditions to help them navigate the complexities and temptations of the modern world. Don't you agree?"

"Well, I…"

"Our church is taking orders for the Bible," I interrupted, anxious to get on with my plan, "new copies of course, as a fundraiser for our mission work in Guatemala. We are seeking volunteers from the college to help us with this worthy undertaking. I understand one of our students lives here in this beautiful home and I was hoping I might talk with… with…"

A wave of panic swept over me. In my hurry to dream up a cover story, I had forgotten to ask Onward his daughter's name.

"Oh, Reverend," she said with considerable relief, "you're here to see Olivia."

"Yes… yes, that's right. Olivia is her name." Sweat beaded on the back of my neck. "Might she be at home just now?"

She vanished without answering. Moments later a young woman appeared in the doorway. My throat tightened. She seemed a younger version of Fie, only her skin shone the color of tea and milk, and her right eye drooped slightly in Onward's sad but thoughtful way.

An image came to me of Fie, young and beautiful, standing only blocks away, pointing a camera at her smiling brothers while my father flirted with Viola Walker. They had little idea the cruel twists the future held in store for them.

I had no words for the young woman standing on the threshold. Pulling off the fake clerical collar, I opened it to Onward's note and handed it across. She eyed me warily. Then she turned her gaze on the paper and read it, glanced up at me, and read it again.

"They told me he was dead," she whispered, taking my hand.

I shook my head.

"Show me where."

Easing the door closed, I led her to the street and pointed at the truck. She pressed the paper in my palm.

"Thank you," she said as she turned to leave.

I held the paper to the light. Onward's tight scrawl read 'Dun is my brother. There's nobody in the world I trust more than him. Listen to what he has to tell you. Please. Your father.' I smiled at what he might say if he knew I hadn't spoken a word.

She approached him haltingly as he waited beside the tailgate, stiff and unmoving. They stood facing each other for a moment. Then he offered his hand but she brushed it aside and instead threw her arms around him.

I turned and started down the tree-lined street. Drizzle drifted from the low-slung clouds in a thin veil, blurring the columned houses into postcard images. Mist hugged the treetops.

I imagined my father roaming the town in the sultry heat of a Mississippi summer. He might have walked this same street, perhaps to meet Onward's mother. Did he love her? Or did he share Augie's prejudice and simply take advantage of opportunity when he had a chance? I realized with dismay I would never know.

Yet I also saw the freedom that lay beneath such uncertainty. Inheritance is not destiny. Onward and I would take from our shared past what we wished and leave behind the rest.

I couldn't help but wonder at my own path forward. Gibson had yet to say whether the publisher approved my book contract. But Whit's rescue of the desk had given me another idea. I only hoped I could pull it off.

Thirty-two

Rows of blue-green swells emerged from the fog, moving shoreward in rippling lines. I leaned my elbows on the rail and watched them move past the pier and then hesitate for an instant before exploding on the inner sandbar. Sea spray hovered feet above the water, milky white against the dark surface.

I puzzled over why I felt compelled to return there once again. Did I hope to find some essence of Griggs, some memory to replace those last moments on Gibson's boat? Or had I yet to say a final goodbye? I could not say.

My still lingering resentment toward him seemed inseparable from my affection. The good and bad in him had mingled like cream in coffee, leaving little room for easy answers. In my own way, I was no different. Still, I cared which held sway over me in a way he never did.

His troubled life reminded me of the manuscript. I had revisited the ending the previous night and immediately seen how I had misread Twain's intent. Huck's return to wandering was not defeat, not the last resort of a jaded and bitter man. Travel for him signaled a new beginning, a return to adventure, a return to hope.

I looked up as a pair of white swans sailed overhead, circled and skidded into the calm water beyond the breakers. Moving together and apart, their necks bobbing, they looped past each other in a strange dance, graceful and mesmerizing. Then all at once they took flight again, circled once and vanished into the fog.

Watching after them, I was reminded of the last time I'd seen Marti. She had come by my apartment late in the afternoon the day after Onward's miraculous return. Breathless, she still had on her white lab coat. The moment she walked in I knew I would not want to hear what she had to say.

Her eyes glinted with excitement as she told me she'd been offered a prestigious fellowship at a teaching hospital in Baltimore. She sheepishly added that her bearded friend had pulled strings to arrange her admission. He'd been offered a position there as well. She would be leaving before the month was out.

I peered into her eyes, unable to avoid all that the opportunity meant to her. Despite my disappointment I gave her a stiff hug and reminded myself I had no claim on her affections. I was about to congratulate her when she glanced at her watch and murmured something about a meeting. Seconds later she was gone. I stood staring at the empty doorway as her footsteps faded down the stairs.

The memory vanished as footsteps sounded behind me, mimicking those of my memory. Out of habit I turned toward the sound. She waited only feet away. Fog swirled past her, beading on the ends of her hair like gemstones. She seemed out of a dream, a dream of my own making, of my own desire. We stood unmoving, as if we wanted to prolong the moment, to somehow capture it.

"You're uncle is looking better," she finally said, breaking the spell. "I went to the store looking for you."

It suddenly occurred to me that the month had ended days before.

"Aren't you supposed to be in Baltimore?" I asked reluctantly.

"Dun," she replied, sounding hurt, "do you really think I'd leave without saying goodbye?"

Her tone touched a nerve. Suddenly I realized I had one last chance to speak my mind, to put into words what I had long wanted to say. All along she had been the only person I could talk to honestly, the only one I could open myself to. But slowly, imperceptibly, pride had silence me. I knew I was too late but I was determined to speak anyway.

"I'll tell you what I think, Marti Finch," I answered, my voice shaking. "I think I'll miss you more than I can say. I made a terrible mistake not telling you my true feelings all along, all the way back to that night outside the dorm. And I'm sorry for it. I'll always be sorry for it. I should've taken my chance when I…"

"Dun," she interrupted, stepping closer. "I'm not going to Baltimore."

I stared at her, unable to believe what I had heard. She took my hand and drew near.

"I turned down the fellowship, Dun."

"But Marti, you can't," I said in spite of myself.

"I have to, Dun. I can't accept knowing I didn't get into the program on my own. I don't want to be beholden to Rob. I don't want to owe anyone that sort of debt. I like my freedom. And, whatever I do, I want to be able to say I earned it on my own. Knowing me better than anyone, I'm sure you can understand."

The wind gusted past us and all at once sunlight pierced the fog, casting the pier in a golden glow. I'd never seen her more beautiful. At that moment I wanted more than anything to be worthy of her confidence.

The manuscript and all that I'd kept hidden out of fear or greed or shame flashed through my thoughts. I peered into her blue-gray eyes, eyes that spoke to me beyond words. Then I leaned close.

"Marti," I whispered, "I want to tell you a secret."